# *River Song*

## JEANETTE GRANT-THOMSON

*River Song*

© Jeanette Grant-Thomson 2025
Published by Armour Books
P. O. Box 492, Corinda QLD 4075 Australia

Cover Image: Elvira Meridy White, 'Mary River';
            hobo_018 | iStock, 'Couple walks down the river beach'

Interior Design and Typeset by Beckon Creative

ISBN: 978-1-925380-93-4

A catalogue record for this
book is available from the
National Library of Australia



Note: Australian spelling and grammar conventions are used throughout
this book.

# DEDICATION

FOR MY FRIENDS THE ROWE FAMILY—
ESPECIALLY JIM AND JENNIFER WHO HAVE
GONE BEFORE US TO THEIR ETERNAL HOME
AND ELVIRA AND JUSTYN WHO HAVE
BEEN DEAR AND KIND FRIENDS
OVER MANY YEARS.

# TABLE of CONTENTS

# ACKNOWLEDGEMENTS

A BIG THANK YOU to my sister Arlene for proofreading and diligent rereading and re-rereading this book, which has undergone many changes of plot and even characters since its original rough copy.

Thanks everyone who read it and commented long before I sent it to the publisher—Arlene (yes, again), Elvira, Jo, and Laetitia. It all helped enormously. A very special thanks to Laetitia, whose fine-tuned brain picked up every little inconsistency and any other timeline issues.

A huge thanks to Elvira White and Justyn Rowe for allowing me to use their former home as the inspiration for much of this novel. Kenilworth Homestead was a wonderful and very beautiful place to stay—and live part-time—back in the 1980s and 1990s. The whole Rowe family were an inspiration and blessing to me.

The lovely cover photo of the Mary River with the hills in the background was taken by Elvira Meridy White and is used with her permission. Thanks, Elvira!

Above all, thank you to my heavenly Father, who gave me the gift of writing when I was about six and I've rarely stopped. Writing has been a source and pleasure and fulfilment much of my life.

# PREFACE

This novel is set partly in the beautiful Mary River Valley in South-East Queensland, on a fictitious property inspired by Kenilworth Homestead, where I spent many very happy days in the 1980s and 1990s. It was then owned by the Rowe family. I loved the place and the people. The Rowes were legendary for their caring hospitality to innumerable people and I enjoyed the company of each one of them—Jim the eternal gentleman, Jennifer with her effervescent joy and encouragement, Elvira with her friendly chats and Justyn who made me laugh at a time I needed laughter. Thank you, all of you. You became my friends for life.

I have rearranged the landscape slightly, focusing on the character of the place, inspired by Louis de Bernieres' *Notwithstanding*. Although parts of the property are depicted a little differently from the Kenilworth Homestead we knew, some of you will recognise the images and hear echoes of the people there.

I have used mainly the slang and colloquialisms from the sixties era when I was at university myself like the *River Song* characters, but have interspersed it with more contemporary jargon for easy reading.

Thank you again to the Rowes for your wonderful hospitality and for letting me use your former home as the inspiration for much of this novel.

*Jeanette Grant-Thomson*

# River Song

## April 1965

THERE ARE SOME DAYS you never forget.

They're etched in your mind in technicolour.

Vivien and I were swimming in the river at her family home on the slopes of the beautiful Mary River. Vivien stretched out, lolling in the shallows at the silty edge while I paddled knee-deep in water, enjoying the smooth stream swishing around my legs. We'd been swimming and laughing for about an hour. Just the two of us. Vivien's father Bert and her sister Ellie had taken the younger ones out canoeing. So Viv and I were alone in the water on this first day of our weekend at *Riverside*, the family property.

After our happy but busy lives in Brisbane, we were glad to embrace the quiet beauty of *Riverside* and let the cool water take the weight of our bodies as we floated or swam in the river. There was a feeling of timelessness there, as if nothing would ever change. As if we'd slipped into eternity. It was always like that and always would be.

Well, that's what I believed then.

The occasional weekend at Viv's parents' property had often proved a welcome break during the three years of our Bachelor of Arts degrees, our Diplomas of Education and now during our postgraduate studies. Back in Brisbane, I was still going out with Mark, a maths lecturer, and my typical choice of a loveable larrikin.

Vivien and I were just beginning to unwind and enjoy ourselves.

Suddenly a storm bird wailed its two haunting notes. Goosebumps prickled my arms. I scanned the sky. Not a cloud.

A strange feeling like a warning gripped me, unlike my usual calm. Was it a premonition? Time seemed to stop for a second.

Perhaps it was the intensity of the midday sun. That brilliant stillness.

I stopped splashing upstream and stood still, gazing up at the dark green pine-clad hills and the sunlight gleaming on the water. A dragonfly glistened as it explored the waterweed. Water gurgled, trickling over the rocks downstream.

The moment crystallised in my mind like a photograph, blue and green and laughing.

It was just as well it did—because I didn't realise I was standing on the edge of a precipice and nothing would ever be quite the same again.

# CHAPTER 1

I could hardly wait to see Mum and tell her. I clattered up the front steps, turned the key in the big old wooden door, and hurried to the kitchen. Mum was nowhere to be seen, so I put the kettle on. A cup of coffee would be good after my second-ever week at university.

This beginning was followed by several colourful, happy years leading up to what I would think of as *The Strange Day on the River*. The day when change began to interrupt and upend our lives. But for now, as I was just starting uni, life quickly slipped into an exciting but peaceful rhythm.

So ... in only my second week at uni I'd just been asked on my first ever date. Ross, an interesting guy in my French tutorial, had invited me to a party on the coming Saturday night.

After my upbringing with two sisters, no brothers, as well as Dad often sick and me at an all-girls school, I'd felt nervous at uni, suddenly meeting so many handsome, interesting men. They all seemed to be staring at me. Very shy at first, I was starting to feel braver and now, a fortnight into the term, I was starting on my real social life.

The kettle was boiling. I was excited and wished Mum would hurry up and appear. '*I could have danced all night, I could have danced all night ...*' I sang as I made my coffee.

'Claire, shoosh!' Mum hurried into the kitchen. 'Your father's got another migraine. He had to come home from work early. I might have to call the doctor and get him an injection.'

*Whoops!* My enthusiasm scuttled away deep inside me. As Mum so often reminded me, Dad had fought for our country in the war and this was his legacy—migraines often bad enough to keep him home from work and to call the doctor. I peeped around his door. Dad lay still and white. He moaned.

'Oh Dad, I'm so sorry you're sick again. Is there anything I can do for you?'

Dad groaned. 'Claire, I'm going to be sick. Would you fetch a bucket?'

Mum overheard and brought a bucket. I scurried back to the kitchen. She sat with Dad most of the night. I tried not to shudder as I agonised for him. He was such a kind, gentle man. A great father—when he was well enough.

It was much later that night when I remembered my earlier excitement. I couldn't tell Mum until the following day and then she was so exhausted, I wondered if she really heard me.

Seeing my tired face a few days later, Mum suggested, 'Claire, all this travelling to and fro. You'd be better off renting a flat near the university if you can find another nice girl to share with. You need to give it your best shot—life here will always be up and down. You need to get away from Dad's migraines for a little while.'

At first I was horrified at the idea of leaving my beloved home. 'Mum, I love Dad. I don't want to leave home to get away from him.'

'Of course not, darling, but just to have a quiet place of your own while you study. You could come home for visits.'

'Well, I don't know anyone there I'd want to live with.'

'Give it a few more weeks, Claire. See who you meet.'

As I lay in bed that night, I thought how much I'd miss my family and this dear old house if I moved out. The familiar rattle of a goods train with its eerie shriek clattered through the darkness. These sounds were friendly parts of my life.

But I knew Mum might be right. The travelling to and fro—a walk, a train and a bus each way—was tiring. Then the often hushed atmosphere in our house quenched my enthusiasm when I arrived home needing to talk about so many new things. I thought about it. Who did I know at uni who seemed nice enough to live with?

A week or so later, I realised there was a nice blonde girl called Vivien in my French tutorial. The guy who had taken me out stayed 'just friends' and livened the French tute. Vivien, too, was funny and often had the group in stitches. Everyone liked her and I often had a cup of coffee with her before our tute, at a time when the refectory was almost deserted and I felt comfortable. Never in the lunch-hour rush.

After a few difficult weeks at home and several coffees with Vivien, I broached the subject. 'Vivien, who do you live with? Or do you live at home?'

She laughed. 'It'd be a fair drive if I lived at home. I live on a farm in Kenilworth. That's a pretty little town inland from the Sunshine Coast. But to answer your question, at the moment I live in one of those mixed households—another girl and a few boys. It's okay. A bit noisy for studying.'

'You wouldn't consider moving to a flat or a small house with me?' *There, I've said it.*

She looked thoughtful. 'Well, I didn't pay any bond or anything and they always have people wanting to move in, so it'd be fine. It'd be nice to have a bit more space for studying and seeing friends.'

'Terrific! So do you know of a house or flat, or should we look around?'

'We'll have to look. How about this afternoon after lectures? We both finish at three, don't we? I drive, so we could take my car and look at any houses advertised on the notice board.'

A girl of quick action! That afternoon we set off with a page covered in addresses of houses to check. Vivien didn't want a flat if we could find a house.

The first place we looked at was a square brick house on a busy corner in Toowong. 'Too much traffic noise,' Viv said. 'I'm a country girl.'

The next one was a dear little house but too far to drive to uni. The third house was just right. A quaint little cottage on the river side of Toowong, quite near uni. It even had a view of the Brisbane River from the kitchen and some of the other windows. Vivien gazed out the window and squeaked, 'Oh, the river! We live on a river at home. The Mary River. I adore it! This'll help me not to miss it too much.'

We arranged to rent the cottage.

Mum and Dad could afford to pay my rent and I'd been lucky to get a Commonwealth Scholarship to pay my uni fees. Presumably Viv's parents looked after any necessary expenses too.

So I packed my essentials, figuring I could come back easily to get anything else. Dad was having a good day, so he drove me and my belongings to the cottage one Saturday morning in early April. The weather was still very hot so I tried to do most of the heavy lifting myself, afraid he might get a migraine. 'Claire, for goodness sake, let me take that.' He grabbed a big box of books from me and lifted it up and carried it into the house. Vivien was already there, smiling as she helped us take everything in.

One bedroom was much nicer than the other. It looked out over the backyard with a jacaranda tree. Beyond lay the gleaming Brisbane River. 'You can have this room,' I told Vivien.

'No way,' she laughed. 'I get plenty of views at home on the farm. *Riverside* it's called. I'd like you to have this one. In any case, this one's a bit smaller than the other one and I seem to create a lot of mess. I'll appreciate plenty of room for my stuff.'

I was glad. This little room felt homey with its pretty view.

Soon I was waving Dad off. *Dear Dad*. He was a sensitive man as well as having post-war trauma. We all tended to walk around his feelings, like walking around the edge of a volcano—a nice volcano. I managed to hold in the tears that threatened, not wanting to upset Dad. I'd miss Mum too of course.

'Enjoy yourself, love, and make the most of this time,' she'd told me. I'd hugged her, then looked out from the old veranda at home onto our lovely big garden and felt a twinge of premature nostalgia. But more than anything I was excited about the future.

So Vivien and I settled in to our little cottage. We enjoyed decorating it.

We studied a fair bit but also managed to fit in parties, some at our cottage. We both went home whenever we had time.

Those three years of our Bachelor of Arts Degrees passed happily enough with just a few dramas. There were times near the beginning when I wondered if it would work out with Vivien. She was very different from me. A country girl from a large family. A pretty bubbly blonde girl who laughed a lot, and went out with almost anyone who asked her. Several guys were in love with her. I was taking it slowly with the boys. I suppose I'm a bit cautious.

I'd delayed having lunch in the refectory, feeling shy among all those handsome men, so for a few weeks I ate my sandwiches with several other girls in the Women's Common Room. At last I braved it. This was before I moved house with Vivien, so I was proud of myself for overcoming my shyness.

The very first day I went into the refectory at lunchtime, I stood at the door hoping to spot someone I knew. I felt all eyes on me. Especially the boys' eyes. I blushed and felt nervous. How embarrassing. But I was used to masking my emotions for Dad's sake at home, to keep a peaceful atmosphere in the house, so I called on my acting abilities and walked in trying to look calm and confident. I already knew Vivien a bit, from my French tute. Across the tables abuzz with chatter and smelling of coffee and cigarette smoke, her bright blonde hair caught my eye.

I waved. She beckoned me. 'Hi Claire, come and join us.'

So after that I made sure I was ready to appear relaxed and self-assured when I entered the refectory, at least until I was used to it. I also knew that Vivien was *really* much more confident than I was. Hers wasn't an act. She was in her element. 'Yes, the guys certainly do check out the girls when they arrive at the refec,' she told me. 'They reckon they can tell a lot about us by looking at our eyes, even from a distance. Cheeky blokes!'

So Vivien and I became friends. I don't think she guessed at first how much I hid my emotions, except when I was genuinely feeling cool, calm and confident.

One night I'd been studying and felt hungry. I went out to the kitchen and began making some milo. 'Want a milo?' I called to Viv.

Silence.

I went to her room and peeped around the door. No sign of her. Only a pile of papers and books on her desk where she'd been working. My heart sped up for a moment. She hadn't mentioned anything about going out. How long had she been gone?

I went back to my study with a mug of milo and tried not to worry. She was eighteen, after all.

The front door opened and shut. I raced out to the lounge. 'Viv, where were you?'

She blushed a violent red. Then laughed. 'Just popped out to check on a friend. She's having a hard time at the moment.'

I was a bit puzzled by her reaction. 'You didn't think to mention you were going out? I was concerned.'

She looked surprised. 'No. I tend to do things on a whim. You'll find I pop out sometimes. Maybe to buy a bar of chocolate even. Don't ever worry about me.'

I found it hard, but I tried to accept that and not worry when, from time to time, she disappeared. Or did something unexpected like having visitors in the middle of a study break.

Vivien was a generous girl and insisted I learn to drive her car. It was a big Ford. 'Dad bought it for me so I could drive home often but we should be able to share the shopping and all that. You'll enjoy being able to get out by yourself sometimes too.'

Not realising I'd need a car, I'd left the little VW beetle I shared with my sisters at home for Julie to learn to drive. Viv's Ford felt enormous and heavy after the beetle but I soon mastered it and was confident driving.

'It's intended as a highway car,' Viv explained. 'It's Dad's insurance that I'll drive home often, I guess. It's a breeze on the open road.'

I always tried to find time to clean the house a bit on Saturdays, when there were no lectures. I was surprised—and a bit annoyed—to find Viv vacuumed whenever the mood took her, even in the middle of pre-exam study. She looked quite glamorous, hair tied in a ponytail and wearing blue shorts and a floral blouse. But the noise annoyed me when I was trying to concentrate.

I asked her about it but she insisted she needed Saturdays free for trips home or outings, and she'd done her study. I realised she had a very quick brain and would do well in exams with minimal study. I had to work hard to get good marks. So I'd shut myself in my room and study while Viv vacuumed noisily.

Most of the time I was really enjoying my life. So far there'd been nothing to warn me that life can suddenly slip out of control and that one day I might face challenges beyond anything I'd imagined.

# Chapter 2

SEVERAL LIKEABLE GUYS asked me out. I had good plainish sensible clothes, bought to last on our tight budget. Mum was concerned about dad's health. Would he be able to keep working? All of a sudden I found myself wishing I had more interesting clothes. More variety.

I was happy enough to buy outfits that would last but I felt like a little brown moth beside a colourful butterfly. I longed to have clothes like Viv's. 'You're lucky you can afford so many new clothes, Viv.'

'I am lucky, that's for sure. Mum loves sewing—she's brilliant at it—and she makes most of my clothes. We can't afford many bought dresses and what-not because there are so many of us in the family.'

I bit back a twinge of envy. Mum had no time or desire to sew much beyond basic mending and altering.

I went out with various boys without getting serious about any of them until, after about four months, I began a low-key relationship with Mark. This was a first. I'd been attracted to several guys from the boys' high school but they had never asked me out. My earlier dates with university guys were fun but not very romantic. Probably my fault. I'd had a few flings in the hope of getting into a lasting relationship but they went nowhere. So my self-esteem plummeted regarding romance until, unexpectedly, Mark seemed interested in me. I was cautious about getting too close to him in case it fell through.

I'd noticed him from my very first week at university. He had a friendly, quite handsome face, he was medium height and skinny and he was always the centre of activity. He was very, very popular. So I thought, *What's an average girl like me doing, setting her sights on a man like that?* But he was the kind of man I liked, and that was that. After my sheltered life at home and school, I was nervous every time I saw Mark. Hardly an advertisement to attract him. I even felt nervous when I thought about him.

I might never have got to know him without Viv and her antics. I admired him from a safe distance. Several months after the beginning of term, Viv and I were sitting at a long table in the refectory. Viv and I sat up one end and this guy came and sat up the far end and lit a cigarette. Nothing unusual about that. Nearly everyone smoked in those days. 'Who's that guy?' I whispered to Viv.

'Who do you mean?'

'The one with the curly brown hair and nice eyes. Hazel maybe, I can't see properly from here. He's good looking.'

She looked at him. 'Mark Singer. His course started a bit later for some reason. I think he's doing the last year of his B.A. with honours. He's a maths whiz.'

'He looks nice.'

'Ooh!' Viv sounded dubious. 'Claire, don't go getting attracted to *him*. All the girls like him. He's mister cool guy here. I've heard some of the girls talking about him. I was thinking of getting to know him myself.'

So I had no hope at all. 'How does anyone get to know him?' The words just popped out of my mouth.

'Well, let's start now.' She giggled, then lit a cigarette. 'Ciggie, anyone?' She was slightly flushed but calm as she held up her packet of cigarettes.

A few of the girls took one. I realised Mark was looking at us. Blow Viv! She was so pretty and looked stunning in her apricot skirt and top. He'd be bound to ask her out if he noticed us.

He did notice us and he did ask her out, pushing his way up to us before leaving the refectory. Viv lit up and blushed while I squirmed. Mark and Viv went out to a movie a few nights later while I stayed home studying and feeling sorry for myself. To my surprise, when they arrived home, Viv called me to join them for supper. She pulled a wry face. 'He's boring,' she whispered. 'Much ado about nothing.'

Trying to hide my astonishment, I followed her to the lounge. Mark sat with his legs slung over the arm of a chair and smoke curling up from his cigarette.

Viv introduced us. Mark sat up straighter. 'Claire! That means *light* in French. You do look like light. Your eyes shine.'

My face felt hot. We talked for about an hour while Viv wandered between us and the kitchen, making endless cups of coffee. I discovered he loved the beach as much as I did and he had a surfboard. And a crazy sense of humour. A bit on the wild side at times, I gathered, but a very intelligent guy majoring in maths. He said he would love to be clever enough to lecture in maths one day as he enjoyed teaching as well.

I figured he'd end up choosing some girl much prettier than I was and more interesting. Someone like Viv. I was just average—pleasant looking, according to Mum. Even if I did, as Mark thought, have shining eyes.

'Would you like a day at the beach sometime, Claire, since we both love the surf?' he asked as we saw him off. 'Maybe we could do a party or something before that though, while it's so windy. Should be nice beach weather before long.'

'Love it!' I had begun to feel relaxed with him.

We waved him off. 'He might have meant both of us for the beach,' I told Viv.

'No way. He and I didn't actually get on well at all.'

I was amazed. 'So he's a surfie?' I suggested.

'Not really. Mark's a muso. I guess he just enjoys surfing too.'

I still hardly believed my luck when Mark first asked me to a party. I was nervous as I dressed, made up my face and tidied my hair. But to my surprise, when the doorbell rang and Viv let Mark in, I felt peaceful and happy. Only later I realised I tended to bury my feelings and act calmly.

We had a fabulous time. Mark was fun and funny. One evening soon after, he asked me back to his flat after we'd been out to a movie. Sure enough, a violin stood propped up in the corner of the lounge room. 'Mark, do you play the violin?'.

He grinned. 'Sure do. I love music. Actually I'm part of a small group. We play at weddings and what-not and people pay us good money. I suppose it'll only ever be a hobby. Maths and other study takes up a lot of time, but I sort of need the balance. You know, there's a strong correlation between being musical and being good at maths.'

'So you're a real all-rounder?'

He laughed. 'I wish. No. I could no more write one of your essays than fly to the moon. But I do enjoy maths—and music.'

I took a deep breath. 'Would you play me something?'

'Another time. I'm not feeling musical tonight.' Perhaps he wasn't at ease with me as a fairly new girlfriend.

After he'd brought me home to the cottage and had another cup of coffee, he left. Later that night in bed, I thought back over the evening and things we'd talked about, wondering if he'd liked me. He'd actually thanked me for having a good time. Such a terrific guy, and so interesting with his music as well as maths-type studies, there'd be lots of girls wanting to go out with him. But ... I was delighted when, a few days later, he asked me out again. And again.

So after a few weeks we went out together often but there was no commitment between us. It was too soon, I suppose. I knew he still dated other girls. He didn't seem to be one for nights at home alone. But we were young.

Even though I enjoyed being free to go out with various boys, I enjoyed my time with Mark the most and often wished there was something permanent about our relationship. I was happy when we were together.

'Who's Viv going out with?' he asked one day as we

climbed into his MG open-top to go to the coast for a swim.

I shrugged, hoping madly he wasn't keen on her. She was so lovely-looking and vibrant. 'Anyone and everyone, I gather. She likes variety.' I paused. Should I mention this or not? 'She goes out a lot, though. Often I have no idea where she is.'

'Oh well, fair enough. She's about eighteen, isn't she?' He accelerated and passed a slow car. The wind whipped my hair into tangles. I loved the feel of it but it must have looked messy. I reached into my handbag, found a rubber band and a little scarf and tied my hair in a small ponytail at the nape of my neck. Mark began to speed up, possibly way beyond the speed limit. He seemed elated as we whizzed along but I gripped the edge of the seat to still my nerves. Sensing my tension, he slowed back down.

We had a great day, swimming and walking on the beach. Mark somehow made me feel relaxed and light-hearted. An occasional joke had me in stitches, yet it was evident he was basically a serious bloke. A thinker but not too complex for me. We ended up at a party in his flat until, quite late, he brought me home.

The first time I heard Mark playing his violin, I surprised him. I decided, unlike me, to pop in to his place on my way home from uni. Viv had stayed back for a tutorial and I'd caught the bus. I got off near his flat, walked up to the block where he lived, and climbed the steps. I knocked at his door. Loud, almost violent-sounding music emanated from the flat. It was beautiful and melodic but it raised goosebumps on me. Realising he might not hear me over his noise, I knocked harder.

The door opened. Mark stood there, his hair tousled and wearing untidy old clothes. 'Claire! This is a nice surprise. Come in.'

'Mark, I've interrupted your violin session. I'm sorry.'

He gave a self-deprecating laugh. 'Probably needed interruption. Maybe the music actually drew you here as my answer.'

'Answer?'

'Oh heck, I was all wound up about a situation at uni. Don't want to talk about it now but it was pretty awful. I felt humiliated. But you know, Claire, I find playing my violin gets all the rubbish out of my system. If I keep on playing whatever tune comes to mind or even make one up, it sort of gets it all out there and I'm good again.'

'That's wonderful. So I'll go and let you get on with it.'

'No, don't go. I'll make us a cup of coffee. Your company will be great now. Just what I need. Thanks for coming over.'

So we talked about everything and nothing. I didn't admit to him that when I became all het up like that, I suppressed it. Used my 'calm mask'. I guess that was immaturity.

At one stage, we talked about Vivien again. The earlier conversation about her had made me wonder. People tended to say Viv would grow up and find a serious boyfriend— but would she? She was so whimsical. I couldn't imagine her settling with one man. She'd be bored. But she was an endearing girl.

As I waved goodbye to Mark, I thought: *perhaps some nice fellow will take Viv by surprise and sweep her off her feet, as the old saying goes.* In 1961 it was still the norm for a girl to marry in her early or mid-twenties if she wanted a typical happy life. I was beginning to think Mark and I probably would end up together after our uni courses. Needless to say, I was plagued by thoughts like: *what if he meets someone he likes better? What if he finds me a bit boring and I'm just a girl to take out? Worse still— what if, when he gets to know the real me, with my sensitivities and strong feelings and definite ideas, he doesn't like me anymore?*

# Chapter 3

THERE WAS SOMETHING SPECIAL about Vivien, apart from her pretty face and trendy clothes. And her bubbly personality, of course. When she arrived at a party, the whole place seemed to light up. Nearly everyone liked her. And she was resilient, in a gentle way. Critical remarks seemed to bounce off her, while I felt them hurt right inside me. 'You're a strong person, Viv,' I commented one day as we drove home from uni.

She looked at me quizzically. 'Strong? I don't know. I guess I've grown up like the second mother in a big family so I've had a lot of responsibilities. Maybe that's made me take things in my stride.' To my surprise, she avoided my eyes as she spoke.

I suppose that was it. The only person I knew who *didn't* like Vivien was Suzanne, a girl in my English tutorial group. I think she resented Viv because she was never invited to *Riverside*. I was puzzled that Viv didn't include her. After several weeks, she not only invited me but sometimes other friends as well.

Several years elapsed before I discovered the reason she left Suzanne out.

Vivien had first invited me to go home to the Mary Valley when a long weekend was coming up. I was unsure about it. What on earth would we *do* in the country?

The lead-up week went quickly. Soon Friday afternoon arrived and we were packing our things into the car.

As we turned onto the main highway, Viv said, 'Oh gosh! I hope you've got your swimming togs in. And something warm. The nights can be cold even now.'

I had my swimsuit and a jumper, luckily. Vivien rarely thought ahead. We were almost on the highway when she mentioned my togs.

'*Riverside* is the name of our place, the property.' She sounded like she was lecturing. 'It's near Kenilworth, a little country town. I come from a big family. Six noisy kids. My elder brother Alan works in the city, then there's me, beautiful Ellie, and the younger ones—sweet angelic Anne, skinny little Lydia and noisy Sam. Sam's the current bet for growing up to look after the property but for now, Dad and Tom do it. Tom's a neighbour.'

'Lucky you. Sounds like fun. Our family's small.' I took a deep breath and told Viv, 'You're lucky. All the guys like you.'

She gave me a brief, quaint look, her eyes barely leaving the road. 'But you're the sort they marry.'

Was I? Really? I definitely wanted to get married but I knew Viv did too. I'd feel awful if I were married and she missed out.

We turned off the Bruce Highway and headed into the country. Tall green mountains towered on one side of the road. On we drove, into the bush with its patches of deep scrub.

The undergrowth soon opened out and broad undulating paddocks stretched on either side of us.

Vivien opened the windows wider, so her fair hair blew across her face. The tangy scent of lantana and bracken filled the car with sharp freshness. 'The smell of home country.' She sighed happily as we swooped over a rise. 'That's our river. The Mary River.'

I glimpsed a patch of water glowing in the late light like a strip of white silk. *They really have got a river!* Delight welled up inside me.

'There's *Riverside!*' squeaked Vivien.

Was it my imagination or just the setting sun? An ancient L-shaped house sat atop a gentle rise. Snuggled among huge fig and jacaranda trees, it was bathed in a glowing haze like something out of a fairy tale. *Just the late sun*, I told myself.

We drove down an avenue of tall, ferny-leaved trees. Silky oaks and jacarandas. The sun was sinking beneath the horizon as we followed the winding track to the homestead. The clouds in the west flamed orange and rose. 'I love this place.' Viv was smiling as if the life inside her had been switched on brighter.

'I can see why.' But I'd only the merest glimpse then. I breathed in the scent of newly-mown grass and just-turned damp earth. A group of cows clustered near a few sheds. Perhaps it was milking time.

An elegantly-dressed woman ran out to the car as we parked outside the long, low building. 'Darling!' She threw her arms around Vivien. 'We've missed you. And you've brought a friend. You said you might. Claire, isn't it? What a pretty name.'

'This is my mum. May Barlow. Call her May,' Viv said.

I smiled. 'I love May for a name too.'

'Come on in, girls, and have a shower after that long drive. Bert's still milking the cows and I've got a chicken in the oven.' A savoury fragrance drifted out to meet us.

'This way.' Vivien led me. 'This is Dad's office. The phone's here if you ever need it. Now, come through the kitchen and you can have this room. It's my old bedroom but I've moved into the new wing with the younger ones when I'm here. We use this room for visitors.'

In the dim, golden light I could just see the walls were a reddish colour, with wide old boards. 'Red cedar.' Viv ran her hand over a board lovingly. 'My' room was long with a lace-curtained window looking out to the hills, where the last pink streaks lit the sky.

'Mum and Dad dress up for dinner.' Vivien pulled strands of long wind-blown hair off her face and gazed at my denim shorts. 'You only need to tidy yourself a little bit and change if you brought a dress—we're both pretty blown about.' Luckily I'd put a dress in, just a navy shift with a V neck.

Viv showed me the bathroom and a brief shower dealt with the dust. I dressed quickly, slipping on the frock and checking my blurry image in the steam-smudged mirror. My hair was a mess so I wiped the mirror, combed my hair, then picked up my clothes from the old tiled floor.

Dinner was set up in an antique-looking dining room. Bert greeted us as we headed for the table. He was tall and lean, with a weathered face. As Viv had indicated, he had dressed for dinner and was exactly my idea of an old-fashioned country gentleman in his good trousers, shirt and tie. May looked feminine in a silky lilac blouse over a long skirt. The younger children were seated around a little table beside us. Bert pulled out a chair for me between Vivien and Ellie.

'Darling, you look beautiful!' May told me.

As we sat at the table, I sensed they were all waiting for something. Bert closed his eyes and said a prayer aloud. The others had all closed their eyes so I closed mine too. 'Grace', they called it. I'd never heard anyone pray aloud before. Surely they weren't those radical sort of Christians?

After a delicious meal, Viv told me, 'Yes, Mum and Dad are Christians.'

I looked at her in horror. 'You'd mentioned it but I hadn't fully realised. Are you?'

She half-laughed. Vivien laughed a lot even though she was often quiet. 'No! I'm finding my own way. I don't want to inherit a belief. Alan's still unsure too. And Tom. You'll get to know Tom if you stick around. He works here a lot in the holidays. The kids sort of believe in God and all that but they'll have to decide properly later on.'

'Who did you say Tom is?'

'My elder brother's friend from a farm down the road. He's my friend too. Not very exciting. Nothing romantic. A great friend, though.' She shrugged, wriggling her skinny shoulders.

I was realising how little I knew about her. We were so busy with study and social life at uni.

'Tom's at Gatton College doing an agriculture degree. His sister Ruth is at boarding school. Tom's best friend Nate's nice.'

Whereupon she blushed a violent pink. *This Nate must be something!*

She added hastily, 'To be honest, Tom is more like my real brother than Alan is. Alan's a city boy. He's great but ... just not part of my life like Tom is. And Sam's only eight.'

'You seem to like Nate.'

She smiled. 'He's certainly nice. He and I went out together for a few months. He's terrific. But not my type for a serious relationship. He's too wild.'

'Your parents are lovely but, gosh, your father's quiet!'

'Dad's shy. Not that he admits it. And he's strict. He'll get used to you and if you ask him anything about farming, you won't be able to shut him up. He loves the property. It's his life.' She paused. 'He can be very strict and stern if the situation arises but you'll never see that side of him, I'm sure.'

In response to her tone of voice, I quailed inwardly and hoped she was right. Viv led me back into the study where I was greeted by the homey smell of furniture polish and old books. 'Choose a book to read,' she offered. 'I hope you don't have to study this weekend.' The walls were lined nearly to the ceiling with temptation, so I decided to have a break from study. I breathed deeply as I looked, enjoying the air permeated with that cosy book smell.

I was glad to have an early night after a busy week. I loved the peace. Once the laughter of the younger children had settled down, the house was quiet. Soon, admiring the quaint lacy valance over my mosquito net, I lay on the comfy old brass-knobbed bed. Beyond the window stretched the sheer blackness of the night sky with a few stars twinkling, bright and clear. Brisbane skies were never truly dark. And the nights were never quiet.

The silence was broken only by the cry of a night bird. A cow lowed. Then all was still.

## CHAPTER 4

A MELODIOUS SONG from a magpie—*surely it's heard Beethoven's Fifth symphony?*—greeted me in the morning. Sunshine streamed through the lace at the window and warmed my face. It must be late. I was tempted to stay in bed and go back to sleep but as I rolled over to face the window, I heard footsteps in the kitchen beside my room.

'Like some bacon and eggs, Claire?' Bert's voice called through the wall with its chinks between the boards.

I was very hungry. 'I'd love some. I just need a minute to get dressed.'

'Want to go for a swim after brekky?' Viv asked over breakfast.

'You mean in the river?' I tried to keep the horror out of my voice. I'd noticed from my window the river was a brownish colour, not at all inviting or shiny white like it appeared in my glimpse from the road.

She laughed. 'Yes. We swim there all the time. It's great. If it looks a bit brown, it's just silt. It's safe. Safer than the ocean and not too cold yet.'

So, soon after we'd eaten a huge, delicious breakfast, we changed into swimsuits and headed off over the paddocks. A narrow track led down through the long grass to a big flattish rock, where we sat and watched the river glide past. The sun warmed our skins. Vivien had tied her hair up into a pony tail on the crown of her head. Mine was not very long yet, although I was growing it. My brown hair seemed very ordinary beside Viv's long blonde tresses.

'Look! What are they doing?' I pointed to the kingfishers. Their vivid turquoise wings flashed blue flames in the sun as they darted into the side of the riverbank.

'They make nests in the mud of the bank.' Viv slid into the river and trod water. 'Come on in. It's not cold.'

I made my cautious way over the edge of the rock into the water. At first I winced at the chill, but my body soon adapted. The river was quite deep and I loved feeling the smooth silky water all over me. When I cupped the brown water in my hand it was a golden colour.

We swam across to the other side and lay in the shallows talking. I felt lazy and relaxed with the balm of the sunshine on my back. We stayed for a while, enjoying the coolness of the water and the heat of the sun in a calm green and golden world. We could see down the river to a pine-clad mountain beyond. Birds twittered and a faint gurgling sound indicated water trickling over rocks. 'So how do you like my home?' Viv asked.

'I love it. I had no idea I'd love the country so much.' I didn't know her well enough yet to tell her the truth: everything felt eternal, almost magical, as if it'd never change—so unlike the city, where there was constant change, activity and noise. 'It's so peaceful.'

She laughed. 'Usually. The kids can make a racket.'

'What do you do all the time, though? I mean, this is like a holiday.'

'Dad works awfully hard most of the day. He's up milking the cows at the crack of dawn. He'd already done that before he made breakfast this morning. Mum looks after the kids when they're not at school and does most of the cooking and the housework. All the furniture needs polishing—and dusting, of course. And we've got several bathrooms. It's a great old place. I love it.'

'Your mother manages to stay looking beautiful. I love her hair pulled up like that. She looks quite stylish.'

'Mum does?'

'Yes.'

Viv looked thoughtful. 'I guess so.'

'Does your father do all the farm work by himself?'

'Tom helps when he's home and he'll work here part-time after he's finished college. Sam'll grow into it, I think. He loves the farm. Tom's got his own property—well, his family's property that he'll own one day. Dad pays a boy from the town to help him during the terms while Tom's at college. Alan could have had this property but he's different from most of us. A city slicker. If I needed a brother to talk to, I'd go to Tom before Alan.'

As the sun grew hotter, we clambered out onto the rock and walked across the paddock back up to the house. The grass was cushiony beneath our feet.

The weekend slipped past in a haze of family games and laughter, swimming, walking in the mellow afternoon light, and eating wonderful meals. Soon we were on our way back to Brisbane again.

Viv always talked when she was behind the wheel. Incessantly. 'So Claire, how's your father these days? You told me he gets migraines since his war experience. That must be hard.'

I sighed. 'It is. He's so stressed. Not that he talks about it. Actually I feel a bit guilty at the moment—you know, spending my free time at your gorgeous property, swimming and what-not, while Mum's stuck at home looking after Dad. He goes to work when he can still, but Mum's got the house and garden to look after. And cooking and all that. My sisters don't help much. Lee's training to be a nurse and Julie's busy studying for Senior.'

'Well, my Mum's busy too. I suppose your mother accepts that as her lot.'

'She does. But you know, there's that girl Suzanne at uni.'

'Suzanne? Not the one ...?'

'The one with the long messy auburn plait. She'd be attractive if she spent time on herself. But she's only doing uni part time so she can look after her father. I gather her mother couldn't cope with him when he came home a while after the war with a roaring temper. So she left. Permanently. Offered to take Suzanne with her but Suzanne said she wanted to look after him. Just a kid then too. Heck, you've got to hand it to someone like that. Her degree will take much longer doing it part time.'

'So don't tell me—are you saying you should be doing that?'

I tensed up. Could I give up my fulfilling lifestyle to look after Dad? 'I'm wondering. I could defer.'

Viv groaned. Then she said, 'Someone told me Suzanne's going out with Nate's wildest friend. A drug dealer. Jeff.'

We were silent for a minute until Viv squeaked, 'Look!' She pointed to the sky—a late silvery sky with curdled clouds sweeping across the north-eastern heavens.

I kept thinking about Suzanne. Whatever her lifestyle, I admired her for the sacrifice she was making for her father. I felt guilty. *Am I selfish?* So when we arrived home, I unpacked, then rang Mum straight away.

'Darling, how are you? What a lovely surprise!'

'Mum, how would you feel if I defer my uni studies to give you a break for a year, say, while I look after Dad?'

'Claire!' Mum's voice was choky. 'Darling, what a kind thought. But no. This is what I want you doing, establishing a foundation for your future, and my life here is what I want to be doing now too. I married Dad for better or for worse and I love every minute of it. Well, most of it anyway. He still works on his good days, you know. The office has been kind to him. And I love him. He's still terrific when he's feeling okay.'

'Mum, you're a champion.' I blew my nose after hanging up the phone.

— Part Two: May —

## CHAPTER 5

MAY WATCHED VIVIEN'S CAR disappear out the front gate and onto the road. *Dear Vivvie.* She would miss her in spite of having the other four children still at home. Viv and Claire had left a warm glow inside her. She sighed. None of the other children laughed like Vivvie.

*So that's Claire, Vivvie's new flatmate.* Although they called their place a 'cottage', not a flat. She must ask Bert about going down for a visit.

It was a relief about Claire. Vivvie sometimes chose odd friends. Like that Nate, Tom's friend. He was a funny fellow. A likeable soul but unusual. She was never sure why he told such strange stories. Was he showing off? Vivvie seemed to think the sun shone out of him. Surely she wasn't attracted to him?

May shivered in the warm air. She sighed, then brightened again as she thought of Claire. A bit reserved but a good, reliable sort of girl. Hopefully Vivvie would bring her back again before too long and Claire would start to feel relaxed around them all.

Strange how Vivvie liked unusual boys. There'd been a few over the years but most of them had come with Tom, who often had helpers on his farm, partly to assist them with their drug problems or whatever else had slowed down their studies. They'd come for a while and then leave, never to be seen again—at *Riverside* anyway.

But Nate kept coming. At first he and Alan were friends but then Alan had backed off. Nate had become almost like family. Except he wasn't.

'I'd be careful about that Nate bloke,' Bert had said last night. And she agreed. She never felt she knew Nate at all, even though he talked about himself so much. Boasting about his adventures.

May sighed and wiped perspiration from her forehead. She felt nervous in her stomach when she thought too much about Nate. Something didn't sit right. She'd ask Bert if that was how he felt too.

It was a pity Vivvie didn't find Tom attractive. He was such a nice young man with fine Christian qualities, but she'd laughed when May suggested Tom as a boyfriend. 'Puh-lease, Mum,' she'd said. 'Tom's like my brother and that's all. He's a bit boring.'

So what was Vivvie looking for in a partner? Surely she didn't have to go as far out as someone like Nate to feel a bit of attraction?

May strolled down to the riverbank to sit and think. She loved the faint murmur of the river as it slid between its banks, gurgling here and there as it leapt over rocks. The sun had disappeared beneath the horizon and the river gleamed white. The girls must be nearly back at their cottage now. May sat until peace filled her mind, then stood up awkwardly and went back to the house.

# Part Three: Claire

## CHAPTER 6

'DID I EVER TELL YOU about how I first got keen on Nate? Because I was genuinely keen on him for a year or so, you know.' Viv blushed as she arranged flowers while I dusted and tidied the bookshelves.

'No.' I wanted to hear her story. It sounded as if she was still keen on Nate.

'Well, Tom brought him over when I was fifteen—Nate rescued me when we went canoeing and I fell in! It was such an amazing feeling, having his strong arms around me in the river. After that, there was always this thing between us. Like we'd sort of connected in that big hug.'

'Viv, you just "fell in"? I bet you manoeuvred that need to be rescued!'

She laughed. 'As soon as I turned sixteen, I was allowed out with guys and so we went together for a while. Mum and Dad weren't all that happy about it. They were cautious about Nate. I thought that was horrible when they'd been so accepting of my other friends.'

'So why did you break it off?'

She took a deep breath. 'He's too wild. He'd try anything at all. Sometimes I was scared. I'm more relaxed with someone who'll look after me. To be honest, I wouldn't totally trust Nate to do that. He's crazy at times. I'll go out with him occasionally because I really do like him. I'm still attracted to him. But ... he takes out more than one girl at a time.' Once again, she avoided catching my eye as she spoke. I was puzzled.

So I decided Nate was fun and attractive, but possibly bad news. Not the man for me anyway. It bothered me that Viv still felt free to go out with him at times if she didn't always feel safe with him. But she obviously liked him. Could that somehow jeopardise her safety? I shivered and changed the subject.

A few days later we sat sipping tea on the sunlit back steps of the cottage. 'Do you ever think about getting involved with church activities like your family?' I asked her.

'No way. Too strict and full of *Thou Shalt Nots*. Well, that's my take on it. I don't view life that seriously.' She laughed.

I frowned at the distant hills. 'I've never had anything to do with the church. Or thought much about God, if he exists. But you know, sometimes I wonder. I can't just dismiss God and all that so easily. When I look at the mountains, the ocean, everything ... I do wonder if someone created it all.'

'But you believe in evolution, don't you?'

'Mmm, I suppose so. But it all had to start somewhere. So I think about it all.'

Viv flicked her hair off her face. 'Well, I don't even like talking about it. Mum and Dad tried a few times to talk me through it all but it just makes me irritable.' She picked up her cup and returned inside.

I sat alone on the steps, gazing at the little garden. I still wondered. Viv's reaction wasn't going to turn me off thinking my own thoughts. Okay, she'd had more exposure to Christianity than I had but I'd like to know more. Perhaps not yet though. I was too busy enjoying life.

I was still timid beneath my calm exterior. Oddly enough, I gravitated to strong, quite way-out boys. They were attractive and fun. So I ended up part of an adventurous, risk-taking group at uni. Most of them were so creative I started to wonder if I were a bit ordinary. I enjoyed acting but hadn't done much about it. I'd done Speech and Drama as a school subject. Perhaps I'd pursue that in the future.

A few days later I was in the refectory before my psychology tutorial. Suzanne came up, balancing a cup of coffee with her books. 'Mind if I join you?'

'Course not. How are things with you?'

'I'm missing Jeff. He's been away for a few days and I get lonely. He's a real support with Dad. I love Dad, and I wouldn't be anywhere else, but it gets a bit heavy going at times. Jeff's great with Dad, and Dad actually likes him. He hardly ever gets in a temper when Jeff's there. By the way, Claire, thanks for caring. Hardly anyone asks me about myself. I guess they're scared.'

I summoned my courage. 'I heard Jeff's into drugs. That's not true, is it?'

She stared at me, puzzled. 'You don't know?'

'Know what?'

'I'd better not say too much. But Nate's the one with the real drug history. Phew! He's a wild one. Pretends he's Mr Cool and takes out all you girls. I don't know.'

*She's covering up for Jeff. Nate might be a bit influenced by Jeff but ... judging from Viv's talking about him, who would know with Nate? And Viv seems unaware of any drug problems.* So Jeff was the 'wild, drug-taking' friend of Nate's Viv had told me about. Maybe Suzanne had her facts biased by her emotions. They were obviously going together seriously. And she hadn't answered my question.

'By the way, call me Suze. I hear you've been up to Vivien's farm.'

*Oh no, here it comes.* She was hoping for an invite to *Riverside*. I couldn't imagine her there but ... maybe?

'Yes,' I replied, avoiding her eyes.

'What on earth do you do in the country?'

'Oh gosh. There are never enough hours in the day for me. But I suspect I'm actually a country girl at heart. We walk and ride and swim and talk around the fire. You name it.'

She looked vaguely wistful and I felt a bit sorry for her. But it wasn't my place to invite her there.

I mentioned the conversation later to Viv, as we drove home. She was silent except for an 'Mmm'. So I was none the wiser. Strange. Viv was usually so friendly and hospitable.

A few days later Viv arrived home radiant and greeted me with her typical, 'Guess what!'

'Give up.'

'I've been changed over to a new psychology tute and the leader, Pete Rogers, is fabulous. Wow! Actually I may have flirted with him—just a teeny bit—but he really is nice, Claire. You'd love him too but I found him first. Hey, I like his looks too. Unusual—red hair, a few freckles, smiles a lot, tall and skinny. Nice eyes. Bluey-green, I think.'

'Has he asked you out?'

'Not yet.'

'Yet' wasn't to be for quite a while. Viv was too busy going around with Nate and various other boys.

The second time Viv invited me home with her, Mum rang May first to check if it was really okay. Mum's a worry-wart. Admittedly she had reason to worry about Dad, but not about me.

'She said they'd love to see you again and to feel free to come as often as you like,' Mum told me, looking puzzled. She would have found it hard to understand, I suppose, as she had to run our home carefully, now Dad was so sick. Several people had suggested he have tests to see if there was anything more serious wrong, but the doctor stuck with his diagnosis of severe migraines.

Funnily enough, Mum and May stayed in touch. They rang each other every couple of weeks to see how their daughters were going. Viv and I had mixed feelings about this.

'Mum's a darling but she likes to keep an eye on me,' Viv told me.

I suppose Mum was like that at times too.

On the second trip to *Riverside*, I was tired after rushing to complete an assignment so I was sleepy all the way there in the car. Still I noticed the entrance to the property straight away this time. As we drove along the avenue of silky oaks, then jacarandas, all my stress lifted and I entered a land where it seemed nothing ever changed. It was like having a familiar dream, so beautiful and happy that I would look forward to falling asleep, hoping to pick up the dream's threads. *Riverside* was a land where beauty greeted me everywhere and life seemed eternal and divorced from the bustle of city life.

After a relaxing weekend of walking, talking, sitting and gazing at the river from under the fig tree, I braced myself to return to the stresses of study and relationship upheavals. Our lives went on—working hard at uni and punctuating our busyness with parties and outings. Going, as often as possible, to *Riverside*. I rang Mum a couple of times a week and sometimes went home to see the family.

Half way through the year, Tom rang Viv. 'Vivien, Nate's missing.'

Gripping the receiver tightly, she frowned. 'Tried the pub?'

'Course.'

She listed places he might be but Tom had tried them all. Nate had disappeared.

Viv went back to her studying but was soon in the kitchen pouring herself a glass of wine. This was often a sign she was uptight. I was surprised she took Nate's disappearance so seriously as she still often disappeared herself. Admittedly she only popped out briefly, but it never failed to unnerve me.

'Claire, this is different,' she assured me. 'He's been gone overnight. I'm nervous about a few of his friends. That Jeff.'

The phone rang. Tom again. 'You can relax, Viv. He's back. He's a bit evasive about where he's been but he's safe and seems his normal self.'

When this little drama was repeated several times, I said, 'Sounds like this Nate's nothing but trouble, even if he's attractive.'

Viv sighed. 'Claire, there's a lot more than all this to Nate, but yes, he's wild and he takes silly risks. But he's musical—a bit like Mark in some ways—and he's a thinker. Specially when he's not on drugs. He said if he hadn't inherited his father's property, he'd study philosophy and see where that took him. He's got depth—like a real philosopher—I know that's the last thing you'd think—but he is. A deep thinker. And there's no doubt, he's an adventurer. He's fun.'

'Sounds complicated. Mark's not really a complex thinker. Sort of deep though. He gets stressed if he thinks too much—except about everyday things. Music's his outlet.'

'I guess that's what he is, yeah.'

Nate continued to disappear for short but mysterious interludes and usually Tom rang us early in the piece, hoping Nate was visiting us. He never was, though. Not in those early days anyway.

I really liked Viv as a 'best friend' and a girl who seemed so open and guileless. Yet there were times when I felt she was hiding something from me and I wondered if I really knew her at all.

# Part Four: Claire

## 1964

## CHAPTER 7

AT THE END OF OUR BACHELOR DEGREES, then Diplomas of Education, Viv and I gave each other Christmas presents before we went our separate ways for our compulsory year of rural teaching.

Viv had often complained about her dry skin so I bought her some very good hand cream and nail polish in her favourite colour, to her delight. She managed to surprise me when I opened my present. It was a length of beautiful material in the autumn tones that suited me. She told me she'd make it up for me if I'd come to *Riverside* every week until Christmas.

*If* I'd come!

'We can have lots of swims too,' she assured me.

The finished dress looked far trendier than my other clothes. Viv glowed as I tried it on in front of the mirror. I'd keep it for parties.

In 1964 we both headed out to country schools to teach for a year. Viv was stationed inland from Kenilworth. I was sent to Tara, a small town in a dry flat area on the western

Downs. I found it lonely although the local families invited me to join their tennis club and other social activities.

I missed Mark. Did he care enough to drive all that way to see me? There was still no commitment between us, after more than three years. Would I see him again?

I loved the current folk singing that had become so popular. The radio blared Peter, Paul and Mary and other trendy folk singers. The music teacher at my school started a group of our own. Knowing I can at least hold a tune, I accepted Shirley's invitation to join them. 'Not imitating you,' I told Mark on the phone. 'It was Shirley's idea.' Soon we were invited to sing in cafes and restaurants, at meetings of groups like the *Country Women's Association*, even at a few weddings. I enjoyed it and became friendly with the others in the group.

One weekend we were booked to sing at a wedding. Then Mark rang saying he wanted to visit that weekend. He must care a bit at least! I'd been missing him so much and wanted him to come. But I'd made a commitment.

I explained my dilemma to the girl getting married. Often country people are friendly and hospitable and, sure enough, she invited me and Mark to her wedding. So Mark brought a suit with him. I decided to wear Viv's creation. We singers abandoned our all-black attire for that night and wore pretty clothes. Hemlines were still going up then, so our dresses came about half way up our thighs. I had golden sparkling stockings.

Mark looked ecstatic when I sang with the group. When we singers paused to eat our meals, I went back to the table where he was tackling a lobster dish. 'So who's not musical now?' He squeezed my arm. 'You led me to believe I was the only musical one of us. I'll have you singing with me when you get back. Just for special occasions, of course, but it'll be fun. Good on you, Claire!'

I was embarrassed at how glad I was to see him. He had finished his initial Arts Degree and was doing his Masters, still hoping to become a maths lecturer.

While he was in Tara, tongues wagged. People assumed we were engaged. I cringed inwardly because Mark still never mentioned getting married. Ever. He continued to date several popular girls. 'A family?' he asked in horror when someone brought up the marriage subject. 'Boring! Can you see me doing the father thing?'

After he left, I tried to get on with life as it was. Ever since my holidays at *Riverside* with the chinks in my bedroom wall, I seemed to have become an expert in over-hearing conversations about myself. One day, as I was heading towards the tennis courts I couldn't help but overhear Lyn and Elizabeth as they watched the game.

'Claire's attractive, you know. I reckon she'll hook Tim. I'm still hoping he'll ask *me* out before too long. I know—we all love Tim—but he still avoids taking girls out. Silly bloke! But you know, Claire's sort of engaged to that guy Mark. They were together at Jilleen's wedding. She's taken. Hopefully we're safe.'

My heart was thudding in my chest. I turned around and hurried back to my car. Hoping they wouldn't notice the sound of the VW starting up, I turned the key and eased it into action. My eyes blurred with tears as I drove home. It was hard in a new town, where nobody knew you.

I'd decided I'd better do as Mark was doing and go out with a few different men. But not the guy those girls were talking about. I planned how to meet suitable guys. My wardrobe was adequate for out here. I tried a few groups— book lovers, a bush walking club ...

Then I met Tim.

Tim was everything Mum had been hoping I'd meet. A nice, friendly man. A farmer with a uni degree. Good-looking. Gorgeous eyes—a deep blue. And we got on well.

Well, I thought we did. He was very polite and always brought out the 'best' side of me. Occasionally I wondered if I had reverted to masking my real feelings, but I brushed that idea away. I was having fun.

I was delighted every time he asked me out. *That'll show you, Mark*, I thought. So, the first time, I dressed up in Viv's Christmas dress and out we went to a local restaurant. I enjoyed talking to him and at the end of the evening he dropped me off and gave me a little kiss goodnight.

We had several outings like that, as well as bush walking. We were getting on so well, I began to wonder if Mum had been right and a man like this was real husband material, more than Mark. A few of the local girls avoided me, obviously jealous. That hurt a bit. But Tina, another teacher, told me she was thrilled to see someone nice going out with him.

After a few weeks, I had a bad day at school. I'd been given a Grade Six, even though I was trained for High School. A few of the boys were there only because it was illegal for them to leave so young. One day they gave me a hard time. They simply refused to obey me. The girls were all cranky because they wanted peace and quiet to work, and they blamed my inadequacy for this disturbance.

When Tim picked me up at the end of the day, expecting to go out for a picnic tea, I was tired and grumpy. 'I just need to go home and get a few bits first.'

'Oh. Okay.'

The phone was ringing when I walked in. It was Viv.

'Viv, I'm on my way out. No time to talk. Sorry. I'll get back later.'

'Okay,' she laughed. 'Only I wanted you to know. I'm going out with Nate sometimes while I'm flatting here, away from the family. Mum's a bit funny about him.'

Nate. What on earth would become of her? Perhaps she and Nate would get married. And I'd be single still.

I was feeling upset but trying to hide it when I went back outside to Tim.

'You must have a lot of bits and pieces,' he laughed, as I got in the car. 'Took a while.'

'I actually got some upsetting news. Could we just buy take-aways for today?'

'Oh, sure. Sorry to hear. Someone died or something?'

'No! Just a worrying situation with my best friend.' Feeling tense, I belted the words out, unable to be the polite, self-controlled girl he knew.

'Nothing for *you* to worry about, surely?'

I thought of Viv, telling me in her 'romantic' voice, about Nate. Something inside me snapped. 'Yes, it's something that will affect me a lot and I'm upset.'

Tim was very quiet. We bought take-aways and ate them while he talked about everything but what was on my mind, then he drove me home.

I was afraid to open my mouth. I'd realised with horror, Tim, likeable man that he was, brought out my mask, never 'just me'. I was disappointed. I longed for Mark's shoulder to cry on. But then I realised Mark would have discussed Viv and Nate briefly and then gone on to something else. We wouldn't have got past my mask with him either.

'Perhaps we'll give our friendship a break for a while,' Tim said, as he dropped me off. 'Till you get over whatever it is.'

I was both devastated and relieved.

The next day I came down with the flu and had to take a week off school. I was miserable and lonely and it was only my croaky-voiced phone calls to Viv that kept me going. She was on cloud nine about Nate.

The year passed with a few nice, but rather boring, men in my life. I never pretended to be serious with any of them. And I missed Mark. I enjoyed classroom teaching but didn't love it like Viv did. Even on my rare dates with other guys, I didn't have that fulfilled feeling I had with Mark.

I went home via *Riverside*, where Viv was already waiting to catch up. We talked and swam and laughed our way through several hot, Queensland summer days, then headed for Brisbane. I tried not to notice the concern in May's eyes. My parents had come to *Riverside* and picked up the VW for

Julie. The visit went well, to my relief. Dad was feeling okay and was talkative.

'Mark's going out a lot with a very trendy girl. Bindy, her name is. She's a bit wilder than you are and they have a lot of fun. So I hope you find Mr Right soon.' Viv gazed straight ahead as she drove us back from *Riverside* again.

So Mark was serious about another girl. I was disappointed. *Why have I let myself feel so deeply for him?* He was nice, that was why. Fun. Attractive. Kind. And so much more. I could only guess at the emotions he sometimes expressed when he played his violin. But he was in no hurry to marry. I would find myself imagining his curly brown hair appearing in the doorway, his eyes twinkling, his ready laugh.

But facing facts, I remembered that after his parents' difficult marriage, he wanted to be very sure of the girl he committed to long term. Worst of all, I'd realised I had yet to let down my guard and express all my real feelings with Mark. I still gave him 'appropriate' responses a lot of the time.

So in some ways, he barely knew the real me. I would have to try to be real with him.

# *Part Five: Claire*

## 1965

## CHAPTER 8

WHEN WE RETURNED TO BRISBANE the next year, we were delighted to find we could rent the same little cottage we'd lived in all through our university courses. So it felt like home.

I hadn't particularly enjoyed classroom teaching. I found it a bit boring, So I studied for Speech and Drama letters. I could teach that while I was learning it; even have my own studio. Viv loved teaching Grade Five in the nearby primary school. I thrived on teaching drama as it gave me an opportunity to express all those suppressed emotions from the years I hadn't felt free to show them. Now I was in my element—at least while I was teaching!

We enrolled to do a few units of literature together in the evenings several nights a week. I enjoyed it—Australian Literature and English Drama. It wouldn't get us through to Masters Degrees but we could re-assess after about three years. It was terrific doing so much together, but Viv was changing. She was still the lively, impulsive girl I'd known, but she had a tendency to make phone calls when I was out. I'd arrive home and she'd hang up quickly, whispering something into the mouthpiece. When I was trying so hard to be my real self with her, this was hurtful.

A few weeks into the year, we were on our way to *Riverside* again. Although I loved Speech and Drama and found my uni subjects interesting, nothing compared with the peace and sheer beauty of *Riverside*. 'Tom's bringing Nate over to see us while we're there,' Viv told me, a hint of excitement in her voice.

In all our four years at uni, I'd always been with Mark when I'd encountered Tom or Nate. I suppose I hadn't taken much notice of them in those brief encounters as I was smitten on Mark. He'd been welcomed at *Riverside* but Viv preferred to go just with me so we could catch up on girl talk. I hadn't even been officially introduced to Tom or Nate at that stage. I'd certainly heard Viv talk a lot about them though.

Mark was an all-consuming person and ... who knows? Perhaps he'd sometimes made sure I had little time with other interesting men despite his own lack of commitment. So this might be the time to get to know the boys. Mark was still the main man in my life, though. Still even after three and a bit years, he wasn't interested in making a long-term commitment. He'd broken off his relationship with way-out Bindy but he was enjoying seeing a variety of girls.

On Friday evening we drove up the highway in bumper-to-bumper traffic. Viv didn't complain about the intense traffic in spite of my frequent groans and comments. She didn't even react when I swore at an aggressive driver who pushed in front of us. It occurred to me I freely showed my real emotions with her now. That was a relief.

I was thankful when we turned off the highway onto the Eumundi-Kenilworth Road. The mountains rose beside us, black humps looming in the darkness. Again Viv opened the windows wide to let the countryside scents fill the car—that damp grass fragrance and the redolence of fresh-turned earth. The wind whistled in the trees above the hum of the car's engine and a gust of wind blew a rattling clump of gum leaves onto the windscreen.

We turned in to *Riverside*, beneath the magic canopy of trees, and drove up onto the flat area outside the kitchen. Bert hurried out and took both of our bags.

'You get my old room again,' Viv said.

I was glad. I looked forward to the view as if it were my very own outlook and part of my real, permanent home. My bag already lay on the floor beside my bed when I walked in and I heaped one side of the dressing table with a pile of books for English reading.

I was prepared to dress up a bit for dinner these days, so I hurried into the shower and changed into a long skirt and an indigo Indian blouse with embroidery and beads. There were even little mirrors sewn into it. I left my hair hanging loose. It had grown a lot since my first visit here and looked much more feminine.

Ellie knocked on my door. 'Dinner's ready. Ooh, you look nice!'

'Claire, you look gorgeous,' whispered Vivien. A guy was standing behind her, barely visible in the dim light in the kitchen now. *Is that Nate or Tom? Or her brother Alan?* Whoever it was looked interesting, if a bit hippyish.

'Claire, meet Nate,' Viv said. 'And here's my old friend Tom. No, not Alan. He doesn't get home as often as we do. He works in Brisbane now and has a fiancée there. Pamela.'

*Wow!* I hadn't noticed in our previous brief meetings. Tom was very handsome. But I wasn't one to fall just for terrific looks, so I told myself to be careful. And I reminded myself I still had a loose but real attachment to Mark. Tom was blond-haired and tanned from working outdoors. He had big blue friendly eyes. Nate had a striking face with dark, longish hair, olive skin and amused-looking brown eyes.

He kissed Vivien on the cheek and even gave me a peck. Tom smiled and said, 'Hello, I've been hearing good things about you.'

Soon we were seated at the dinner table, extended to its full length, in the antique dining room. A cool chill had crept in with the evening and Bert had lit the fire. Light and shadows flickered over the walls and across our faces. May asked, 'So what have you been doing since we last saw you, Claire? I was hoping you girls would come here more often but I realise you're busy.'

I hesitated. *What if the subject ends up turning to religion?* So I talked about my uni subjects, and mentioned how I loved reading the Australian novels, even the plays and poems. I was passionate about Judith Wright's poetry. 'Have you read it?' I asked her.

To my surprise, she had. 'I've got a lovely book of it in the bedroom. *Five Senses*. Would you like to borrow it while you're here?'

'I'd love to, thanks.'

May moved on to Nate, who didn't need much encouragement to talk about himself.

He laughed loudly, his dark hair flopping onto his face. 'My usual antics, May. You don't want to know!'

'Yes, do tell us, Nate. Within reason!' She glanced meaningfully at the younger children.

'Well, I was over at Straddie—you know, Stradbroke Island—last weekend. A mate dared me to swim across to the blowhole. Helluva lot of sharks there so I wasn't sure. But I did it. It was great.'

'Why did you do that?' Bert asked, almost angrily. 'You could have been killed.'

I suspect he was concerned his younger children would want to try dangerous antics too, thinking they were brave. Young Sam appeared to idolise Nate.

'Why?' Nate looked surprised. 'For kicks. And I never— well, hardly ever—turn down a dare.' His face looked defiant in the warm golden light from the dim electric lights and the fire.

Tom avoided everyone's eyes and focused on his dinner, loading roast lamb and peas onto his fork. I wondered if he'd been with Nate. Perhaps he was even the 'mate' who dared him. He looked very sensible, though. Perhaps even a bit boring? Not my type anyway.

Dinner was a delicious roast with lots of baked veggies, gravy and greens. I'd been missing home cooking. I went home only once a month and Mum was often busy looking after Dad and had no time to prepare elaborate meals. Dad still suffered severe migraines. He went to work most days but often wasn't well enough to have dinner with the family when he came home. And at this stage my own cooking skills left much to be desired.

'Leave room for dessert,' May told us. 'It's apple pie and custard.' She watched the boys eat heartily. 'Ellie and Anne are on washing up tonight. You've all been travelling for hours. You can give a hand tomorrow, if you like. But this is a holiday for you.'

Soon we were sitting around the fire while Nate entertained us with tales of his latest exploits. He leant back in his chair in the shadows while firelight danced over the rest of our faces. May ushered the younger ones off to bed. Ellie came back after doing the dishes, so only the five of us sat in comfy chairs in front of the fireplace.

Nate was funny. Hilarious. He was quite a rough guy, and that made me aware of Mark's subtly refined demeanour.

'You swear an awful lot at the moment,' Viv told him indignantly. 'I don't mind a bit of language but honestly ...'

'Your father swears. I've heard him,' he said.

Viv laughed as usual. 'Dad swears at the cows. That's all. He says it's the only language they respond to. He's a devout Christian.' I looked intently at the fire. Nate snorted. Tom was silent, frowning a bit. Ellie wriggled to get more comfortable.

As I settled into bed that night, I heard May and Bert come into the kitchen. I could hear clear conversations through the wide-spaced boards, whether I wanted to or not.

'I'm worried about Vivvie,' May murmured.

'What about her? Surely not her studies at this stage?'

'No. She still seems to have her eye on Nate after all his coming and going. I like him well enough. You'd have to like

Nate, he's such a lively, entertaining soul. But I worry about him. All these risks he takes. It's not quite normal, is it? He's always got some new story about how he cheated death. I think he's telling the truth. But why does he feel the need to do all these silly things?'

Bert grunted. 'Yeah, I s'pose it's a bit of a worry. But it can be pretty normal for a young fellow to enjoy showing off and taking risks. That's just who he is, I reckon. I do need to discourage him from saying too much in front of the young ones, though. They're impressionable. Sam thinks he's the ants' pants.'

'But Bert, he never ever mentions his parents or any family. Has he got parents? He seems to consider this like home. He's even here for Christmas. Ever since Alan met him in Year Eleven when he was staying with Tom. Not that I mind having him here. Oh, I don't know. I just somehow feel that underneath all that bravado, he may not be happy at all. He seems to be drifting through life. I feel sorry for him. I really do. But I'd rather see Vivvie with a different young man. She's only in her early twenties. He's late twenties, I think.'

I was wide awake by then. Oddly enough, I shared May's feeling of unease about Nate— unusual for me. After all, I'd been out with some quite wild guys and usually had fun with them. I tried not to think about Nate as I rolled over and settled down to sleep.

# CHAPTER 9

SO AT FIRST THE YEAR progressed happily. We loved having 'our' little home again. We hadn't exactly expected that, although we'd both secretly hoped for it. Viv had even prayed for it. We'd come to love its cottagey garden and its views of jacaranda trees. I still enjoyed looking out the side, too, where the Brisbane River gleamed in the late sun.

Dad and Mark had helped us to build in a room under the cottage, much to the owner's delight, and with his permission. I used it as my studio.

One of Mark's dreams had come true and he had a job as a lecturer in maths. He was stoked.

Three nights a week, Viv and I drove to uni for our lectures in English Drama and Australian Literature. Sometimes Viv was tired after a long lecture and asked me to drive us home. I'd taken the VW out to Tara, then lent it back to Julie, so Viv's Ford felt big and heavy again. Still I soon felt relaxed driving it once more.

From time to time, we'd throw a party. Any excuse. Viv's birthday, my birthday, anything we thought warranted celebration. Viv would decorate with flowers plus sprigs of foliage and I'd clean the cottage and put out some nibbles. I'd set up music, still favouring folk songs. After an hour or so, someone would change it to faster music, often the Beatles, and everyone would start dancing.

For the first month or so, our lives were busy but happy. 'Hey, it's fun being back here all together. Well, a lot of us are back anyway,' Viv said one morning. I was going through lessons to teach later that afternoon while she hastily applied her makeup.

'Mmm. We don't see much of the ones who've left uni properly, though.'

'Well, let's have a party. Hey, let's do something special. I think Mum and Dad would be okay with it. Let's have a house party at home. At *Riverside*. Like in those old English country houses. You know, you read about these weekend house parties. All sorts of romances start there!'

'Shouldn't you check with your parents first?'

Vivien crinkled her face. 'Oh, I guess so. They won't mind. I'll ring them.'

I could hear the conversation as I was tidying my hair in the bathroom just around the corner from the phone. Presumably her father answered. Viv dangled the phone cord towards the bathroom and pulled a wry face in my direction. Her father was strict. Then she put on her sweetest voice and asked him about the group weekend party. 'Ask Alan too?' she almost shouted. 'Why on earth? He doesn't know most of the people who'd be coming. Only Nate and Tom.'

Silence and a serious face, then: 'Nate doesn't need an eye kept on him! You see him often. He's fine. I don't know what you're talking about, Dad. Alan'd be a real wet blanket.'

She listened a bit longer. 'Okay, I'll ask Alan. But he can be very high-handed and he'd better keep that side of himself to himself. The others wouldn't be impressed. Thanks, Dad. Love to Mum. Bye.'

She hung up with a scowl. 'Dad and his scruples! He's so old-fashioned. He never trusts Nate even after all these years of having him stay there. I have to ask my bossy brother, Alan, would you believe?' She sighed. 'To keep an eye on things!'

'Wouldn't Tom be able to do that, seeing he often works at your place?'

'Dad wouldn't expect Tom to be the boss. Alan's a city boy and he'll never take over the farm. But it's still his heritage and his home, so Dad sees him as having a sort of authority over visitors.' She sighed again. 'Darn Alan. I love him but he's heavy-handed.'

Never having met Alan, I didn't have a clear opinion. It might take the edge off some of the fun if he were very bossy, though.

Viv sent out official invitations, including to Alan and Pamela; so about twelve of us set out on the highway for a weekend at *Riverside*. To my dismay, Viv asked Mark to give Marilyn a lift as she lived near him. Viv asked me to go with her as she needed my company. At times she puzzled me. She'd invited Jen and her boyfriend Greg, several of our uni friends, and needless to say Nate, Mark and Tom and his current helper, Chad. There was still no mention of Suzanne.

I took a deep breath. 'Viv, you didn't want to invite Suze?'

'No. Not at the moment.'

'She feels left out, you know. But it's your home.'

Viv shrugged. 'She'll be all right.'

I looked away, feeling awkward. I rarely saw this flippant side to Vivien. She never used it with me. Was it Nate's influence? Or was she shallower than I'd thought?

The weekend began with an outdoor meal. The days were still warm enough to enjoy the balmy air as the sun sank beneath the horizon, leaving great golden patches on the paddocks. Nate, needless to say, recounted several of his own exploits. I suppose they were true. I was never sure. He'd stand behind his chair with one foot on the seat and wave his arms as he talked. I think Jen was a bit nervous of him. A few times I caught Alan looking at Nate with sarcastic eyebrows raised. Even Mark, who seemed to like him, was soon cheesed off.

'Come on, Nate, for goodness sake. It can't have been that dangerous or you wouldn't be here,' was Mark's response to a story about mountain climbing at Carnarvon Gorge.

'Ha! Don't you believe it. Okay, I'm a walking miracle but it was even worse. I've been sparing the chicks' feelings but we had to climb down through a dark, slippery cave with water running through it and bats flying everywhere. They were chittering and pooing all over the cave and I felt one brush my head. Urk! I don't like bats myself.'

I shuddered. He'd had a friend with him so I could always check with the friend if I wanted to. Jen gave a nervous giggle.

'Did you bring your violin, Mark?' I asked him.

He shook his head eloquently. 'No. Not this time.'

I was disappointed but realised how personal his music was for him.

We stayed up and talked around a fire until late, then headed for bed.

'Claire,' May called, 'I've put your things in your old room. All the boys can sleep in the new wing. The girls can sleep in Ellie's room. It's huge.'

I was glad. I loved 'my' old room with its view of the hills and the river. I talked to Mark for a few minutes before we went to our rooms. He was enjoying the group. He kissed me goodnight and I thought, if only he'd decide to propose to me in this beautiful place—a place where dreams could surely come true. But he didn't.

As I settled into the big old bed, turmoil kept me awake. Did Mark love me? Or was it just a convenient relationship? He still took out other girls sometimes. I decided I'd been fooling myself in expecting him to propose, and rolled over and slept.

The next day we took several canoes up the river and paddled down. The last part was the best. We could drift on the current and watch the huge, bulbous, grey and white cloud reflections skimming along the surface of the water beside us. I sensed a glimmer of that foretaste of heaven feeling but it was different with a group of us laughing and talking. Fun, though.

That evening after dark we spread rugs out in a paddock near the homestead. We lay on them, staring at the deep black sky with all the brilliant sparkling stars. Most of us were city dwellers and had never seen the sky like that—so dark with the stars so bright. At *Riverside* the sky seemed endless.

'That's the Southern Cross,' pointed Tom. The stars were so clear. He knew the names of various stars and we enjoyed letting him tell us about them.

'How come you're a farmer so young, Tom?' Jen asked.

Tom cleared his throat. 'Well, I'm not all that young. I'm nearly thirty. I've been working on the farm since I was a kid, except for when I was away at College. I love the land. We're so blessed here in coastal Australia. It's so rich and fertile here on the rim near the sea.'

'Didn't you ever want to—well—make something of yourself?' Jen asked hesitantly.

There was an awkward silence. Then: 'Jen, to be frank, I feel I *am* making something of myself in as much as I'm developing the land I'm inheriting. It'll be mine. And I'll work hard to keep it as productive as possible. To me, that's fulfilment and making what I'm meant to of myself. I've never had any ideas about being a doctor or anything although I highly respect those professions. I'm fulfilled where I am.'

'You wouldn't meet many nice girls here.' Jen was persistent.

He laughed. 'Well, here I am surrounded by beautiful girls and nice blokes. What's the problem? I meet plenty of girls I like. I don't have a huge amount of time for social activities but that's okay. I do make some time for that sort of thing.'

Viv said, 'Nate, you hardly ever go to your own land. I don't know much about it at all.'

Nate groaned theatrically. 'I've got a bloke managing it for me at the moment. It's a dry, flat piece of land out near Dalby. It's so darn dry. You guys here don't know how lucky you are.'

'So you'll move out there sooner or later and make something of it?' Viv sounded anxious.

'Dunno. I might. But it's depressing. Haunted by bad memories. No wonder it's arid. It's spooked. You know, I reckon I'll end up selling it and going more into music. I might study philosophy too. Might even make a career out of that instead, if music doesn't come together. Make my bucks discussing the whys and wherefores of the universe.'

'What instrument do you play?' Jen asked.

'Flute.'

'How come you hardly ever have your flute with you?' Jen continued.

Nate gave a cynical laugh. 'Who wants to hear me playing it? I'll join an orchestra or something that's all about music. I take it seriously and it's not part of my partying and whatnot.'

Everyone began joking about their parents or telling us things they'd done. I noticed Mark was unusually reticent.

'Mark! Have you got perfect parents?' Jen asked.

Mark sighed loudly. 'No. They're definitely not perfect.' And that was it. He turned over and gazed at the sky in silence. *What are his parents like?* I wondered. I'd only been to his house briefly in our years going out together. I'd met his mother, a normal-looking rather tired woman who greeted me in a kind manner. I'd quite liked her.

'Count ya blessings, mate,' Nate said, suddenly angry. 'Mine don't even live together anymore. And any problems you ever think *I* might have, just take a look at the old fella. Hell! I mean ta say, I'm not perfect but I'm not too bad compared with him.'

There were a few seconds of embarrassed silence. Then Tom said, 'This is one of my favourite things to do—when I have time. Just relaxing, staring at the sky.'

Everyone echoed his sentiment.

On the Sunday morning Viv waved the family off to church, then she and a few others went swimming. Mark and I walked along the bank, holding hands while we watched the swimmers and enjoyed the countryside.

It seemed only an hour or two until we all piled into our cars and Mark took off in his MG. To my delight, he wanted me to go with him as Marilyn had become friendly with one of the others, but Viv insisted she needed me to help negotiate the traffic. She and I talked all the way, although I was sleepy. Our driveway was a welcome sight. We laughed about the various things people had shared, and Viv said again how she felt sad for Nate about his parents. I was more concerned about Mark and his home life.

Viv laughed at me. 'Mark's doing brilliantly. And he's got you for a girlfriend. More or less, anyway. He was cross with me for saying I needed you in the car with me. He's sort of claimed you. He'll be fine. But Nate ... he's gorgeous but ... I just don't know.' She didn't elaborate.

# Chapter 10

I frowned at the mirror. I was putting on weight. I wasn't actually fat, but my clothes were all getting too snug.

'Why don't you take up a sport?' Viv suggested. 'We're too sedentary. I'm going to go bushwalking. Do you want to come too?'

'I love tennis. I was in the A team at school. I'd just need to find someone to play with.'

Viv jumped up. 'Nate! He's a tennis player. Only he never seems to get to it these days. But you know, that way you could become friends with him ...? You know, just platonic friends.'

It was one of Viv's 'good ideas' and I thought it might actually work. I still barely knew Nate and Viv seemed keen on him.

'I'll have to get my racquet next time I'm home.'

About ten days later when I arrived back from a visit home, Viv announced: 'I've asked Nate and he's quite keen. He'll arrange it because I've told him our hours and he'll go for your Thursday afternoons while they're still free. That works for him too. Except when he's up at Tom's, of course.'

I'd never have picked Nate as a tennis player. Surely he wasn't the type? But perhaps Viv was trying to make our relationship as normal as possible to make me accept him.

He arrived to pick me up for our first game. We talked all the way. Not just chat but discussing the Vietnam War and the whole concept of war. Nate was angrily against Australia's involvement. 'Hell,' he flicked his dark hair out of his eyes, 'some of the guys mightn't even come back. It's not our war.'

On the court, Nate was clever and fast. Agile. I suspect he was kind to me, often letting me beat him, but he would never admit it. I was surprised to see skinny Nate move so quickly and accurately. But I enjoyed the game and several following ones. To my surprise, he was good company and more considerate than I had expected. Perhaps Viv had had a word with him?

'You hear about Merle Thornton?' he asked one sunny day as we arrived at the court.

'No.'

'Chained herself to the bar in the *Regatta* as a protest against women not being allowed to drink in bars. Good on her, I reckon.'

I was a bit shocked. Merle was the philosophy secretary and brought her baby, Sigrid—later to become a famous actress—to uni in a basket.

'I reckon, good on her,' Nate said again.

So Nate became my source of a lot of information. He was rough and ready compared with Mark, who was kind and courteous in a traditional way despite some of his ebullient outbursts. I found it hard to reconcile, at times, the considerate Mark who took me out with the Mark who apparently had wild nights with girls like Sally and rode crazily with a bikie group.

Nate was just Nate. He let me open my own car door and in general acted as if I were one of the boys, but I felt more comfortable with him like this. I never felt he had any romantic ideas about me.

Some days he was quiet. 'What's up, Nate?' I would ask.

But he was elusive and full of excuses. A late night. A hard exam. A run-in with a tutor. And so the 'reasons' went on. I had the odd feeling he was sitting on something big and secret. Surely Suze had been lying about the drug issue? I felt sick when I thought about it. It was hard to imagine so I dismissed it from my mind. Nate was clear-thinking and kind. His longish hair was often a bit messy, flopping over his face, but that was just Nate. He wasn't fussy. But nor was he a down-at-heel druggie. At times, though, when I was puzzled or almost afraid about his behaviour, I'd think about Viv. She seemed totally unaware he might be into drugs. Suze *must* have been wrong.

So I dismissed the more sinister ideas and summed him up in my mind as an interesting man, good-hearted, but a bit of a mystery. Someone who was a good friend. A bloke I could talk to easily, to my surprise. As he tended to be untidy and 'take me as I am' in his appearance, I let my mask down more with him than with most people. I'd become quite fond of him.

# Chapter 11

ONE NIGHT ABOUT TWO WEEKS later, Viv went to a dinner party with some friends I didn't know. I planned to stay home and study. I'd just begun to read some notes on *My Brilliant Career* when a loud knock startled me. I looked at my watch. Seven o'clock. It could be anyone. I ran a comb through my study-tousled hair and went to the door.

'Bout time!' Nate stood there looking impatient.

I didn't feel I wanted to ask him in without Viv there. In spite of our early-stage friendship, in some ways he was an unknown quantity. 'Viv's out, Nate. I thought you might have been at the dinner she's at. I'm studying.'

He shrugged. 'Home alone, eh? Poor Claire. Let's go out and have some spaghetti and a glass of wine at the *Milano*.'

'Sorry, I've had dinner.' I felt uncertain about it anyway. Certainly, he was involved with the Barlows, specially Viv, but just friends with me.

'Come on, Claire. Let's go and have a glass of wine somewhere and just a bit of cheese or something. You can't study all the time. All work and not enough play makes Claire a dull girl.'

*Ouch! Dull!* My old enemy. I still tended to worry I came across as dull compared with colourful Viv and her sisters and some of the uni crowd. So … 'Okay. Just give me a minute to change out of my house clothes.'

'Right. Hurry up, though. You girls …'

A few minutes later I'd changed into a good pair of jeans and a pretty top and I let myself into Nate's old car. I noted again how he didn't open the door for me, whereas Mark always did. We drove down to the *R.E.* at Toowong and sat in the beer garden under a tree. Nate bought some wine and savoury snacks. I quite enjoyed the time there. We laughed over a few of Nate's exploits and chatted with another couple from uni. Then Nate stood up. 'Time to go, I s'pose, or we'll be chucked out.'

As we parked outside the cottage, I thought, *I don't want to ask him in.* 'Nate,' I said, 'I'm very tired although it was fun, thanks. I'm glad you took me out but I need an early night now. Thanks again! And good night!'

Before I knew what was happening, he had clasped me in his arms and begun to kiss me. It was no gentle, courteous good-night kiss either. I wriggled free and opened the car door. 'Night!' I called again and hurried into the garden. Nate's car screeched and roared away down the road.

I went to the bathroom. My face in the mirror was flushed and my eyes looked unnaturally bright. I hoped Nate would forget about this evening as fast as possible.

A few nights later, Viv said, 'Claire, we need to talk.'

My heart sped up. She must have heard about us being at the pub together. She might feel betrayed.

We sat at the table and Viv said, 'Claire, I got an unpleasant surprise the other day. Nate told me you're what he calls "a good kisser" and he enjoyed your company the other night. What was that all about?'

I sighed. 'Viv, the only thing is to tell you the whole story.' So I did. And I told her I wasn't impressed with his behaviour.

She ran her hand through her hair and pulled it off her forehead. 'I realise Nate's a very attractive bloke. Any woman would jump at the chance to kiss him.'

'No way! Not me. I'm not attracted to him in that way at all,' I said crossly. 'And I didn't actually want any of what happened that evening. I certainly didn't want him to kiss me. And as for being a good kisser—I didn't actually kiss *him* at all. And I'd always just considered him a friend. I would never, *not ever*, think of him as husband material. Or even as a boyfriend.'

Viv looked me in the eye. 'Well, I can sort of understand but I'm disappointed you felt okay about going out with him at night. It's not like playing tennis in the daylight. I thought I'd more or less let you know I'm interested in him still. In spite of all my reservations.'

'I only meant it as a very low-key fun evening, Viv. Companionship. He all but insisted I go.' I took a deep breath. 'And he told me I might be dull if I stayed home and I'm awfully scared of being dull, compared with all you super trendy girls.'

'Oh Claire, you're not dull. You're you and I like you. We all do. But please don't go out with Nate again.'

'Of course not. I hadn't realised you were that serious about him. But what about tennis?'

She shrugged. 'Maybe we'll see how he's going before you play with him again.'

'But I did enjoy his company, you know. Not in a physical attraction sort of way but he's interesting. I enjoyed our conversation. Same as when we played tennis.'

'Yes, he's nice, that's for sure.'

We had a cup of milo together and Viv hugged me. 'All forgiven and forgotten.'

As I lay in bed that night, I thought about Nate. So much for my 'just friend'. I liked him as a person in spite of the kiss. And yet ... there was still something about him that made me uneasy.

# Chapter 12

A few weeks of teaching, study, lectures and parties followed. Then Viv suggested another weekend at *Riverside* while it was warm enough to swim. Just the two of us.

And so we came to that day when we were at *Riverside* again, swimming peacefully until I suddenly felt ... was it a premonition? It was still April—calm, sunny and balmy, but carrying in its wings something ominous. That pivotal day arrived, interrupting my peace with a strange, puzzling feeling.

The weekend had started out sun-kissed and perfect ... we had no idea our lives would never be the same again. That weekend life handed us the tip of a spool of dangerous thread that would unwind, again and again, until we were tangled in its confusing and frightening end.

Anyway—Viv lay in the shallows sunbaking while I sploshed my way upstream, watching the tiny birds in the river oaks. It seemed nothing could disturb us, yet as soon as a storm bird called, I felt that odd sense of unease. Something unnerving. I tried to make myself believe everything was normal. After all, we had Nate and Tom arriving soon for lunch. We were looking forward to seeing them. I missed Mark, though, even more these days. Nate and Tom were real country boys and were often here as part of the *Riverside* scene. And the tennis games had worked—I'd become quite attached to Nate. Despite the kiss, he was part of the fabric of my life now.

Suddenly ...

'Viv!' A yell sounded from the high bank. Startled, I looked up. Tom stood there, waving his arms frantically, unlike his usual calm self.

'What's up?' Viv called.

He beckoned. Viv began to swim across. 'Come on, Claire,' she called.

I began a reluctant breaststroke to the bank. Viv slipped lithely up onto the big rock and I heaved myself up after her, envying her slim body. I wrapped my big yellow towel around my old green swimsuit and waited for Tom to explain his summons. Viv stood, pretty as always, her floral towel dangling over her blue swimsuit. We both shivered as a sudden gust of wind swept up from the southern hills.

'Nate's missing,' Tom announced grimly. Nate had been staying with Tom, working on his farm in a part-time paid job. 'Really missing this time. Not a trick. He went out to meet some friends three nights ago, said he'd be back by midnight so I went to bed and slept after a big day on the farm. Next morning there was no sign of him. I kept expecting him to show up as if nothing had happened but he didn't. It's three days now and still no sign of him.' Tom looked haggard. 'I've rung all his local friends.'

Vivien's wet skin was covered in goosebumps. 'Should we ring the police?' Her voice shook.

'We can try. Gotta start somewhere.' Tom sighed. 'I'll go in and see the cops now.'

'Gosh I hope he's okay,' I said to Viv. I wished Nate wouldn't play these crazy tricks and scare everyone. Surely he'd be all right. He always was. I'd certainly miss him if anything serious had gone wrong. I'd been saving a bit of news about one of my tutors to discuss with him.

Viv turned, tears in her eyes. Tears over Nate. Nate who specialised in tricks and scary antics. He and Viv were not all that close at the moment as far as I knew. I shrugged inwardly and glanced at her again. She looked peculiarly fragile.

My mind was still imprinted with the brilliance of the sunshine on the river and the chorus of little birds twittering in the river oaks. For a moment I resented this interruption to my weekend. But what if something serious had happened? Could Nate have taken one risk too many and had an accident?

When we were back in the big old kitchen, Viv grabbed a tissue and wiped her eyes. She averted her face, apparently embarrassed about being upset. At times like this, she was a mystery. She was so easygoing most of the time, yet she had these sudden outbursts of emotion. Much as we both liked Nate in our different ways, I thought: *all this over the wild way-out guy who's still studying part-time, rather erratically, at Gatton College and often staying with Tom and helping on his farm. Not as if he's one of our boyfriends, I don't think. Although Viv ...? He'll turn up again, like always. This is just typical Nate.* He was different from most of the others in so many ways. He had taken his time with his study, preferring to work at the same time. But he never seemed short of money. Quite the opposite.

You'd think after Nate's regular exploits, even disappearances, it wouldn't upset us that he was missing. But it did. Vivien was tense and moody. I could tell she wasn't sleeping. One evening soon after, back in our cottage, she rang her mother to see if they had any news. She cheered up visibly as she talked.

'Any news?' I asked when she clunked the receiver down.

She shook her head. 'I'm not worried, though. Mum and Dad think it's just another prank. You know, like scaring the heck out of everyone by swimming across to the Blowhole at Straddie. They're not worried.' She pulled her hair off her forehead. 'I'm sure he's fine. He's a bit like a cat with nine lives, you know. This will probably be just another giant Nate-sized adventure.'

I remembered Nate sitting at the dining table at *Riverside* and recounting his antics at Straddie. The result of a dare. I shuddered. What now?

That night I couldn't sleep. I lay awake watching the cars' headlights illuminate my bedroom wall, then make those grotesque shadows bouncing off the furniture. And I thought about Nate. Likeable, attractive, funny Nate. Nate the philosopher. The musician. The adventurer. My tennis partner when he made it. The one who initiated all sorts of pranks, usually harmless.

I imagined him running along, his dark hair flopping over his forehead or flying back in the wind, with someone chasing him.

Where was he? Was he okay, as always before? Or was this serious?

Just as I was getting sleepy, I realised I was hungry again. Perhaps a hot milo would help me go to sleep. I crept out to the kitchen and began to heat some milk.

'Oh, it's you!' Viv's sleepy voice came from her doorway. 'Have you made enough for two?'

I stirred in some more milk and soon two fragrant, steaming mugs of hot chocolatey milk sat on the bench.

'I know I made light of it before,' Viv said, 'but there could be something seriously wrong. I'm concerned about his friendship with Jeff.' She sniffed. 'I'm still worried about him. No matter what, I still care about him. What if he, say, had too much to drink and lay unconscious somewhere? I do know he drinks far too much.'

'Someone would have noticed him and reported him after a day or two.'

'Yeah, I suppose so.' A tear trickled down Viv's cheek. 'I'll pray for him. That he'll be found and safe. He's like a brother to me.'

I stared at her. 'But you don't believe in praying and all that.'

'I know. But I'm desperate and I'll try anything. Sorry.' She stifled another sob.

'It's fine. If praying helps you.' Perhaps praying would make Viv feel she was doing something helpful, even if it accomplished nothing more.

I never ceased to be surprised at Viv's odd combination of frailty and strength. How could this disappearance—for the tenth or whatever time—make her so miserable? Admittedly he'd never before been missing for this long.

The following day Viv walked around the house looking pale and exhausted. Silent. She sat on the sofa and played with the cushions. Increasingly she wore a calm, determined expression, ready to face whatever. Another anxious day passed and the next morning I went to the corner store to buy some milk. The day was clear and sunny so outwardly I began to feel relaxed, yet an inexplicable apprehension was growing inside me. My stomach churned.

As I stepped up the dusty old wooden step into the shop, I stopped. My heart thudded in my ears. There was Nate staring at me—gazing out from the front page of the *Courier-Mail*, the daily Brisbane newspaper. His dark hair was messy as usual and he looked straight at the camera as if to say, *Yes, it's me.* I found myself clenching my hands into fists.

Taking a deep breath, I bought a newspaper. My hands shook as I gave the shopkeeper the money. I hurried out and sat on the old wooden seat outside the shop. My hands still shook as I read the article.

> 'Nate Gordon, aged 29, was arrested for possessing and dealing thousands of pounds worth of marijuana and a small amount of heroin. Gordon declined to give any details of his contacts but it is thought he is connected with another source from an Asian country and, according to Gordon, paid only a "couple of hundred" for the drugs. The haul might have fetched almost a million on the Australian drug market. It is alleged another young man, Jeff Gascoigne, was involved also.'

The article went on with less important details but I'd seen as much as I could cope with. How could he betray us like this? Just when I was starting to trust him. How could he lead a life like this behind the scenes and get on with being our close friend? My mind screamed, *How will Viv cope?* For that matter, how would I cope? But Viv had had all those idealistic views about Nate being like a brother and I'd even heard her hope he'd be Mr Right for one of the Barlow girls. So much for Viv's flippant side, assuming he'd always be fine, no worries.

I had been starting to trust Nate, almost as a good friend. *How can I have been so wrong? So gullible? This man, this criminal, is part of my life.* And, on a superficial note, *There goes my tennis playing.*

I'd never told Viv about Suzanne's claim he was into drugs seriously and I knew she had no idea about it. I'd tried to protect her but it had backfired. Assuming Suzanne was lying and trying to make Nate look worse than he was, I'd all but ignored her words. She must have been telling the truth. So—I dragged my fingers through my hair—*he really was living a double life.* Which accounted for that elusive streak in him. The big mystery.

I'd always prided myself on being a good judge of character but I'd been way off with Nate. Had his charismatic personality disguised his dishonesty? Had Suzanne's boyfriend Jeff sucked him in and used him? Had Viv guessed some of this and that was why she never asked Suze home?

Questions bombarded my mind and my head began to ache. *Poor Nate.* Regardless of what he'd done, he was still the fun-loving guy I'd had so many good times with at *Riverside* and here. Perhaps he was an addict. *What will become of him? Will he have to go to jail?* I shuddered. *Handsome Nate in jail. Will they be lenient because Jeff's the leader?*

How was I going to tell Viv? I began to walk slowly back to the house. I'd have to make a cup of tea and tell her over a cuppa. Perhaps I should buy a chocolate to have with it. Definitely a time for comfort food. Not that it'd soften the blow but ... I went back and bought one of Viv's favourite chocolates, milk chocolate with caramel filling.

Just as I began to walk up the steps to the house, I realised I'd forgotten to buy the milk. I turned around and hurried back to the shop yet again and bought milk. The shopkeeper gave me a puzzled look. 'Not with it today, Jim,' I spluttered with a sorry attempt at a laugh.

I continued to ponder the Nate situation. *What about Tom? If I've been so wrong about Nate, is Tom just as bad?* I could no longer trust my own judgment. *And*—my stomach tightened—*is Mark okay?* All that turmoil he expressed sometimes in his music. But I soon pushed Mark to the back of my mind. I saw a lot of him. He never disappeared without telling me exactly where he went. Or Viv or Suze told me if he took other girls out.

I let myself into the house and put the milk in the fridge. 'You home, Viv?' I called. My voice come out high and a bit croaky, to my embarrassment. I cleared my throat and tried again. 'Viv?'

Viv emerged looking half-asleep, with swollen eyes and a white face. 'It's okay,' she said in a flat voice. 'I know. I can see you do too.' Tears shimmered in her eyes.

'How do you ...?' I began.

'Tom rang me. He's devastated.'

'That rat Jeff,' I said. 'Leading Nate into all that.'

Vivien looked sad. 'Claire, Tom told me he'd discovered Nate was the leader. Jeff was just a pawn. Nate was a full-scale drug dealer, selling drugs to farmers and their teenage kids at the local pub.' Viv began to cry quietly, tears trickling down her face. 'Claire, I knew he was doing drugs but I had no idea he was selling them to young people. I sort-of coped with his drug-taking but I can't handle the rest of it. I'll have to back off a bit, I suppose.'

'I didn't know there was much of a drug problem in Brisbane,' I said. 'I know it's an issue in Sydney. A lot of the arty people down there are into drugs, I hear. I'd been thankful we'd escaped it. So I thought.' *Nate, the leader. Selling drugs to teenagers.* My legs felt like jelly so I sat down. 'Viv, is Tom involved with all this?'

'No! No way! He was upset about it. I think he's had an occasional joint—marijuana, you know—but he values his brain being clear. And he's got strong opinions about leading young kids the wrong way. He even brings a few needy kids from a drug rescue place out to his farm sometimes, to give them a break and teach them some farming skills.'

I was relieved. Tom was so just-plain-nice.

I went to my room to study, only to find myself staring at my books and pondering the situation. Would Viv and her family remain Nate's close friends? They'd have to forgive him because of their Christian beliefs. But wouldn't the parents worry about his influence on the children? Was he still 'one of us'? How far did acceptance go? Maybe in this day and age with morals shifting, it didn't make much difference—unless he proved a bad influence on Viv's younger siblings. I stared at my study notes for *The Tree of Man* and sighed. *What a mess.*

Later that evening, after tea, Vivien went back to her room and I went to mine and studied. After a while, I heard a strange, awful sound. Like muffled sobbing. I listened carefully. It was probably the sound of someone crying into a pillow. *Vivien.* Better to leave her in peace.

Later, when the sobbing sounds had stopped, I made a cuppa and knocked on her door. 'Cuppa, Viv?'

'Thanks.' Viv's voice was thin and tight.

She looked up from her study. 'Oh Claire, how could he? That's going way too far.' She sniffed. 'We trusted him. Tom trusted him. You did, I assume. And Mum and Dad had him to stay over and over again. They treated him as family. Gave him a place to live in the holidays, nice meals, you name it.' She paused and blew her nose. 'And yet part of me still likes him. He's so much fun and interesting. Oh gosh, I suppose he's in jail.'

'We don't know all the facts yet, Viv. Some other character's probably behind it all. And Nate mightn't have to go to jail. A big fine perhaps. I have no idea.'

'I feel as if I don't know anything at the moment.' Vivien sniffed and blew her nose again. Her wastebasket was half full of used tissues.

'Actually,' I said, 'I always thought I was a good judge of character. But apparently not. It's a lot worse for you, of course.' So much for Nate's good sharp mind. How sharp would it stay with this sort of abuse? And it hadn't served him well in drug-related decisions.

'I need to see him and talk but I don't know how to do that.' She grew frantic. 'How could he? How can an intelligent man be so dashed stupid?' She kicked her wastebasket across the room and damp tissues plopped everywhere. 'I'm not going to forgive him. He doesn't deserve it. I've taken as much as I can. Blast him.' She burst into loud crying and threw herself across her bed, shaking with sobs.

'Would you like me to get you something to eat with your tea, Viv? Chocolate has soothing properties, I'm sure.'

She subsided. 'Sorry.' She sniffed loudly. 'It's such a horrible mess. Just tea's great for now, thanks.'

I gave her a hug and left her to drink her tea. After trying to study for a while I went to bed, but I found myself awake and thinking far into the night.

I went out to the kitchen to get another drink about midnight, only to find the entire lounge room covered in cushions and mess where, presumably, Viv had thrown everything around. She certainly knew how to express her emotions. Unlike me.

To my astonishment, she had rallied by the next day. She emerged from her room already showered and dressed when I came out. 'I didn't get a lot of sleep but I'm ready to face it all now.' She gave a cynical laugh and still looked droopy as she began to clean up the mess in the lounge. 'Sorry about this.'

'He betrayed me too, you know. He and I had begun to share all sorts of things because I trusted him. More fool me.'

Viv gave me a peculiar look. 'Well I've forgiven him now. I thought it through during the night. I'm going to fight for him. I'll even ask Dad to pray for him to get completely free from drugs. And to be more honest and caring. I love Nate, you know. This is just a weakness he has. Okay, it's a really serious one, but I'm fighting for him.'

*Love?* Was she putting on a brave face? She was standing very upright, almost as if going to war. I found it easier to relate to her when she let it all hang out. *But that's the pot calling the kettle black*, I thought.

I was troubled by the awareness that Viv had known all along Nate was into drugs—although she'd been unaware of the seriousness of his activities—but had never told me. She'd encouraged my friendship with him, but I'd had no idea the type of guy I'd been befriending. And yet, she was such a dear, generous girl.

Viv went home for the holidays. She went knowing she wanted to discuss Nate with her parents but realising she might not brave it yet. I tried not to envy her, holidaying for perhaps weeks in that beautiful timeless place. My conscience niggled me into going home to my parents and I really enjoyed catching up with them at length.

Mum was concerned about me. 'This Mark,' she said, 'he seems a nice enough fellow but Claire, love, he's not asking you to marry him, is he? I mean to say, you'd better go out with a few different young men and see who comes along. Darling, don't let life pass you by.'

'I have started seeing other men, Mum,' I said in a choky voice. 'But I still like Mark best. He's just not ready to settle down.'

'He might never be at the rate he's going. You get those men. And I've discussed it with May. You've been keen on Mark all through your BA degree and your Diploma of Education. Surely that's long enough for him to make up his mind. And May agrees with me.'

'Oh Mum. It's not a good time for May. She'll be upset about all sorts of things, I imagine.'

Mum looked faintly puzzled. She had never met Nate and knew nothing about our current drama. In theory I agreed with Mum. I was ready for Mark to propose to me but it hadn't happened. An independent streak rose up. 'Mum, I'm not in a hurry to get married. I'm only twenty-two. What's the rush? There's lots to do and I'm enjoying it all. If I get married, next thing I know, I'll be having children and I'll be tied down.'

I ran to my room and cried.

# Chapter 13

A few weeks later I managed to catch another fluey bug. Perhaps I was a bit strung out after the Nate drama, as I became very sick. Viv had returned from *Riverside* for a special friend's party. She seemed concerned about me and threatened to take me to *Riverside* for her mother to look after. 'No way! But thanks, Viv. Your mum's got enough on her hands if she's heard about Nate.'

I was concerned Viv might catch my bug. I was too sick to make my own meals for a few days and Viv happily prepared them and brought them to me in bed. She even made chicken soup. I hadn't realised she could be so housewifely as she rarely showed any evidence of it.

As I began to feel almost human again, I found myself thinking through the events of the past months. To my embarrassment, I was seriously distressed and cried over Nate and his plight, and the pain he'd caused Viv and her family.

It slipped into my mind as the aches and pains lifted and food began to appeal to me again that I was a bit irritable after spending about five days in bed with a fever. Still I wouldn't dream of grumbling about it or reacting irritably. Was it that cover-up thing again? The protect-Dad mask? I'd created a persona of a sensible girl who rarely had any ups or downs in her emotions. And I suppose, quite honestly, I *was* sensible and stable—most of the time.

Had I been right or wrong? Would Mum and Dad have been just as relaxed about me if I'd had normal teenage ups and downs? I would have to ask Mum.

I waited until I'd recovered properly and went home for a weekend.

'Darling!' Mum flung her arms around me. 'You've lost weight. I can feel your bones.' She squeezed my shoulders. 'I hope you weren't too sick. I didn't risk visiting you because of Dad. His immune system's very poor. It's amazing how much that war affected him. So ... how are you now?'

'Getting there, thanks Mum. Still a bit tired, but I'm okay.'

We chatted for a while and then had tea—a hearty pea and ham soup as Mum hadn't been sure what I could eat. Afterwards we sat in the lounge to talk. 'Mum, how would you and Dad have coped if I'd been an average tantrum-throwing teenager with all the ups and downs some of them have?'

'Well, for goodness sake, Claire. That just wasn't you. I'd have been thinking you'd had a personality change or something.'

'No, I mean if I'd always been like that. How would you have coped? Would my ups and downs have upset Dad? And made it harder for you?'

Mum frowned. 'What a funny question, Claire. We would have loved you just as much, no matter what. I'm your mother, for heaven's sake. And Dad adores you. Julie sometimes loses her temper, if that's what you mean, but it soon blows over. I don't often have to speak to her about it. She's not quite as close to your father as you were, though. You were always a Daddy's girl.'

She hugged me and later tucked me into bed as if I were a little girl again. 'Now sleep tight, darling, and don't be worrying about all sorts of things that might have been or might not. You need to use your energy to get well properly.'

*Dear Mum.* I don't think she fully understood where I was coming from. But I was convinced now about my mask theory and that it was often wrong. I'd tiptoe around Dad with his migraines or if he were tired and stressed. But I began to think I should save that behaviour for home and let myself go more outside. When I was half asleep, I thought, *what if Viv's got a mask too? She's usually so open—but not about Nate and drugs. What else? There are times …*

I fell asleep.

Viv returned to *Riverside* again. She told me before she left, 'I'm hoping to discuss the Nate situation with Mum and Dad. I wasn't ready last time. They're pretty good at getting things in perspective, although I can guess where Mum will be at. Tell you more when I see you.'

I wondered if her parents would be understanding. Surely they'd be hurt at least, after all their kindness to Nate.

I missed Vivien's lively presence in the cottage. Suzanne came around a few times but, although I enjoyed her company, I no longer fully trusted her. 'I guess you know Jeff got a big fine.' She laughed. 'At least he's not a candidate for jail like Nate. I'd miss him too much. Nate was a bad influence on him.' She settled into a lounge chair. 'I suppose you'd like to know a bit about it all.'

I cringed at her attitude but my curiosity won out. 'Yes, of course.' Viv and I had very skimpy knowledge about Nate's situation. Perhaps Tom was trying to protect us.

'Nate had been on probation for a while for dealing heroin in his early twenties. This time they refused him any lenience. Said he's made a farce of the system. He's a smart bloke, Nate. He managed to get hold of the heroin and sell it while he was theoretically under their eye. He still had to report to the police in Brisbane regularly and they sometimes came out and checked on him out of the blue, but he managed to slip the system. Until now. If he's actually in jail, I think they plan to give him only a short time if he behaves well, and then put him on parole again. Who knows, though? Maybe a longish prison stint.'

I groaned. Knowing Nate and his acting ability, it'd be only a few weeks in jail. If that. Not that I'd wish jail on him, but how would he learn?

'This will be upsetting for Vivien,' Suze half-laughed. 'Assuming she's got the guts to keep going with Nate after this.'

'Viv's not going with him at all,' I protested. 'And she's got plenty of guts, but she and Nate are only friends.'

'You reckon she's got guts? I always think she's a wimp.'

'No way. She's tough. Just a gentle type of tough. She's strong, not loud and domineering. She—well, she's different.'

Suzanne gave an unconvinced grunt and flung her plait over her shoulder. 'That giggle of hers sounds like a darned schoolgirl.'

I shrugged. 'That's just a mannerism. She's a basically happy person. More so than you or me. Maybe that's why she laughs so much.'

Soon I waved Suzanne off.

*If I lived at Riverside, and all my cares fell away like they do there, I reckon I'd be as happy as Viv. It's like a foretaste of heaven, if such exists.*

I was lonely without Viv. Mark dropped in a few times but I was still tired and felt embarrassed about my lack of bright, happy small talk. Mark seemed fine about it and chatted on cheerfully but I still felt surprisingly tired after the flu. I went out with Mark a few times. 'To cheer you up,' he said. Still I continued to feel flat.

Just as I began to feel thoroughly bored, Vivien rang to say she was coming home. *At last.* But I felt, quite irrationally, disappointed in her. She'd stayed away such a long time when she knew I was still recovering after being really sick.

I remembered my resolution to be more open with my feelings so now was the time to start. What if this was the reason Mark hadn't become more serious with me? I'd better get on with being more me.

I went to Viv's room as soon as she'd arrived. As she unpacked her overnight bag, I leant against her doorpost. 'Hi Viv, good to see you again. You were an awful long time, though. And you took a week off teaching.'

Vivien looked astonished. 'Stress leave. What's got into you?'

My face felt hot and uncomfortable. 'Ah, um, well I was starting to get lonely and I still don't feel a hundred percent. I know you had very serious things to discuss but ...'

'Claire! This was a major family drama! I thought you had your head around that.' She burst into tears.

I was appalled. All I'd managed to do was upset Viv at a difficult time in her life. So later, as we sipped a glass of wine to welcome her back, I explained my theory to her. About how I'd been masking my true feelings.

She looked dubious. 'You seem sincere enough to me. But I'll tell you what: Mum's terrific for talking through things like that. She's talked me through a few beauties.'

Consequently, a few weeks later I found myself sitting with May in the comfortable old kitchen and sipping coffee. I explained the situation to her. She was such a loving, patient lady, I found it easy to tell her all my silly foibles.

She looked at me earnestly. 'Darling, you're starting at the wrong end. You may be a Speech and Drama teacher but you don't do well at acting in real life situations. You're too sincere for that. You need to start at the beginning and let yourself *feel* your feelings. Stop suppressing them and telling yourself you're a calm, unemotional girl. You *are* quite a calm person as far as I know but we'll see how you go when you let yourself feel your emotions properly.'

I stared at her, thinking I'd been an idiot.

'It's an understandable response to your home situation,' May continued. 'You'll gradually find, as you let yourself feel more, there'll be some people you're comfortable to share your feelings with and just a few where you'd be better off keeping that mask so you're safe. I doubt you'll want everyone to know everything you feel.'

It sounded sensible. I thanked her and said I'd try it.

I found it hard at first. I felt angry with Viv for speeding a bit on the way back to Brisbane but I realised this was not the time to tell her when she was so uptight herself. Then I settled down as I thought about how well she was coping in the face of her situation. I was beginning to understand that, in a way, she might genuinely love Nate, problems and all.

'Sorry,' she said out of the blue. 'I was speeding.' She pulled back to the limit. I smiled inside myself.

## CHAPTER 14

MAY DIDN'T BOTHER with rubber gloves for washing up these days. She always seemed to be in a hurry. She lathered her hands with expensive hand lotion several times a day and before bed at night. That would have to do. She frowned out the window at the hills, gentle humps lying peacefully shoulder to shoulder. All hazy blue today. There'd been a mist this morning. It was always nice when the trees emerged, branch by branch, from the white haze and she could enjoy their friendly green shapes.

She frowned. Vivvie was in a mess. She must be in love with Nate who, sure enough, had turned out to be on drugs. She'd never felt comfortable about him. Worse still, he'd been selling drugs to younger people. What would her lovely daughter want with a man like that? How could she trust him? Vivvie could have had her pick of so many nice young men.

Bert walked in from work on the tractor. He hung his old army hat over the knob at the top of a chair and sat down. 'Cuppa tea, love?'

'Sure.' She sounded flat.

'What's wrong, May? Tired after Vivien's antics?'

May sighed again. 'Well, I don't know, Bert. If it's not one thing, it's another. When we were their age, you were off to war. They were terrible times, all right. I never did learn to enjoy milking the cows while you were away. There I was, a young woman with a baby, running the place with all those farm girls helping. I'd done my nursing training but I put my professional life on hold. Then it was a juggling act when you came back from the war and I had a baby to look after. The young people who came to work here were a mixed lot. A few lovely girls, a nice young man, and a few silly young things. I never knew from one minute to the next what they'd be doing. But we got by. I think they found me a bit dull. They liked to get out to town, such as it is, a tiny place, but Alice Baker told me they got drunk most nights. She said the noise was something terrible.'

'Well, all that's over now, love. We got through and I came home in one piece. Okay, you say I never had this grumpy streak before but, May, I got off lightly. Some of the blokes, if they came back home at all, left parts of their bodies in the war zones. Worse still, parts of their minds. We've done well, love. And got six beautiful kids.'

'The thing is, Bert, it's *not* over. World War Two is, but people seem hell-bent on destroying themselves. If it's not war, it's drugs. Look at Nate. And now it's war again with Vietnam. Not that I understand why we have to take part. It's their war, not ours. I'm praying Alan isn't called up. I think he's too old. Please, God! I think it's the nineteen-year-olds.'

She clicked her tongue. 'Just out of school.'

'This National Service! I like the idea of freewill, thank you very much.' Bert heaved himself out of his chair and put an arm around her shoulders. 'You *are* wound up, aren't you? I suppose it's Vivien who's started all this. And I don't know if Claire's much better.'

'Bert, I'm afraid Vivvie's really fallen for Nate. She might even be thinking she'll marry him. I keep encouraging her and Claire to get themselves serious boys who really do want to get married but it's no use. Vivien's always had a soft spot for Nate.'

'Well, love, aren't you forgetting what I was like when I was around his age? I was a real rascal. Gave both my parents some grey hairs. And you fell for me. Even though I was on the wrong side of the law for a little while there. Nothing serious, mind you—but you remember when I helped myself to some cigarettes from the local shop? A friend dared me to and I was never one to ignore a dare. Not in those days. And you used to find me attractive when I was at my craziest. You were a bit of a wild one for a year or so there.' He frowned. 'The war was hell but it actually knocked some sense into me. I'd never encourage someone to do stupid things like that again. One thing leads to another. It's a no-win way of life.'

'Well, Bert, I don't see Nate being called up to war, the way things are. He wouldn't make much of a soldier. He's too old anyway. The thing is, love, people need a purpose in life. This friend of Claire's, Mark, he's dithering around and stringing her along. Got a good job at the university but he doesn't seem to feel any purpose in it. I don't get the feeling he knows what he wants in life. And there's poor old Claire, madly in love with him, faithful all the way, and he could be just playing with her emotions. Such a lovely girl. Vivvie was lucky to find her to share their living place. But I don't know—and who can tell how Claire and Mark's relationship will pan out?' May untied her apron and hung it over the rail beside the oven. 'It's more than that too, you know, Bert.'

'What?'

'There's something different. Young folk these days seem to think they know better than their elders. They'll try anything. They're searching for meaning. Do you think it's because most of them have tossed religion overboard?'

'It'll be part of it, that's for sure. But God's bigger than all that and He'll get through to them in His own way and time. Actually, you might be right. It could be the root of the whole thing. Well, one of the roots anyway.'

May looked at Bert with a puzzled expression. 'People do seem to have changed. This Vietnam War's making them all angry. All these protests and what-not. I remember "our" war, Bert. It brought out the best in everyone. Remember how your mother helped me run this farm? She still looked quite a lady even in gum boots. She had all the girls jumping to her tune. But they loved her. And I was up at the dairy milking the cows every morning and evening and trying to act the lady of the house. I learnt to handle it, well, more or less. And I'd help your Mum in the house during the day. All that furniture to keep clean and in order. Baking for all those working girls. You know, I miss the wonderful veggie garden Nancy and Maud made.' She pointed down towards the river. 'We had our own fresh veggies every night and salad for lunch. For a while we even had a stall out the front to sell vegetables and a bit of fruit. People loved buying fresh produce and it was hard to get at times. But this is so different. Not that it affects us much here.'

Bert grunted. 'That's why the kids are angry about it. A dirty war, they call it. And in one way it is. Like you say, it's not our war. God alone knows if we're meant to be in it, helping those blokes, or not. It's messing our boys up, that's for sure.'

'But, Bert, it hasn't really touched Vivvie. She shouldn't be so up and down. Claire's a lot more stable and she's got that father who came home from the war with crippling migraines. Her mother's worn out looking after him at times. Nice woman, too. I don't know. Vivvie was such a lovely child. Bright as a button. I never thought she'd be the one to bring me grief.'

'Don't jump your fences, May. Vivien hasn't done anything too bad yet and I'm praying it'll stay that way.'

Later that day May was out under the riverside fig tree with a cup of tea and a scone straight from the oven. She loved relaxing there, looking down at the river, gleaming white in the late afternoon light. She couldn't get Vivvie off her mind. She couldn't understand it—why on earth did she keep going back to Nate?

Bert's heavy footsteps crunched on the big fallen leaves behind her. 'Mind if I join you?'

'Please do,' she smiled up at him.

He put a loving hand on her shoulder. 'Still thinking it all over?'

'Mmm. Sort of. You know, when we were young, we didn't have the choice Vivvie and Claire have with all those nice young men at the university. Goodness me, you and I had been best friends ever since those bus rides to high school in Nambour.' Her eyes twinkled. 'Remember the day you asked if you could sit with me?'

Bert laughed and squeezed her shoulder. 'How could I forget it? It took me a while to get up the courage to ask you and I was holding my breath to see if you'd let me.'

'Bert, Vivvie's got so many fellows to choose from. Do you ever wish you'd had a lot of nice girls to pick from? I think I was just there, wherever you were so often, you got used to me.'

'Used to you! I used to get butterflies in my stomach every time I knew I'd be seeing you. I was attracted to you and you were such a nice person. I felt like I could talk to you and that was important to me then. Mum and Dad were having a bit of a hiccup in their relationship—they got over it—but it seemed like my world was falling apart and I needed a friend I could trust. May, if I had all the girls in the university, I'd still have chosen you. Anyway, I did meet a lot of nice girls. All my friends at Gatton made sure their sisters met me. Some of them were beautiful girls. But there was never anyone I gave a second thought to. You were always the one for me.'

'Oh Bert, I don't deserve you. I was a bit of a flirt when I went nursing. We girls all went out on group dates sometimes.

I liked lots of boys. But I always knew I could go running back to you. You were my best friend. Maybe that's where Vivvie gets that flirting from. It's my fault.' She sighed.

'Well, you turned out all right. Fantastic. And I have no complaints. You chose me when you were only about twenty or thereabouts.' He put his arms around her and kissed her cheek. 'Vivien will find her way.' He stood up and stretched, then strode over to the tractor.

May wandered down to the riverbank. Here she could stroll along and talk to God. She needed His input as well as Bert's at the moment. She listened first to the peaceful, murmuring river song, then sat under a camphor laurel tree and watched the water run quietly by.

## ~ *Part Seven: Claire* ~

# CHAPTER 15

WHEN WE ARRIVED HOME at our cottage, I was dying to know the outcome of Viv's discussion about the Big Issue with her parents. I'd left them alone, except for my own one-on-one time with May. And meals, of course. I didn't want to upset Viv while she was driving on the busy highway so I waited until she'd unpacked. Then I made a cuppa and sliced us each a piece of chocolate cake.

'Time for a cup of tea, Viv,' I called at her bedroom door. She sat amid an untidy pile of rumpled clothes, looking a bit lost. Several messy curls poked up from her hair. She stood up and followed me into the kitchen. She looked calm enough so I asked, 'So how did it go?'

'Oh Claire, it was heart-breaking.' She sniffed and grabbed a tissue. 'Dad was predictably angry and worried about the younger kids. Sam's a teenager now—spunky kid— and he seems to like Nate. But Mum was her typical self too.' Viv sighed. 'She was so sorry for Nate, would you believe? Honestly, Claire, this is Mum: "Oh Bert, we should have realised. I'd wondered why he spent so much of his holidays here instead of with his own family. And I never could get him to talk about them. He joked about it if I asked. But the poor boy was hurting—he must have been—to get into such terrible things. I wish he'd shared with us and we'd been able to pray with him. It might have made all the difference." And she kept on about how she had failed Nate and he was our friend and all that.

'So I said, "Well he still is our friend. He'll probably get out of that scene now. And he's fun. We all enjoy his company." But Dad said, "I don't want his influence on young Sam. Sam's just at that stage. I won't have it." And they went on and on about it. So I took a deep breath and said, "Well, I'm still friends with him. And I won't be taking drugs."

'Dad looked grim. And he can be grim, Claire, oh boy, can he! He said, "He's not coming here, at least until he's had time to prove he's off drugs and stopped that shocking behaviour selling them, and cut all those influences. If you're silly enough to see him, Vivien," and he gave me a funny look, "you'll have to see him in Brisbane or elsewhere. He is not welcome on this property for now."' She giggled. 'I probably had tears in my eyes.'

We chatted about other things for a while, then I went back to do some lesson prep for my speech pupils.

Viv's head poked around my doorway. 'I nearly forgot to tell you. Would you believe I'm going out to dinner tomorrow night with Pete Rogers? You remember him from our early uni days. That yummy nice psych lecturer and tutor. I'm looking forward to it.'

'Great.' An attractive man who wasn't Nate might be a good thing. Viv still tended to prefer going out with a variety of men.

'Who's this girl Sally who keeps asking about Nate?' I asked Vivien later.

She shrugged. 'I don't know anything about her. Oh—you don't mean that untidy, hippyish girl with the long brown hair?'

'That's her. She's in my Australian Literature tute. When she turns up, she is, anyway. She's not very with it. But she asked me if I knew what was happening to Nate. I barely know her and she's a bit far-out so I just said I didn't know.'

Despite our disappointment and disillusionment with Nate, we both felt oddly defensive if other people criticised him. For so long he'd been one of us. We felt unable to break the tie completely. Yet I would never be able to trust him again.

Despite her initial excitement, Viv was curiously subdued after her evening with Pete. 'Everything okay?' I asked her.

She shrugged. 'He's ready to get married. He wants kids NOW! Says he won't go out often with anyone who doesn't take the relationship seriously, meaning, hoping it leads to marriage. Claire, I'm not ready for that. An engagement might be fun—a nice long one. Years.'

'Is he interesting to talk to?'

Viv blushed violently. 'Very interesting. Oh gosh, he knows what questions to ask. He ended up knowing more about me than Nate or maybe even you know. I actually learnt things about myself while we talked. He's into personalities and why people make choices and all that. I felt embarrassed about my relationship with Nate. I mean, I suppose it's based mainly on attraction. Emotional and physical. That's fine but there has to be a lot more. And of course there's heaps of fun with Nate but ...' She paused. 'I always assume he's got real depth because of his talk about philosophy and all that. But I am just assuming. So Pete's got it more together in all those areas. I only told him a little bit about Nate and our relationship but he switched modes and became like a shrink and I felt like a worm.'

'Well, at least you know he's not the man for you.'

Viv blushed again. 'I guess not. He's attractive, though.' She shrugged. 'He didn't even give me a proper good night kiss. Only a bit of a peck.'

She went to her room, then came out in her pyjamas and put on a saucepan of milk to heat. 'I'm having milo. Want one?'

'Thanks. I do feel like one.' We often had a hot drink before bed at night now.

'Let's invite Sally to dinner one night and check her out,' I suggested.

'Okay. Might be fun. We should be friendlier towards her anyway. We see her nearly every day but we barely know her.'

After our next tute, as we packed our briefcases, I asked Sally, 'Are you free next Thursday evening?'

She nodded quizzically.

'Like to come to dinner at our place?'

'Yeah. Love to. Thanks.' She looked brighter as she hurried away. Perhaps she'd actually be nice once we got to know her.

On the afternoon of her visit I decided to skip the tute

and bake a homey meal for once. Viv was busy showering, then getting ready in the bathroom. So I began putting out the ingredients to make an interesting version of shepherd's pie. Lots of herbs in the mince.

Viv came out, and announced: 'Just slipping over to the shops.' She headed down to the garage.

A knock sounded at the door. Surely Sally hadn't skipped the tute as well and come this early? I hurried to open it.

Suze stood there looking miserable. She never called in. Claimed she didn't feel welcome with Viv there. Talk about bad timing. 'Come in, Suze. I've only got a minute or two, though. We've got visitors to tea.'

I dared not invite her to tea as well, assuming Viv would react.

'I'm just needing someone to talk to,' Suze said in a low voice. 'Jeff's having coffee with Ophelia, would you believe.'

*Yes, I'd believe anything of Jeff.* 'So...?'

'He's my *fiancé*, Claire. I love him. I don't trust Ophelia.' To my dismay she began to sob loudly. She said Jeff had told her he needed to sort out a mix-up about something discussed in a tute group. Suze was unsure whether to believe him.

*Oh dear.* Viv would be back any minute. The shepherd's pie needed to be in the oven. So I patted her shoulder and tried to calm her down. After a little while, she stopped crying. Her face was a mess with mascara everywhere. I hadn't realised she wore mascara.

We had a quick cup of tea and then my conscience made me tell her, 'You'd better go and wash your face before you go if you want to impress Jeff.' I pointed her to the bathroom.

She ducked inside and splashing sounds emerged, then she came out looking red-faced. As I waved her off, I said, 'At least he's being honest with you. If there was a real problem, he wouldn't have told you. He must have had a genuine reason.'

She thanked me and drove away.

I returned to my chopped veggies. Soon the mince and potatoes were cooked and by five o'clock I put a delicious-looking shepherd's pie in the oven.

Viv came clattering back in. 'Mmm! Smells great! Veggies too!' She rushed around, hoping to be ready on time.

'Yes. Even ice cream and home-made chocolate sauce for dessert.'

Sally arrived right on time but still dressed hippy-style. She had combed her hair for the occasion. We talked about *Riverside* as an easy starter. Sally had obviously heard a lot about it but Viv didn't invite her for a visit. I must admit, I was relieved.

'So who are you going out with at the moment?' Viv asked her. I cringed. Would Sally be ready to discuss this? But sure enough Sally laughed and told us. 'I've got a long-term man. Blake. But we've agreed that I'm free to go out with other men while I'm at uni. Just to get it out of my system, you know. So I'm getting to know as many blokes as I can. Just so I'll be sure Blake's right for me before we settle down. So I'm actually going out with several guys at the moment. It's fun. Most guys are nice if you give 'em what they want.'

Viv gave a tight smile. 'I guess so.'

Sally took a deep breath. 'But I've met a bloke recently. One I really like. I'm actually feeling unsure about Blake at the moment because of this guy.'

'Who is it?' Viv looked tense.

Sally gave a seductive smile. 'Ask me no questions and I'll tell you no lies.'

'Oh. Okay.' Viv's terse speech always meant she was angry. She changed the subject to talk about the Beatles and their songs, which she loved.

Soon afterwards, Sally left. I shut the door quickly and said, 'She'd better keep her hands off our guys.'

Viv pulled a face. 'She's doing the rounds of the guys. She even said so. I've told my parents I'll only see Nate occasionally. But that'll make him more vulnerable with Sally and those girls.' She groaned. 'I'll stay away from him for a while, though.'

I would have run a mile.

'I feel sorry for Sally,' I said. 'She's had a harder life than either of us. Her mother doing the single mum thing in a society where you didn't do that. They would have been ostracised.'

'She's doing all right for herself now.' Viv made a snorting noise.

I laughed but felt uneasy. Later when I was half-asleep, I remembered Sally asking about Nate.

The following evening Viv was dressing for a party. 'Claire, have you seen my bracelet?'

'No. Sorry. That pretty one your father gave you?'

'Yes. And I had a little gold squiggle added to it with Nate's N and my V in a knot. I like to think we're sort of joined. But Claire, I can't find it. Would you keep an eye out for it?'

'Sure.'

# CHAPTER 16

THE NEXT TIME we spent a weekend at *Riverview*, I was keen to spend some time relaxing and thinking about our complex life. After an enjoyable evening, I went to 'my' room but was too sleepy to think about it all. I reminded myself of my decision to spend some time alone in my favourite spot near the river. There'd been a few times now when I'd sat under the jacaranda tree beside those fragrant camphor laurels, breathing in their sharp freshness, listening to the whisper of the wind in the river oaks. Sitting in that peace, I'd felt I understood some of the situations facing me. Our lives had become so complex. It had begun with that mysterious feeling as I stood in the river sensing something ominous, and Tom had told Viv about Nate's disappearance.

I woke early the next morning, dressed quickly, had a glass of milk and slipped out the side door and down towards the river. I sat where I was hidden from the view from the kitchen window, and tried to think. *Blank!* So after a few minutes, I relaxed and enjoyed watching the early glow on the river.

Perhaps inspiration would come. Enlightenment about Viv's messy situation? What on earth would she do really? Not that she'd do what I suggested. I watched the kingfishers diving in and out of the muddy bank on the far side. I breathed in the fresh scent of camphor laurel. I was none the wiser, yet gradually I sensed a scary feeling. A feeling I shouldn't trust Nate at all.

I sat for a bit longer, enjoying the peace and the little birds. Watching the river. Then I said to myself, *Well, that'll be easier said than done regarding Nate.* He was in our lives even when he wasn't there bodily. Viv lived and breathed him most of the time.

I wondered if the various feelings I'd experienced on the riverbank were somehow a mysterious, intrinsic part of that place or ... what? Perhaps I relaxed enough to access some inner part of my mind or emotions I usually squashed out of the way? One thing was for certain: I wouldn't tell Viv about these feelings or even my secret times by the river. She had enough on her plate—and she did seem to love Nate.

So I strolled back to the house and made myself some breakfast. May had told me to help myself, so I took a jug of milk from the fridge, then reached into the old wooden cupboard and pulled out some Weetbix and honey. The kettle was already boiling so I assumed someone would join me soon.

Sure enough, Viv walked in after a few minutes. She looked happy and relaxed, ready to enjoy the day.

We were tidying the cottage a few days later when out of the blue Viv said, 'Suzanne looks amazing when she takes the time to tidy herself. That gorgeous red hair. Tom loves red hair. He's got a real thing about it. We reckon he'll marry a redhead.'

'No kidding. Well, why don't you invite her home? I realise you don't like her but she's got a nice side. I know she's a bit of a rough diamond.'

Viv looked away. 'It's not that. I wouldn't like to see Tom involved with her. And he'd love that hair. That'd get his attention and it might go from there. But Claire, she's not right for him. And it'd be my fault they got together if I asked her home.'

'Would it matter? As long as she gets free of Jeff and the drug scene. Oh, I suppose Tom deserves someone who hasn't been into that yuck. I'm not sure where Suze is actually at.'

Viv shrugged her skinny shoulders and changed the subject. Suddenly the thought dropped into my mind: *Viv wants to keep Tom for herself in case it doesn't come together with any of her current guys. And Nate's blown it as a husband for her.* And yet, she loved him. I hoped she'd get over it.

Viv interrupted my thoughts. 'You know, I never did find my bracelet. You don't think Sally might have—um—well, stolen it? She went to the bathroom. And I think I left it on the bathroom bench while I got ready.'

My stomach tensed. 'I'll see if I can find a way to mention it to her.'

The next day, sure enough, Sally sauntered up to the table where I was sitting. I was nervous about approaching the bracelet subject but Viv implied that Sally had been more my guest than hers so I was responsible.

I breathed in deeply and reached out to any god who might be up there. 'Sally, Viv can't find her bracelet. I don't suppose you took it home by mistake?'

She looked astonished. Then: 'Are you implying I stole it?' She swore. 'How could you? I trusted you and came to dinner there. Now you're accusing me ...' She was furious and I glanced around quickly to see if anyone was listening. Everyone seemed involved in their own conversations.

'I'm not actually accusing you at all. But it has disappeared. And you were the last one to see it, I think.'

She looked me in the eye. 'No. Sorry about the bracelet but I never even saw it.'

I told Viv.

Viv frowned. 'She's lying. It's definitely not here.'

A few weeks later while I was making coffee, the phone rang. I put the cups on the bench and went to answer it. To my surprise, Viv beat me to it, grabbing the receiver with a slightly shaky hand. I shrugged and left her to it.

She was blushing while she talked to whoever had rung. *One of her admirers?* There were several of them.

She hung up.

Not that this was any of my business, I asked curiously, 'Which of the boys was that?'

She laughed. 'Nate, actually.'

'Gosh! You'll have to be careful if you're going to see much of him. He can't go home with you. And Viv, how can you know when he's telling the truth?'

She wriggled her bony shoulders. 'I'll know. He's been my friend for years. He's in a flat at the moment but he's going back to work at Tom's place soon. Part-time anyway. He's worked there for years so I've seen lots of him. Even when I was at home, I often slipped over and met him there. Nate's okay, Claire, but he's made mistakes. I think he's hooked on some of these drugs he uses. But he'll get over it.'

'I wouldn't be able to trust him after the last drama.' I poured boiling water onto the coffee and stirred it. 'He's done something dreadful.'

'Honestly, Claire, he's a lovely guy on the inside. When you get to know him better, you'll see. He's sensitive and thoughtful. And fun, of course.'

And so I watched Nate become one of Vivien's men. At times I remembered the feeling I'd had on the riverbank, not to trust him *at all*. But Viv went out with him as often as— or even more than—the others she liked. She was usually flushed and bright-eyed after her times with him. I tried not to worry about them. Well, about Viv. She seemed very gullible these days.

She still took off without warning to visit friends while I studied. She studied too but her top-of-the-class type intelligence enabled her to sail through her exams with minimal work, while I had to study quite hard to get good results. 'You'll be just like Nate if you keep this up,' I said a bit nastily one night. 'Disappearing like this.'

Viv looked surprised. 'It's only visiting friends. No big deal. Certainly not drugs or anything. I guess Nate and I are both spur-of-the-moment people. We don't like planning. I like surprises.'

'I don't. I like to know where I'm going.'

The next night we were at a party at John's place. The air vibrated with loud Beatles' music. A softer song floated through the room and several couples were dancing. John had rigged up a light covered in multi-coloured material so the walls swam with soft blues, reds and purples. *Psychedelic*, they called it now.

'Don't look!' I whispered to Vivien as Mark and I danced past her. I'd spotted Sally with an arm around Nate. Sally was in one of her hippyish outfits, a long semi-transparent Indian cotton dress with very little underneath it.

Of course Vivien turned and saw them. She looked tense but continued dancing with a med student she'd met only that night. Nate looked up and saw her. He wriggled free of Sally and grabbed Viv from the med student's arms. Viv was flushed. They were theoretically only friends but if Nate wanted to take out both Sally and Viv, he was playing with fire.

Later at home, Mark wanted to come in but I was tired and felt concerned about Viv. Mark was grumpy with me for saying I was tired but he kissed me goodnight in the car.

There was no sign of Viv or Nate at home but soon after I began sipping milo, I heard the key in the door. Viv's giggle. Then she came in alone.

'I didn't know if you'd be comfortable having him come in,' she told me.

'Well, it's not a matter of me feeling comfortable or feeling anything at all. It's you. Where's all this going? Viv, Nate's a dear—sometimes—but he's not long-term partner material.'

'Says who?'

'Says me. Honestly Viv, you must realise that. He's on parole, for goodness sake.'

She sighed and tears filled her eyes. 'I know, I know. But I've always been very attracted to him. And he's so affectionate.'

That was obvious. Feeling worried about her, I decided to go for her vulnerable areas. 'What would your parents think? Your father with his strict side.'

She shrugged. 'It's actually only my business. I want to go out with him for a while anyway. I'll still go out with other men occasionally. But I want to see how Nate and I get on if we try taking it a bit more seriously. A loving relationship might get him off drugs. I reckon that'd be all he needs. He comes from a messed up family, you know. And he's fun. Gosh Claire, you can't talk. You and Mark often do crazy things. Mark's just about as wild as Nate.'

'Vivien, Mark's not on drugs and he's not in favour of them. He's got a brilliant mind and he plans to look after it.'

'Well, good for him. Claire, give Nate a chance. Please.'

*So what else can I do?* 'Okay.'

'By the way,' Viv said, 'I still haven't seen my charm bracelet. You know the one? It's special because my parents gave it to me. It's gold.'

'No! Sorry.' If Sally was lying, she had it. But knowing Viv, it could be buried under a pile of clothes.

She shrugged. 'Oh well, it'll turn up. But I still think Sally has it.'

# Chapter 17

Mark's heavy steps rattled the front stairs of our cottage a few mornings later. He looked wind-blown and elated. 'You home, Claire?'

I tidied my hair and went to the door in my old jeans and a striped t-shirt. Fortunately Mark was used to seeing me in casual clothes. 'Hello! This is a surprise. I thought you were going out with the boys today.'

'I've got something to show you.' He grabbed my arm and led me downstairs and out to the roadside. There stood an old Harley-Davidson with a sidecar. I'd never seen one up close in real life before.

'Anytime you need a lift—or if we're going out—you get to ride in the sidecar,' he announced proudly. 'In the daytime anyway. And in fine weather for now. Come and have a go of it.'

I climbed into the big old sidecar and Mark swung his leg over the bike and started the engine. We roared down the street. My hair whipped around my face but I'd have to wear a scarf to get to uni or anywhere like that. I laughed involuntarily as we skidded around a corner and pebbles scattered everywhere.

We came back up the street and I asked Mark in for a cuppa. 'You're not joining any of those bikie gangs, are you?' Concerned, I looked him in the eye.

Mark shrugged. 'Not yet, anyway. I've got my hands full enough but I enjoy riding so I may take it further after a while. Still getting used to it myself. I'll probably use the car at night and the bike in the daytime.' He paused. 'By the way, how are you managing teaching your drama without driving Viv crazy? I mean to say, she'd just be getting home from teaching *her* pupils and *your* pupils would be arriving here.'

'It's fine. The room you helped us renovate under the house, you know, the ex-tool shed, works really well for a Speech and Drama studio. Viv hardly knows anyone's there. She goes straight up to the kitchen or her own room. The kids are probably a bit noisy at times but not often. And she enjoys seeing them here—well, so she says.'

'Takes all types. Couldn't handle it myself. If you lived with me, you'd have to build a shed in the backyard away from the house.'

*Oh no. Doesn't he like having children around?* That didn't bode well for my hopes of marrying him and having a family.

'By the way,' he said, 'that chick Sally looks interesting. Quite appealing, actually.'

'Mark!' My heart sank.

'Well, she does. You're good-looking but you could make more of yourself and try to look more attractive to guys. You dress so sensibly. You always look nice. Always. But too old for your age.' His forehead wrinkled in a concertina of folds. 'But look Claire, you're great. You're lots of fun. You just don't try much with your appearance.'

'I don't want to look any more *attractive to guys*, as you put it, thanks. I get plenty of compliments.'

He shrugged and soon went down and roared the bike into action.

*Fun but not appealing-looking like Sally? Is that who I am?* I just didn't care as much as some girls about my clothes and I had to watch my spending. But 'fun'? Mark was the one who was fun and we enjoyed our time together but, most of the time, I took life seriously. I wished he did a bit more, too. He was a serious guy but he felt free to avoid so many issues. Like marriage. I put the issue of my appearance on a shelf in my mind to think about later.

So began a new chapter for me. Sometimes I loved riding in the sidecar but occasionally Mark took crazy risks and I was nervous. It was a vulnerable position, sitting there with no sides or top, the road whizzing along under us and the wind and other cars whistling and roaring around us. Sometimes gravel flew up in a hard spray.

One day Mark turned up with his violin. 'Time I played this with you and even Viv around.' And off he went soaring into beautiful melodies and all sorts of dramatic tunes. Although he played in a group at times, he was quite private about his own compositions, and about his tendency to get on the violin and play whatever his mood dictated. I sensed our relationship was much closer now. He trusted me.

We had one particularly cosy evening at his flat. He slipped out to the nearby shop and bought some Chinese food to bring home, then took a bottle of wine from his pantry. We ate hungrily, then he serenaded me with his own creation on his violin. The melody was beautiful. He was obviously feeling romantic as he played, so I ended up relaxing in his arms once he'd stopped playing.

'At least it's not like my parents, with you,' he told me.

'What are they like, Mark? What's the problem?'

'Oh hell, Dad came home from the war with one heck of a lot of bad moods. He gets mad and blasts Mum at home and in public. Humiliates her. And she's learnt to fight back so she yells at him. It's awful. And he hates my violin-playing.'

Some father. I snuggled in to Mark.

'Claire,' he sounded surprisingly tense, 'I'd feel better about you if you saw less of Nate.'

'What do you mean? The tennis we used to play? When he made it. Which is not at the moment. He's a bit erratic and he's in deep water now.'

Mark gave a heavy sigh. 'Nate's fun. But he's not the friend I'd choose for my sister if I had one. There's just something ... hard to put it into words. I don't feel you're safe sometimes when you're with him.'

*Oh.* Maybe Mark didn't know about Nate's drama. Or maybe he thought we didn't know. Perhaps he didn't have time to read the papers or listen to gossip. He'd soon find out.

And a *sister*? Was that how he thought of me? *Oh dear.* Had I let my emotions run away with me for years? And of course he was right about Nate. More right than he seemed to know yet. I wriggled away from him.

Later that night at home, I thought, it's nice that he cares about my wellbeing. But ... a *sister*! Really?

A few days later Mark rang me. 'Claire, I'll be away for a day or two. I've joined up with a few other bikers and we're doing a ride up to Bargara for a swim. Just for fun. Test out the bikes.'

My heart thumped in my chest. 'Oh, Mark, be careful.'

'It's okay, Claire. I need a few risks for my brain's sake. Keeps it alert. I've been getting wimpy in my old age. Gotta get myself up and running again.'

I shuddered.

When I told Viv, she smiled. 'He's always been like that, as far as I know. A bit like Nate at times. A risk-taker. Actually, he seems a lot milder than he used to be. He had a reputation for taking awful risks. It must be your influence. Hmmm!'

I put my calm face on and went to my room.

'Is Mark ever going to ask you to marry him?' Viv asked one Saturday morning as we cleaned the house.

I flinched. This was my sore point now. Of course I still hoped we'd marry. Sometime. But if he felt I was like a sister? I was embarrassed. So many of our old friends from our Bachelor of Arts days were already married. I'd been a bridesmaid twice now.

Mark turned up at the door and we asked him in for a cuppa. 'Would you like to come on a three-day ride with me and the gang, down the Coast and up into the mountains?' he asked me.

I shivered. 'Mark, I'd love to, but maybe just not yet. I'll find it a bit scary, you know.'

Mark laughed and gave me a squeeze.

Viv seemed happy to keep going out with several men, although she gave most of her free time to Nate. I wondered again if she would ever be able to settle down. She had lots of admirers. And Viv deserved admirers. She was so pretty, light-hearted, kind—and to add to it, her mother was a brilliant seamstress and Viv often appeared in a lovely new dress, different from the styles in the shops but trendy all the same.

I remembered something Mark had just told me, and passed it on to Viv. 'I hear Suzanne's getting married soon.'

'She'll have a hard life with Jeff. I don't envy her at all.'

I laughed. 'She's been going with Jeff long enough. She must know what she wants by now.'

Viv stopped sweeping and wiped perspiration from her forehead. 'Do you think she loves him?'

'Apparently. Jeff's a bit of a surprise package in spite of the drugs. He's promised to help with her father. She's thrilled.'

'But her father's been nothing but a heavy load for her, with his post-war problems. I thought she'd want to get away from him.'

'She loves him. She blames the war for his tempers.'

Viv still looked flabbergasted. 'Well, live and learn. By the way, horrors! Guess what!'

'What?'

'Dan Jones has been called up. You know, National Service. It can even end up with going to Vietnam. Celia's devastated. They're engaged. Gosh, it's scary.' Vivien swore. It always surprised me when she swore as her parents were sincere Christians and she seemed to have their basic values. Viv was still undecided about Christianity, as was I.

Stories were filtering back from Vietnam. It was hard. Dirty. What were we Aussies doing there anyway? That was the catch cry. It seemed plain cruel to separate a newly engaged couple. What chance did that give their relationship?

I sighed. 'Yeah, hellish,' I said. Viv began to sweep again but I noticed her eyes sparkled with tears.

Vivien's parents were still concerned that neither of us was married yet. Not even engaged! Needless to say, we kept it a secret about Viv and Nate's close relationship. 'They'll only worry if they know,' Viv assured me. 'And Mum says your mum feels like she does.'

I refrained from telling her I was concerned myself.

We were at *Riverside* for a weekend when the husband subject came up yet again. 'When are you girls going to settle down?' Bert asked. He seemed almost angry. 'You've got into the habit of having fun all the time and I don't know if you take life seriously. What are you getting up to?'

I gazed at him, his face flickering light and shadows in the firelight. He was sitting in one of the antique comfortable chairs but he had tensed up and was leaning forward. I'd never seen him angry before. Well, perhaps he was not angry but worried. My insides knotted up.

'Dad,' Vivien said, 'for goodness sake! We're not up to anything. Claire will no doubt marry Mark sometime soon...'

I flinched.

'...and I haven't made up my mind yet. Yes, I'm having a lot of fun. Better to have fun now than to crave it after I settle down, isn't it? And we're only in our early twenties still. Everything was different when you were our age.'

May sighed. 'I suppose it's good to enjoy life while you're young. But I'd more or less expected you'd find a nice man to marry at the university. You know, I never lacked for fun after I'd met your father and we weren't even twenty when we started going out together. Do be careful, Vivien. There are a lot of men out there who want to use you and then walk away.'

Presumably hoping to change the subject, Viv asked, 'Do you like the music we play?'

May laughed. 'It's all right, I suppose. I can see why it appeals to you. The words are clever too. By the way, I think that flimsy-looking dress you wore yesterday is not at all ladylike, Vivien. It's certainly a pretty dress but you can see right through it.'

'Only the outline of my legs, Mum. There's nothing wrong with that. It's Indian cotton.'

'You could wear a petticoat, Vivvie.'

'Mum! Can't you see, Mum and Dad, you've got a carefully controlled little community of your own here with all your own values and, well, rules more or less. It's not like that in the big bad—wonderful, exciting, changing—world.'

'Well, don't end up like Nate,' Bert said. 'What a mess.'

'Dad, as if we would. But you have to give us the space to find our own way. Life's just different now. It really is.' Vivien flicked her hair off her face and yawned.

As we headed away from the lounge, Viv whispered, 'Maybe it was the war. Like your Dad got migraines. I don't know if Dad always had this super-strict streak. It could be a reaction to the war and all that trauma. You know, Claire, Dad never talks about the war. Not a word. Well, not to us kids anyway. I think he and Mum talk a little bit about it. Mum was farming here to help out then. I think they might have even been married. Not sure. It's silly, but I'm sort of scared to ask.'

Elegant May farming! It was hard to imagine. I had vague memories of Dad's brief allusions to the war but he never actually discussed it with us. A wave of sadness hit me. That was a whole part of Dad I never knew. Did he think I was too weak to cope with it? But then Mum was always so keen to protect him against unrest, even noise, in the family. It was puzzling. I must ask Mum.

Just before midnight I slipped back through the study with its dear familiar book smells, back to my old room with its lacy curtains and bedspread. I thought about anything and everything as I lay there listening to the occasional cry of a night bird. Soon I began to drift. Fragments of thoughts flitted through my mind. The folksong was right. The times were a'changing.

# CHAPTER 18

I WAS SIPPING coffee in the refectory when Suzanne came up. 'Mind if I join you? You looked deep in thought.'

I laughed. 'Course you can join me but I've only got a few minutes before my drama tute.'

'Well, I wanted to ask you something. Something important.'

*What on earth will she ask me this time?* 'Sure. Fire away.'

She looked happy as she told me, 'Remember I told you we're getting married next month?'

*Married. Suzanne.* I tried not to envy her—although I certainly didn't envy her Jeff. 'Everything going all right with Jeff now?'

She smiled. 'Of course.'

'What about your father? Still all good?'

'Oh, that's all fabulous. Jeff's happy for us to move into the house and for Dad to have the granny flat. He'll cope okay with that. And Jeff will mow the lawn and do any of the heavy jobs. Knowing Jeff, he'll even cook the odd meal for Dad if I'm at uni. Dad likes Jeff so it'll all be good.'

'Well, congratulations!'

She paused. 'Claire, I haven't got any sisters I'm at all close to. My sisters are older and live all over Australia. And

I haven't had time to make close friends with Jeff needing my time apart from work and uni. I don't seem to make friends easily. I don't know why.'

I could have told her. Her abrupt manner and her relationship with Jeff scared most of the girls away. Even— dare I say it?—her usually scruffy appearance.

'Anyway,' she continued, 'I wondered if you'd be willing to be my bridesmaid. I really want a proper wedding.'

For a moment I was shocked. I hadn't seen this coming. Then: 'Sure. As long as the wedding's at a time I can do.'

She named a Saturday in a month's time. She paused. 'Um, don't they have weddings in the garden at Vivien's place in the country? It's meant to be incredibly beautiful.'

I nodded reluctantly, knowing Viv wouldn't want her to have her wedding there, although I couldn't see why not. Some of the people who had been married there were only slight acquaintances of the Barlows.

'I'd love to do that. To have my wedding there. Jeff says it's gorgeous. He saw it when he was staying with Nate at Tom's place.' I felt unhappy at the idea of Jeff mixing with Tom and the *Riverside* crowd. But I told myself it didn't concern me. Suzanne continued, 'Do you think ...?'

I shook my head. 'It's only for close friends, Suze,' I part-lied. Her face clouded over and I felt sorry for her. 'Sorry, Suze.'

'Well, it'll have to be in the Botanic Gardens. There are a few very pretty nooks. I guess you have to book one. And, Claire, would you come shopping with me for a bridesmaid dress, one we both like? I've already got my wedding dress.'

Suzanne never ceased to surprise me. She presented so scruffy at uni, I couldn't imagine her going for all the frills for her wedding. We went shopping together in the city and, after trying on a few dresses that made me feel ridiculous, I found an indigo dress that suited me well. The colour highlighted Suze's hair too.

'How will you manage all the expenses?' I asked as we sipped coffee in a little shop in an arcade.

She laughed. 'Dad's got plenty of money now. He inherited heaps. He's really happy about us getting married. So he'll pay whatever for the actual wedding and the reception.'

'Wow, you're lucky!'

She nodded, glowing.

So when the day came, the wedding was in the Botanic Gardens on the river. Suze wanted it done differently from the usual so I stood at the front of the group, waiting for her to arrive. The violin trio began to play a romantic song and there was Suzanne in ivory satin and a long veil. She held a bouquet of trailing blue and white flowers. Jeff had been looking nervous. Perhaps he was wondering what he'd got himself in to. But he relaxed as soon as he saw Suzanne. His face lit up and, for one treacherous moment, I wished I was getting married. Not to Jeff, of course, but Mark was standing in the group, wearing a suit and looking just so handsome.

The service was short and simple but they vowed to love and look after each other until death parted them. To my astonishment I felt my eyes fill with tears. I glanced at Mark. Did he feel as moved by it as I did?

After the service we headed towards the restaurant for the reception. I had to sit at a table with Suzanne and Jeff and his best man but, as soon as we'd finished the first course,

Mark came over, grabbed a chair and sat beside me. His hazel eyes twinkled and his strong, well-shaped hand rested on the table. Hearing Suze talking, I looked towards her. And froze. There, glittering in the light from overhead, was Viv's bracelet on Suzanne's wrist. The memories flashed back. She'd called in for a cuppa just before Sally had come to tea. She'd gone to the bathroom after we'd talked. Goosebumps prickled all over me. I was horrified but I could hardly say anything about it at that moment.

'Nice wedding,' Mark whispered. 'She scrubs up well and you look stunning. Fantastic colour for you.' He paused. 'You're looking a bit tense, though. Everything all right?'

I nodded weakly.

Jake came up and joined us. 'So ... another wedding soon, eh?' He grinned at us.

I blushed. Mark was silent. The crease between his eyebrows deepened and he avoided my eyes. *If only ...*

'Where's Viv?' he asked.

'She wasn't invited.' I tried to make it sound low-key.

'No kidding!' Mark's eyebrows shot up towards his hair.

As we drove home later, my own life seemed a bit flat. All these friends getting married. And I was still chugging along with Mark. No commitment and no assurance there ever would be. I shivered in the evening air, feeling suddenly very alone despite Mark's presence beside me. *Could Mum be right?* And Viv's mum as well, for that matter. Could Mark be one of those men who would never marry?

One afternoon Viv arrived home while I was in between pupils, and I noticed she had been crying. 'What's up, Viv?'

She sniffed loudly and grabbed a tissue from the lace-covered box. 'I'm sick of all Nate's moods. I don't know how I'll cope with him if we actually get married.'

'Married?' I was shocked.

'He mentions it sometimes. It's what I want. Well, mostly I do. But when we have a day like today, I just feel it's all wrong and I want to marry a man like Dad. He and Mum have been so happy. He looks after her. And he makes good decisions. I don't know. I just sometimes feel I need someone who makes me feel safe and relaxed. Cosy. Not having to worry all the time about where things are going.'

What could I say? I, too, would like a man who looked after my emotions as well as his own. Someone who would make me feel safe and peaceful. Would Mark make me feel secure and happy? Sometimes he did. 'Heck, Viv,' I said, 'you need to take it slowly and think about how you really feel.'

'I have a lot of fun with Nate. And you know, I love him. I always will. Even when I have these doubts, I always spring back. I need him.'

I swallowed a sigh.

The next day Viv was out with Nate again and came home radiant.

# CHAPTER 19

AFTER SUZANNE'S HONEYMOON, I summoned my courage and went up to her in the refectory. She was glowing. 'Suze, have a good time?' I was dreading my real subject.

'Fabulous, Claire. You ought to try it.'

*Ouch!*

'Suze, I noticed you'd borrowed Viv's bracelet for your wedding. Did you ask her to lend it to you?'

She looked me in the eye. 'It's not Viv's, it's mine. These things are everywhere. Has Viv lost hers?'

I was floundering. 'Yes. It disappeared after you'd been over for a cuppa that afternoon.'

'You're not implying I took it, I hope?'

'Well, I just need to ask you about it.' I was wracking my brains to think if I'd seen the little squiggle with N and V on it. I hadn't noticed, I'd been so shocked. Perhaps I'd been wrong and it hadn't been Viv's bracelet at all.

'Look in the shops,' Suze said. 'They're everywhere. And so much for trusting friends.'

I felt sick.

I was beginning to feel awkward again about Mark's silence regarding long-term commitment. He was late-twenties now. But, I asked myself, wasn't it normal for a guy to wait until his late twenties? There'd been a rush of young couples marrying in their early twenties, but they must have been very sure of their relationships. The problem was I felt sure about Mark. If he proposed to me that night, I'd accept. I was certain I loved him. I felt complete with him.

Viv had invited him to join us at *Riverside* for a weekend, but only if he was happy for me to come up with her in her car. He jumped at the chance and rode his bike up. Invitations to *Riverside* were highly coveted. It occurred to me I'd love to arrive well before Mark and go and sit in my special place by the river again to see if my feelings clarified in that peaceful atmosphere.

'What's the hurry?' Viv asked.

'I'd love just a little time to myself before Mark arrives. Your place has ... well, healing properties, I guess you'd call it.'

'Oh yes! It sure has. Go for it, Claire.'

So as soon as we arrived, I hugged all the family, had a quick cuppa, then headed down to the riverbank. I sat, watching the water. There had been a bit of rain and the river had risen. The water swirled in brown currents, no relation to the familiar calm, glowing white surface. It rushed along, splashing up the far muddy bank, gouging and scouring out chunks of earth so it reshaped the whole riverside. It was like watching a potter at work. Fascinating. Scary. Most of the birds were quiet but a shower of light rain prompted a whipbird to call its sharp, sweet cry.

I let the scenery soak in. There seemed to be no wisdom for me as I sat there that day. I was dominated by my desire to hope, even pray, that Mark would do something definite. Even if we only discussed it. I felt left out of the flow of life.

A shower came over, splashing sharp camphor laurel scent onto me. As I didn't have a raincoat, I hurried back to the house. Mark had arrived! He jumped up from the kitchen table and hugged me. I laughed, feeling a bit embarrassed with everyone there but I was so glad to see him.

An hour later another car roared into the spot beside the kitchen. 'That'll be Alan,' May told us. 'He's bringing a friend. A psychology lecturer he met at a function and they're friends now.'

I could see Viv battling nervousness and almost hear her thinking, *Well, there are plenty of psychology lecturers. It won't be Pete.*

The kitchen door swung open and in walked Alan. He grabbed his friend's arm and drew him into the kitchen. 'Meet Pete, everyone,' he said, and introduced us all.

Pete was unfazed. 'I already know Vivien,' he told everyone. Viv went scarlet all over her face and even her neck.

Fortunately Pete was easy company and the dinner conversation went well. After dinner, Mark and I sat and talked for a while with Viv, then I was tired and opted for an early night. Just as I began to drift off to sleep, I heard voices. Alan and Viv. Viv was angry. 'Didn't you know I knew him?'

'I thought you knew him slightly but no big deal.'

'Well, you could have checked to see if I was okay about it. He's sort of my friend too. I've been out with him.'

'Well, this is a great chance to get to know him better, isn't it? He's fussy about his women and currently hasn't got a girlfriend.'

'I don't like being manipulated and you know Nate's my man.'

'Well, it's high time you looked a bit further afield. You can do better than Nate, Vivien. Pete's a great guy.'

'He'll think I rigged this.' Viv's voice was high-pitched.

'No, he won't. He's a genuine friend of mine. Relax! Enjoy getting to know him.'

'Well, I'm going to bed. You can have supper by yourself.'

'Don't be silly, Viv. But an early night's a good idea anyway.' And the voices faded.

The next morning, Mark asked me to go for a walk with him. Vivien nodded and grinned. She hadn't been able to invite Nate who was still unwelcome on the property.

Mark grabbed my hand in his strong grip. We walked along the winding gravel path to the bitumen road and headed towards the river with the big bridge over it. Mark seemed reticent to open the conversation, so I tried. 'Suzanne seems happy now she's married, doesn't she?' Subtlety was never my strong point.

'Yeah. Right bloke for that chick, I reckon.'

'Lindy and Bob seem incredibly happy too.'

Mark cleared his throat. 'Um, yeah, they do. It's a matter of knowing it's the right one, isn't it?'

'I take it I'm not the right one, even though we've been going out for years?'

Mark raked his long fingers through his brown curls. 'Oh heck, Claire, what's the hurry? We're still young. You might meet a bloke you like better than me in the next year or two. You know, I don't know if I'm the marrying kind. You're great company and I really like you a lot but ... I'm just not sure.'

I sighed. 'So, are we meant to be going together seriously still?'

Mark avoided my eyes. 'You know, Claire, I like you a real lot and I find you very attractive. But the funny thing is, even after all these years, I don't feel I know you properly.'

I winced. It was the mask thing. Still. I'd been trying so hard to be the girl I thought Mark would want. And it had backfired. I would have to let him in a bit at least. In to my real feelings and ups and downs. He mightn't like me anymore then, but I'd have to take that risk. I took a very deep breath. 'I'm sorry, Mark. I'll try to relax and let you see my real self more. I've been trying too hard to be super woman, I think.' I tried to make light of it and laughed. 'You might decide you prefer super woman.'

A long-beaked water bird swept near us and alighted on a branch beside the river. Feeling embarrassed with Mark, I stopped and gazed at it. Finally, I gathered my courage. 'Apart from that, I know we're fairly young but I want to get married before too long. I want to have a family.'

He looked uncertain. A frown flickered over his forehead. 'Yes, I realise that.'

'I've always wanted that. If you don't want that as your future, we'd be better off splitting up.'

Mark's eyes widened, then he frowned again. 'Hell, Claire, you make it hard. I'm not ready to think about this. And yeah, you'd better let me see who you really are if this has all been you putting on a front.'

I cringed inwardly. *A front?* Surely it hadn't been that bad?

The late morning sun suddenly seemed too hot and draining. I grabbed a tissue from my bag and wiped my forehead. Then I took a deep breath. 'You're nearly thirty, Mark. A lot of our friends are either married or travelling.'

He wiped perspiration from his forehead with a big crumpled handkerchief. 'I do want to travel one day. Not yet though. I'd like to save a bit more money first. I've only been working a few years. I love my job but I'd like to save a bit more before I take off from Oz.'

'So are you planning to travel alone?'

'Hell, Claire, I'm not planning any of that right now. We'll see what happens. It'll be good, however it all pans out.'

We walked carefully across the bridge, listening for cars. The bridge was quite narrow for two cars to pass—and if there were people walking as well—I felt sick when I remembered what Bert had said: 'If that ever happens, just *jump*! Yes, into the river.'

On the other side was a neighbour's property. Lush, vibrant green grass stretched out beside us.

There was the awkward feeling of our unresolved relationship hanging around us as we went back to *Riverside*. Mark headed straight for the shower, while I stopped and had a cup of tea in the kitchen at the old wooden table with Vivien. 'You okay?' she asked.

I shrugged. 'More or less.'

I felt confused about my feelings for Mark now. I tried to push the conflict out of my mind.

How was Viv reacting to Pete, I wondered, but decided not to voice it. Pete must have known about Nate because he made a point of avoiding one-on-one time with Viv. But he was a likeable, interesting man and obviously Viv thought so too. He seemed to like her but kept himself at a distance. Viv had sprung back into her usual lively mode and appeared to enjoy his company in spite of everything.

The following day Mark announced, 'Just going to have a walk and a bit of a think.'

He disappeared, presumably wandering along the riverbank. Then I heard the roar of his bike starting up. A few hours later, he arrived back, hot and perspiring. He came over to where I was sitting reading on an old armchair outside the kitchen.

'Surprise!' He handed me a small square box.

My heart leapt. He hadn't proposed or anything. In fact, he'd said almost the opposite. So surely ... I opened the box, which had been gift-wrapped by the shopkeeper by the looks of it. Inside was a pretty gold ring. On it were engraved my initials and Mark's.

'It's a friendship ring. At least that's one thing I'm sure about. You're a great friend and I want everyone to know it. You're not up for grabs with any old bloke who comes along.'

*Wow!* My initial response was delight. The ring was elegant, made by local jewellery-craftsmen. I pushed down the feeling of disappointment it wasn't an engagement ring. Mark was a great guy and I planned to accept if ever he got around to proposing.

To my surprise, Viv was angry. 'Where does that leave you? You're not about to get married but you're not available for anyone else to ask you out and get to know you on a serious basis either. That Mark, honestly!'

So there I was, still going out with Mark, but with no future I could see in the relationship.

'Why don't you break it off and meet some new guys?' Viv asked me.

I sighed. 'I couldn't do it right now. Not just after he's responded to my talk about our relationship by buying me an expensive ring.'

Viv snorted. 'It's like keeping you on a string.'

'Oh, not really. He just didn't think. It's his way of showing he does care, I think. Well I hope so, anyway.'

'Nice ring, though.'

'By the way,' I took a deep breath, 'speaking of jewellery, I noticed Suzanne was wearing a bracelet like the one you lost. I mentioned yours and she said there are lots the same in the shops.'

'No way! They're not the same as mine! I need to see it. I had that little piece made of gold—I told you about it. A combination of my letter V and Nate's letter N.'

'Well, you'll have to ask to see it. I've done my bit.'

'I will. Don't you worry.'

# CHAPTER 20

'How's Nate managing, on parole and all that?' I asked Viv a few days later.

She flicked her hair off her face and frowned. 'Hard to tell. He's a bit distant. Maybe he's upset but doesn't want to show it. Or cheesed off that everyone knows about his drug problems now. You know Nate. Likes to always be on top of things, or at least to make people think he is.'

'That's a pity, you know. If he was more open about his stresses or whatever's going on, he might get some moral support from his friends—like us—and not have to resort to drugs.'

'Maybe. I don't know if that would work. I think it's almost like a game to him. Outsmarting the system. He's not your average guy. Nice. Gorgeous. But he is who he is and I don't know if he takes input from anyone at all. Anyway, he doesn't view drugs as a problem. He likes them.'

'Dangerous pleasure.'

'Mark took out that pretty blonde girl in your tute last week,' Viv informed me.

I winced again. *Helen.* She was an attractive but easy-to-please girl. Maybe that's what most men wanted in a wife.

Easy going. Go with the flow. And all that would entail. *What about me, wearing his friendship ring?*

Viv became anxious, almost miserable, about Nate's situation. I tried to talk her out of it. 'He's not worth this, Viv.'

She looked me in the eye. 'I love him.'

*Still? Love? Nate?* 'Viv, you could do much better. He's got a drug problem. Your life might end up like Mum's, looking after him half the time. You're intelligent, pretty, vivacious, lots of nice things. You're a real catch for a terrific guy.'

'Thanks, Claire. But so is Nate for a girl. Claire, I love him. I always have.'

A few weeks later, Nate was allowed back to Tom's farm to work. I realised Vivien would make sure she went home again soon to see him.

# Chapter 21

After some serious thought and a few angry moments, I decided to talk to Mark yet again about his commitment to me—or lack of it. Perhaps I'd simply read more into our friendship than he had intended. Perhaps he meant a friendship ring as exactly that and nothing more. *Just friends.* My stomach churned at the thought.

'Mark!' I hurried up to him one evening as he was walking to the Psychology building. We went and sat on an old seat away from the rush. 'Mark, I'm not comfortable with you taking out other girls while I'm wearing your friendship ring. I love wearing it and I realise you're not ready to take things any further but if I'm going to wear it, I honestly think you should stop all this seeing other girls.'

Mark sighed deeply. 'Hell, Claire, you make it hard for a bloke. I don't know what I'm ready for yet. I love you as my closest friend but I'm still attracted to other girls too.'

'Mum told me guys often get attracted to other girls, sometimes even after they're married. They just have to ignore it and stay faithful to the one they've chosen.'

'I'll give it a go, just for you.' Mark sounded reluctant. 'We'll see how it goes.' He looked at his watch. 'Gotta go. I'll catch up more next time. I'm taking a tute now and then a lecture. This is supposed to be my big career.'

I felt annoyed—yet also proud of him. He'd done so well in his exams and had been offered this job as a lecturer and part-time tutor. Mum always reminded me that men were often focused on their careers. If only he'd managed to get our relationship sorted out first.

I walked slowly back to the refectory and I told Viv about it. Shrugging, she said, 'You know what I reckon?'

'What?'

'Mark's too sure of himself. And of you. He needs to get a good fright to get him moving.'

'Like what?'

'Well, you really could go out with another guy and act like you're seriously keen on him. Get a new dress and everything. And make sure Mark sees you. Go on, Claire, you can act. Act as if you're in love with the other bloke. That'll make Mark think in a hurry.'

'I'll think about it.' *That would make me as bad as him. Just when he said he'd try harder. But Viv's often right about these things.*

We were just finishing our coffee when Viv exclaimed, 'Gosh, look at that!'

I looked where she was staring, near the doorway of the refec. There was a stunning girl with auburn hair tied on top of her head, good jeans and a multi-coloured blouse. It took me a few seconds to recognise Suzanne. She'd had a makeover.

'Suzanne!' I exclaimed. I waved to her as she looked in our direction, searching for familiar faces.

'Gosh, married life must agree with her,' Viv said.

'Yeah. She's lost that hard-done-by look. And apparently she still helps her father and Jeff does too. I don't know where they get time to get into the messes they do with drugs.'

'Hello, Claire, Vivien. You're both looking great.'

A few seconds ticked by while we both scrutinised Suzanne's immaculate hair. We'd only ever seen it straggly and her clothes a bit untidy. Apart from her wedding, of course. 'You're looking terrific too, Suze,' I said. 'I gather marriage agrees with you.'

Her face lit up in a radiant smile. 'How'd you guess? I'm so glad to be away from all the pressure of drugs and Jeff wanting me to try them. He's more or less off them now. Got a fright, I guess. He's amazing now. He looks after me. He loves me.'

I didn't find Jeff at all interesting and didn't trust him. 'That's great,' I lied. 'So do you genuinely love him?' I found it hard to understand.

'I wouldn't have married him if I didn't.'

Viv sighed as Suze walked away. 'You know, I sometimes wondered if marriage was a bit of a rut. Although Mum and Dad are genuinely happy. They enjoy life. Well, I've had lots of fun with blokes I've been out with, but I'd like to be as happy as Suzanne.'

I thought about Viv's idea of giving Mark a fright. I'd even planned who to ask out. But then I thought about Mark. Imagined him being hurt and disappointed. And I couldn't do it. He trusted me—and whatever the future brought, I wanted to keep his trust.

Viv grabbed my arm. 'Let's head to *Riverside* for a few days and go for some nice long walks and get some fresh air into our systems. It might give us a new perspective on all this mess. We're still young, you know. All this silly stress over getting married.'

A few days later we were winding our way beyond the turn-off to Kenilworth again. The weather was cooler and Viv told me there was a drought. The vivid shades of green had been replaced by stretches of golden grass and dry-looking brown areas. The trees looked smudgy with dust in the air.

'Mum and Dad will have settled down a bit about Nate now, but it's still a sensitive area to put it mildly. Do you mind not mentioning him?'

I groaned. 'Course I won't, but it must be hard for you.'

She gave a funny little hiccupy noise and sniffed, but kept her eyes on the road.

As we followed the driveway into the homestead, dust flew up in clouds around the car once we emerged from the avenue of trees. Viv peered at the property and sighed. 'As Dad would say, "We need a good flood now."'

I shuddered. 'Sounds awful. It's very dry, though.'

'Look, Claire, some of the trees are wilting. Only a flood will get right down into their roots.'

We pulled up outside the kitchen area. May, eager as usual, ran out to meet us. She hugged us both warmly. I was, apparently, like family to her now. 'Oh, you've got pretty hands, Claire. That ring just sets your hand off. It's lovely. So when's it going to be an engagement ring, or hasn't he said anything yet?' May sounded anxious.

My throat tightened. 'We're taking it slowly. I'm not sure where it's going, to be honest.'

May enfolded me in a loving hug. To my embarrassment, tears ran down my cheeks.

'Darling. There's a time for everything. Don't worry about it. God has it under control. And Vivvie here's still as free as a bird.' She had certainly changed her tune but it may have been just to comfort me. She was like that. Perhaps that's where Viv inherited her whimsical streak.

I doubted God had my life under control when I didn't really believe in him.

Soon we were sitting at the dining table eating another delicious roast meal. May realised we didn't manage to find time for any elaborate cooking back in Brisbane and she went to a lot of trouble for us.

After dinner a curious sense of emptiness filled me. Relaxed and peaceful, for sure, but missing something. *Someone?* Well, I'd be fine once I'd been for a walk tomorrow and let the peaceful atmosphere of *Riverside* soak into me. That would start to put perspective into my complicated relationship. Surely I wasn't missing Mark, considering all the uncertainties between us?

I didn't know how Viv felt about Nate at the moment as he'd backed off the relationship for some reason. It was the most turbulent romance I'd ever seen. But Bert had told her they all needed to give Nate a 'bit of a break to get free of drugs' before he was allowed back to *Riverside*. He had no idea how deeply Viv felt for Nate.

'Phone for you, Claire,' May called.

'Mark! How are you?'

'Missing you. Can I come up and join you girls?'

'Well, I guess I'll have to ask May or Bert. Hang on a sec.' *Wow!* Had he heard my thoughts? So much for our fresh air and solitude with time to think and get things into perspective. I laid the receiver on the pile of papers on Bert's desk and hurried out to the kitchen. May was tidying up the dishes. 'May, Mark has rung and asked if he can come up here and join us. He's lonely!'

May laughed. 'Of course he can, darling. When would he arrive?'

I groaned. 'Knowing him, late tonight. But if you were to say it had to be tomorrow morning, I'd be fine with that.'

'Oh, let him come tonight, if he's that keen. You never know what might come of it.'

I knew what May hoped.

So I told Mark he could come. 'I'm on my way,' he said. 'I was out riding the bike and I stopped at Caboolture for a drink. I'll see you in an hour or so.'

My wonderful relaxed, unwound insides—okay, admittedly I'd felt empty—began to speed up. So much for my escape to this timeless place. Viv pulled a face and went off for an early night. I had another quick shower and slipped into a better dress, just an oldish rust and gold one with an autumn pattern on it. Those colours seemed to suit me.

Then I propped myself up on a mound of pillows on my bed and resumed reading *Catch 22*. I was enjoying it, occasionally giggling as I read. Suddenly there was a knock at the bedroom door and May's gentle voice called through the cracks between the boards, 'Claire, you're getting ready, are you?'

'Yes,' I called. 'Well, in a fashion.'

'Can I come in for a minute?'

'Sure.'

'Claire, I wanted to talk to you about your future, just briefly for now but I wanted to say something.'

My heart rate galloped. I nodded as her face peeped around the door.

'Darling, you've been coming here with Viv for several years now. We love having you. But you girls should be thinking about getting to know the kind of boys who'll marry you.' She cleared her throat. 'I mean, I'm not at all happy about someone like Nate as a partner for Vivien and I don't know if this Mark of yours is much different. He's had you on a string for all these years. Don't get me wrong. I'm delighted to have him here. But I'm concerned that he has no plans to marry you—or perhaps anyone.'

I sat bolt upright. 'Mark's nothing like Nate,' I said indignantly. 'He's a bit on the wild side but he's terrific and kind and I'm in love with him. We have a lot of fun together. And I feel sort of "right" when I'm with him.'

May sighed. For just a moment she sounded like Vivien in one of her down moments. 'Well dear, I felt I had to say something. You're about to see him. He seems to enjoy your company. You're a very attractive girl and there are a lot of nice boys out there who'd love to go out with you, I'm sure.'

Surely she wasn't hinting I should go out with someone like, say, Tom? Tom was a pleasant, kind, good, hard-working man but I didn't find him very interesting. There were plenty of those men around, certainly.

I pulled a distasteful face.

May looked at me and sighed again. 'Oh well, dear, as long as he makes you happy. But I hope he does something more than buy a friendship ring soon.'

'May, you're trying to get rid of me!' I half-joked. 'You think I should get married and stop needing to come here.'

May looked shocked. 'We all love having you here, Claire. But we do want to see you have a happy life. Sometimes I think you and Vivien are a bit too comfortable without being genuinely happy and fulfilled.'

She kissed me on the forehead. 'Good night, darling, sweet dreams. I won't wait up for Mark. You can let him in.' Then she had gone and I was left with a myriad of emotions swirling around. Was I happy? I'd thought I was but ... a proposal from Mark would have helped. And I had no feeling he was coming here to propose.

# Chapter 22

I WENT OUT TO THE KITCHEN as soon as I heard the Harley roar into the yard. For just a moment I wondered if the atmosphere here affected him too. When he rode along that beautiful avenue at the entrance, perhaps he felt all his cares lift off like I did. Perhaps even his cares about where our relationship was going.

My heart began to race. Mark was here! The bike parked outside the kitchen and I hurried over to it. Mark swung his leg off and gave me a hug, then kissed me. I made us a quick cup of coffee and we headed out to the table overlooking the river. The water lay black with touches of moonlight gleaming on it.

I'd been thinking about May's words—which perhaps was a mistake. They seemed to cement inside me, dispelling the *Riverside* timelessness and that carefree feeling.

I knew what I should do. I was glad Mark had come. The gentle loving atmosphere here made me feel secure enough to do what I now believed was necessary. Yet, as we sat on the old wooden seat, gazing at the river glinting silver-white in the moonlight, an errant feeling of romance washed over me. Tugged at my heart.

I needed to speak first, before anything stopped me. 'Mark, I really care about you—but I need to break it off.'

'Claire! You *what?*'

'You heard. I need to find the right man and get married. Have children. Like I said. That's what I want while I'm young enough to enjoy it all.'

'Hell. After all this time. Not "Welcome to *Riverside*" but "I want to break it off".'

'Sorry. But yes, *after all this time*, we're still just friends. Not engaged or anything.'

Mark made a peculiar croaky sound. 'Claire, I don't know if I can cope without you.'

'Well, you don't want to get married and we're not getting any younger.'

He swore again. 'To think I came up for a relaxing, romantic weekend.'

'I'm sorry, Mark, I truly am. But this relationship has had long enough to show its true colours. I need to stop playing at life and start living it the way I want, big picture.'

Mark put his head in his hands and sighed. Then he sat up. 'How about if we try a short term "separation". Say, three months of not going out together at all. Hardly seeing each other. Then see how we both feel about things.'

A weight lifted off me. 'That might work. Again, Mark, I'm awfully sorry. But I need to do something.'

He put a gentle arm around me and stroked my hair. 'It's okay, Claire. I guess I've been a chicken. My parents have got that lousy marriage and I've been scared stiff of getting trapped into the same thing.'

'Oh, Mark. I keep forgetting about your parents. You never mention them.'

'Huh! Well, I never talk about them. They don't even live together some of the time. Don't worry, Claire, we'll sort it out.' He took my hand and led me back inside. I showed him to the room May had designated for his bedroom and went back to mine. My head was whirling.

I gazed out the window. The moon was gleaming white, that eerie unnatural light on the trees and shrubs. I shivered, feeling more alone than ever before, even with Viv and the family in nearby rooms. Then my face felt wet and I realised I was crying.

The next morning I was exhausted after a sleepless night. A note for me lay on the old oval kitchen table.

*Dear Claire,*

*I've gone back home. I'll miss you like hell and I'll actually miss having a weekend here.*

*See how we go for three months.*

*Love, Mark xx*

I must have dozed for a while after all as I hadn't heard him leave. He'd disappeared into the night while I slept. Blow it, I thought, and went back to sleep in some more. That was the plan, anyway. However, soon after I went back to bed, I heard May's voice whispering in the kitchen beyond the wall. 'Now everyone, no shouting. Don't forget Claire's asleep in the next room.'

Several voices giggled.

I rolled over and closed my eyes.

'Vivien, you can't wear that short skirt to church. They'll wonder what you're up to. Haven't you got something to change into?'

Viv whispered back fiercely. 'Does it matter what they all think?'

May's voice, a little louder now. 'I'd prefer to be proud of your appearance. You're a lovely-looking girl and you're my daughter. Some of these people haven't seen you for years.'

A sigh, probably Viv. 'Okay, I'll find something, I suppose.' Footsteps hurried away.

A few minutes later, I heard: 'That's better, Vivien. That blue suits you beautifully. The purple one was a bit too bright for you.'

Then the sound of scuffling as, presumably, they left for church.

By this time I'd given up on sleep and had propped myself up on a pile of pillows. Vivien was going to church. Was it just to keep May and Bert happy? She never went to church in Brisbane. She claimed not to be a Christian and had been annoyed when I said I was open to belief. How could she possibly be going out with Nate one moment and going to church the next? Admittedly Nate was off the scene but ...

I crawled out of bed and washed my face, then dressed and went to the kitchen. Tea and toast would be nice. Mark's face intruded on my thoughts. I dismissed the image.

After I'd eaten and cleaned my teeth, I wandered down to the river. It was a bit too cool to swim so I put on my sneakers and walked to the riverbank. There flowed the Mary River, gleaming silver-white in the morning sunlight, a skinny, shining gash in the parched land, splitting it in half, *Riverside* on this half and the neighbours on the other. It would look stunning from the air, I imagined. I sat down in my special spot and gazed at the water.

I leaned against the jacaranda trunk, stretching up tall, grey and bare, its branches poking bony fingers into the wintry sky. The camphor laurel leaves around me rustled in the faint breeze and crackled underfoot. The air was redolent with their tangy scent. Bigger birds twittered and hopped from branch to branch. Tiny birds sat quietly on the stalks of long grass by the river. Fairy wrens, Viv called them.

If I sensed anything at all as my emotions unwound, it was just an affirmation to be very careful with Viv regarding her religious beliefs. It seemed important, as I mused on it. I felt quite small when I considered the possibility of God's existence. I was dwarfed by the hulking mountains to the north and the hills crouching on the western horizon.

I tried to relax and soak in the beauty, but my break from Mark and then Vivien's sudden attendance at church dominated my mind. Had Viv made a decision to live as a Christian, since she could not have the man she wanted? Or was she pleasing May?

I'd been hoping to feel some clarity about my future or lack of it with Mark. But there was silence inside me and all around me when I thought of him. Silence and peace.

As I heard the Barlows' two cars drive back in and park near the kitchen, with happy voices mingling loudly, I stood up and walked along the narrow track to the house. My mind was filled with the river's song—the peaceful swishing sound of water slipping along the banks and gurgling over the rocks. The dry grass scratched my feet. Even the weeds were wilting. Part of the soil had contracted into splits. Great dry fissures, ugly gashes in the land, like parched mouths screaming for moisture.

'Hi Viv,' I called. 'Did you go to church?'

She blushed. 'Yes. I did. I enjoyed it.' And she began to talk to one of the younger children, so it was clear that was all she wanted to say about church for now.

That afternoon we drove back in the fading light. 'I saw Mark's note,' she said. 'Sorry, I didn't have time to discuss things.'

'Well, there's not a lot to discuss.'

'Gosh, did you have a row? I heard him leave last night. He roared out. Must have been angry.'

Presumably he left during the one time I was asleep in that interminable night. I explained to her we were having a three-month break from our relationship to see how we felt when we weren't going together.

She looked appalled. 'Gosh, that's a waste of time. You'll go running back to him as soon as the time's up. And he'll just go along with it. Nothing will be any different.'

'Viv! That's negative for *you*.'

She shrugged. 'You've spoilt Mark. He's too sure of himself with you. Like I said, he needs a good fright, like ... to see you all over some sexy guy. He just assumes you'll always be there for him.'

'Is that so bad?'

'Well it hasn't got him to propose to you.'

Maybe she was right. I sighed. In my efforts to be sincere, I might be making it too easy for Mark.

Vivien's face lit up. 'Why don't you go to a party with a terrific-looking bloke, a party Mark's going to be at, and act like you've fallen for this guy?'

'Who on earth would be willing to be part of a game like that?'

'Grahame! You know, that guy who obviously likes you. He'd do it.'

'He likes all girls.' Well, I hoped he did. He'd made it clear he liked me, to my embarrassment.

'Well, that's okay. I'll be seeing him in a tute tomorrow night. Would you like me to ask him?'

I would never do it myself. I knew that. 'All right, I suppose.' Doubts nibbled at my insides.

Viv flicked her hair out of her eyes. 'See you later,' she smiled over her shoulder.

And so it was that Grahame picked me up the following Saturday night. I'd taken Viv's advice and worn a pretty dress, fairly low-cut and one that made me look a bit appealing. Well, I liked to think it did.

'Wow!' Grahame greeted me. He opened the car door for me, just like Mark always did. A fleeting image made me wish it was Mark but I dismissed it.

As we walked in to the room where everyone seemed to be dancing and talking, Grahame turned to me and I noticed his intense dark grey eyes. Unnervingly intense. His gaze made me feel too vulnerable. Exposed. Would people think we were going together? That I'd fallen for him? Importantly, would Mark think it?

I caught Mark's eye, then quickly pulled my gaze away. For just a moment I almost gave up and went over and hugged him. But I had to see this through.

'Come on.' Grahame grabbed my arm and we began to dance to Beatles' music. I felt his gaze, almost as if it pierced my mask and saw me, the real me.

The Beatles were singing *Ticket to Ride* and the lights were dim. The smell of incense filled the air. My skirt swirled around as I danced. Grahame's eyes seemed bright and alive when he gazed at me. He clutched my shoulder, leant over and whispered in my ear. 'Claire, you're the only one in this charade who's pretending.'

Giant butterflies flapped inside me. *Did he mean ...?*

'I'm not pretending,' he whispered.

My stomach jolted. Did he mean he was falling in love with me? He barely knew the real me. Cups of coffee, discussion in a tute group, and the occasional dance at a party—that was the extent of our relationship. But then ... I'd been very keen on Mark after one outing. What if Grahame really fell for me and got badly hurt? Because I loved Mark. There was never any doubt in my mind about that.

What on earth would I do? And was Mark feeling hurt tonight after seeing me with Grahame? After letting him kiss me goodnight and making sure he realised I wasn't too attracted to him, I lay awake wondering how to handle this.

At last I knew and the next day I bought a nice card and wrote him a friendly letter, explaining that I was still in love with Mark and this was only a temporary break from him. I hoped with all my heart it was temporary.

The next time I saw Grahame he waved to me but avoided talking. *Oh dear.* I hoped he'd be all right.

'He'll be fine,' Viv said. 'He's taking Jill to a party tonight. She'll give him a good time.'

Viv seemed very content now. I had no idea if she was seeing Nate. She continued going to a local church and apparently enjoyed it. When I had time to think in this crazy time, I wondered about it all.

# CHAPTER 23

I ENJOYED TUTORIALS, especially getting involved in interesting discussions. Viv and I went to different tute groups so we could share various perspectives at home. Several guys took me out but I tended to feel flat afterwards. I missed Mark. And if he'd been at a party with another girl, I'd feel quite jealous. So I willed myself to try harder with other men but to avoid guys I knew were seriously attracted to me.

There was a bit of awkwardness, now, between me and both Sally and Suze. Hardly surprising! I'd be so frustrated if Viv found the bracelet in one of her drawers. But I still felt the one Suze wore at her wedding was the real one.

One night I arrived home from my tute group to find Viv looking a bit concerned. 'What's wrong?'

'You'd better be feeling tough,' Viv announced.

My stomach clenched. 'Why?'

'Mark's taking Ophelia out tonight. And apparently he took Sally out last week. He's having a fantastic time. Well ... let's say he's pretending to.'

*Ouch!* Over the following few weeks, I watched as he turned up at parties with several different girls, all very attractive and popular with the guys. My heart ached.

'Don't let it worry you,' Viv said cheerfully. 'He's just trying to make you jealous.'

'Well, he's succeeding. I *am* jealous.'

'It's just his way of coping with losing you,' Viv said.

'I don't want to *lose* him. I'm just having a break from him to see how it works out.'

'Well, you'd better get it straight in your head what you want, because he could come and ask you out again any time, you know.'

'No. Look!' I stretched out my hand. *No ring*. I'd removed his friendship ring from my finger and kept it in my top drawer among my scant pieces of jewellery. 'It's over for these three months at least.'

'I admit, now I know him, he's a great bloke, Claire. But he needs to get his act together. Hopefully he's having his fun now so he should be ready to settle down after your three months.'

That was about Viv's third different opinion of Mark. I had enough conflict inside myself without getting more from her.

A few weeks later I went home for the weekend. I wore my ring, hoping Mum wouldn't say anything about Mark. It was good to see the old house again. Lee was on night duty so she slept mostly while I was awake but Julie was there, bouncing around the house telling me all about her latest crush.

I was helping in the kitchen after dinner when Mum suddenly asked, 'Are you still going out with Mark?'

'I was. Very much so. But I'm having a little break from him just to clarify things. Have I shown you this?' I showed her my ring.

My heart sank when she frowned.

'What's wrong, Mum?' Although I suspected she was doing a 'mother reaction' like May had.

'Nothing's wrong, love. It's just—well, he's been taking you out for years now. Isn't it time he came up with more than a friendship ring?'

My throat tightened. 'Mum, like I said, we're actually having a break at the moment. You know, to see how we feel when we're not going out together all the time. He's a great friend though, and I have my hopes about how this will turn out. And Mum, it's all okay, you know. I'm young.'

We chatted for a few minutes about various types of relationships but Mum seemed anxious. As I untied the old floral apron and hung it on the hook by the stove, she said in wistful tones, 'Darling, I know I've said it before but don't let life pass you by. It's easily done if you're having a good time. Don't let this Mark blind you to all the nice men you meet so often. Men who want to settle down.'

I swallowed an urge to cry and soon hurried back to my room. Had the two mothers been discussing Viv and me again? 'I think our mothers have been discussing our futures,' I'd moaned to Viv only recently.

'Well, it might have been about how you don't dress to attract,' Viv had said.

'Have you been talking to Mark about that?'

'No! As if I would. Just saying. I know I'm lucky with Mum making most of my dresses but Mum's just as keen to make me look attractive as I am. She might have said that to your mum. Men do notice, you know, even if they couldn't tell you later what you were wearing.'

I'd shrugged. I dressed sensibly. I liked clothes and I loved Viv's pretty, stylish outfits. But she was very slim and slightly taller than I was, so the clothes looked terrific on her. I'd always been content to have dresses I liked, even if they weren't anything special or attractive to guys. I assumed the right man would like me for who I was, not for how I looked all dressed up.

Vivien disagreed. After thinking about it, I agreed to buy one new very pretty dress for starters and see what effect it had.

My new dress was a rusty colour, cut lower than usual for me, and with a shortish skirt. I felt feminine in it and wondered how Mark would react. But it was about two more months before I'd see much of him.

I decided to wear it to the next party. Bob and Lindy were having a get-together I was invited to, and I knew Mark would be there, no doubt with one of his current women. I decided to see if he noticed my dress at all.

'You look terrific,' Viv announced as we left. 'The dress is beaut.'

Mark noticed me as soon as we arrived.

'Nice dress,' he commented as he walked past me to get a drink. I felt great. A lot of people looked at me with what I hoped was admiration. As for Mark, that was it. He didn't say anything more to me. Perhaps he felt it would be inappropriate. As Ophelia drifted past in one of her long, flimsy Indian dresses and Mark gazed admiringly—*lustfully*, I thought angrily—at her, I realised I never would meet his standards. Not in my dress code anyway. He liked my dress but Ophelia's definitely caught his attention.

So I'd decided then and there just to be myself. With or without Mark in my life. Emotions out for all to see—although I realised this might take time. Clothes I felt were 'me' and not some chick who was out to attract all the men.

# Chapter 24

'CLAIRE?' SUZANNE LOOKED a bit dubious as she approached me in the refec.

'Mmm?'

'This is confidential. Are you okay with that?'

'Sure.' I said, hoping she wouldn't talk about Viv or the bracelet.

'Jeff needs a bit of help in staying off drugs. He's done well so far but he's struggling. I'd heard someone say that guy, Tom, out near Vivien's place, takes in blokes who are finding it hard and helps them through it. Is that right?'

I hesitated. Viv had gone to so much trouble to keep Suzanne away from *Riverside*. I was both curious and uncertain about the reasons. Was it really about Suze's red hair? Surely not now she was married. Would I be violating some unwritten law of Viv's or her family's? I had no idea but my stomach tightened with unease. And yet—this was Tom, not Viv or *Riverside*—and Tom loved to help blokes get off drugs. I felt torn.

Finally: 'Yes, he does.'

'Well, how can I contact him? Vivien and I don't seem to hit it off for some reason.'

I had Tom's phone number and gave it to her. Surely I could trust Tom to make the right decision and, if there was anything I didn't know about, he would probably know.

'Thanks, Claire.' She took the number and put it in her wallet and soon let me know Jeff was planning to stay with Tom for a while. 'It'll be hard for me, even for Dad, but it shouldn't be for long.'

As luck would have it, Viv and I were at *Riverside* and had popped in to see Tom—when Jeff arrived. *Oh no!* He had Suzanne with him. Viv had noticed them arrive and was looking tense.

'Come in, guys.' Tom welcomed them in to join us.

Jeff was casually but neatly dressed. Suzanne wore jeans and a pretty golden-brown blouse that highlighted her immaculately combed red hair. Needless to say, she looked beautiful.

We all talked for a short time, with Viv sitting on the edge of her seat and sometimes wriggling her shoulders. I expected she would soon get up and go back to *Riverside*. Instead, Jeff said, 'Well, we need to go and buy some bits and pieces and Suze will drop me off and drive the car back to Brisbane after that. I'll settle in here for a few weeks.'

'Great.' Tom looked happy but puzzled.

As they drove away, Tom stared at us. 'Vivien, what's wrong? Is there something I should know about these people? Have I made a blunder?'

Viv sighed. 'No. It's okay.'

'Fabulous-looking chick, isn't she!' Tom said.

Viv stiffened. 'Well, you always were a sucker for redheads.'

Tom laughed. 'Yes. I love red hair. Shame she's not the kind of girl I like but ... there you go. She's already taken, anyway.'

'Would you have liked her if she wasn't taken?'

Tom laughed again. 'No. She's not my type. You have to admit she's a good looker, though.'

Viv blushed. And suddenly all the missing pieces fell into place. My suspicions had been right. Viv wanted Tom to be available for *her*—even though she was so keen on Nate. As we drove home, I asked, 'Viv, are you keen on Tom?'

'No way. He's not my type at all. But I'd hate to see him with Suzanne or anyone like that.'

So I remained uncertain what she felt. I still suspected she was keeping Tom in reserve in case the Nate relationship didn't work out. But she refused to talk about it.

She slipped her head around my bedroom door later. 'By the way, Tom really has got an obsession about redheads. It'd be good if we didn't extol Suzanne's virtues too often when he's around.' She frowned. 'Anyway, she's married.'

'Is Tom the reason you haven't invited Suze here?'

Viv looked shocked. 'No way. Claire, I knew they were all into drugs. Who knows what she might've said to Mum and Dad? I couldn't risk it. And then there was too much bad feeling between us.'

I should have realised that. But I still wondered if she hoped Tom would be there for her—or even one of her sisters.

# CHAPTER 25

LATE ONE SUNDAY MORNING back at our cottage I was studying but I could tell Viv was bursting to talk. About religion, perhaps. She had maintained her silence about religion although we normally talked about everything. She'd just come in from church.

'Have a good morning?' I prompted.

Her face lit up with a huge smile. 'Great! Thanks.'

'So you enjoy church? Or you've been somewhere else?'

'Both. I enjoy church and, you'll never guess, I ran into a girl from my Drama tutorial there. She's a full-on Christian, just like Mum and Dad. So she asked me to have a cup of coffee with her and we talked our heads off. She's nice.'

'Oh.' I felt out of it all. 'That's great.'

'She's invited me to go with her to a group that meets on Tuesday evenings at another girl's place. I'll go. It'll make me a bit busy, I guess, but no more than going to a party.'

'Sounds good.' I returned to my desk in my bedroom.

Viv's head poked around the door as I picked up a pile of books. 'You could come, if you'd like to, you know.'

'I'd feel out of it, thanks, Viv. I don't believe in all that Christian stuff.'

'But you told me ages ago you were open to it all, but hadn't made up your mind.'

I tensed up. 'That was ages ago. I'm still open-minded but I don't feel ready for church or anything like it. I've got enough on my plate with Mark taking other girls out.'

Viv laughed. 'Well, you didn't expect him to sit at home and wait for three months, did you?'

'I don't know what I thought. I didn't think much at the time. It was a surprise. I suppose I should keep my end of this break from Mark and get on with seeing other guys.'

'Well, make sure Mark sees you with someone else again or at least hears about it. Who's asked you out? Apart from Grahame ...' She giggled and I winced. '... and a few guys you weren't keen on.'

I heaved a sigh. 'Nobody to speak of. Yet, anyway. I may have to tell a few more people I'm not going out with Mark at the moment.'

Viv grinned. 'Tell Suzanne. She'll tell a few people.'

'Good idea.'

'I'll make us some lunch. It's nearly midday.' She disappeared and I stared gloomily at my books.

Over lunch, to my dismay Viv picked up the church topic. 'Claire, this girl I met, her name's Carolyn, she reckons I should be more open about my beliefs now.'

I flinched. *What will that entail? Being Bible-bashed?* 'Meaning?'

Viv smiled. 'Meaning I need to tell Mum and Dad I've actually become a Christian and to tell you and my other friends too. So—there you go, I've told you!'

'Well, it's obviously a good thing for you as it makes you so happy but it's not for me. Not at this stage anyway.' I stifled a giggle. 'Can you imagine Mark's face if I did?'

'Mark! Forget him, Claire. For now anyway. I'm sure there's someone nicer than Mark for you. And to be honest, God's more important than that guy. You know, I'd be surprised if Mark ever gets married.'

There we were again. Viv changed her mind about Mark depending on her latest encounter with him. I changed the subject in a hurry and tried to forget how much I missed Mark. 'Anyway, I don't want to think about church and meetings and all that sort of thing at the moment. It's just not *me*.'

Vivien wriggled her bony shoulders and tried not to look disappointed. 'Maybe you'll get a surprise one day.'

I laughed. 'You're a try-hard. Viv, don't waste your religious zeal on me. I'm a tough nut in some ways.'

She looked at me quizzically. I served some more salad and ate it heartily, avoiding her glance. Fortunately she and Nate didn't seem close at the moment, I thought, as he wouldn't cope with religion either. None of the way-out guys would.

I mused on the fact that Viv never suggested I go out with Tom. I still thought that, in spite of her love for Nate, she was keeping her options open. Tom was the opposite of Nate— quiet, stable. He was also handsome and likeable. Viv liked him. So did her sisters. It had taken me ages to be sure about it as Tom was not Viv's usual type at all.

1966

## Chapter 26

Society was changing. Moral values were less rigid and I was fascinated by groups like the hippies. At university, many of the girls followed the Mary Quant style with their hair cut short and sculpted close to their heads. It looked trendy—and very nice if they had the features for it. Viv tried a modified version on her hair but was not happy with it.

'I'm going to grow it out again,' she frowned as she walked in from the hairdresser. 'It's just not me.'

I wasn't brave enough to try a very short cut. It needed a stylish demeanour, usually accompanied by a very slim figure, to carry it off. I didn't qualify. I was always 'just me' although people often told me I looked great, so most of the time I wasn't worried. I'd spent years growing my hair long, too, so I didn't want it short again. I sometimes envied the girls who stood on the walkway, showing off their new hairstyles. They were nearly all slim too. Trend-setters like the model Twiggy were very thin and led the way in fashions—except for the hippies and beatniks, with their long hair and long, loose clothes.

One morning I stared grumpily in the bathroom mirror. I was still a bit overweight. I'd never get Mark's full attention if

I continued to look so uninteresting. But I couldn't see myself with a mega-short haircut. My weight had always been a challenge. Not that I was fat. But I wasn't very slim or trendy-looking either. I was average. My legs, shown off in miniskirts these days, were not skinny. They were quite shapely though, people told me.

'You just need to break out a bit,' Viv told me again and again. 'Go out with a few new guys. Try different clothes. Experiment and see what works for you. Would you like Mum to make you a dress?'

'Oh Viv, your mother's got enough on her plate without sewing for your friends.'

'She loves sewing. She makes nearly all my clothes. And you're just about family now.' Viv twirled around like a model. 'I'll ask her. That way, you won't have to feel embarrassed if she's too busy and doesn't have time to do it.'

My face was growing hot as Viv headed over to dial the phone and ask May. 'Well, I suppose it's okay. If you think she wouldn't mind. And of course I'd buy the material.'

'How about letting Mum buy it and you can pay her if you want to. She'll have lots of ideas about what to buy for the sort of fashion you and she choose.'

So before I knew where I was, Viv had me on the phone with her mother, discussing styles. I was nervous. What if she thought I wanted dresses like Viv's? I couldn't carry them off. Viv was skinny and pretty.

A few weeks later I was standing in 'my' room at *Riverside*, being fitted for a half-made dress. The material was gorgeous—a muted maroony red in a silky fabric. I felt embarrassingly glamorous.

'You'll wow the guys with it,' Viv told me. 'Mark might get his act together and propose.'

'I wouldn't want a re-run of the Grahame episode,' I told her firmly.

To my surprise Clyde, whom I barely knew, asked me out the following week. He'd heard I wasn't going out with Mark. He was a nice guy but quite casual. Clyde and I had fun, starting with a delicious meal at the *Milano*, then going to a party at Jake's place. Jake had lots of parties and they were good. Terrific music, colourful lights, lots of people I liked. And a few I struggled with, like Sally and Ophelia. *A Hard Day's Night*, sang the Beatles. I liked that song.

Clyde thanked me, with a kiss, for a great evening and asked me out again. I hoped Mark would hear about it. He hadn't been at Jake's party.

I went inside after a theoretically great evening, made a milo and went to my bedroom, where, after an hour or so, I cried myself to sleep.

'Guess what!' Viv was beaming as she greeted me a few days later.

'What?'

She all but jumped up and down. 'Nate and I are going out again. It's all sorted out.'

'Are you sure that's a good thing?'

'Claire! Of course it is. I love him. I'm only ever totally happy when I'm with him.'

Where would it all lead? A lovely girl like Viv from a Christian family—could she make a go of it with a guy who'd been a drug dealer? Would Nate actually marry her? One good thing from my point of view: at least she'd told me and hadn't gone back to hiding it all.

For the next several weeks, Nate visited often. He was still working spasmodically on Tom's farm so we saw him when we were at *Riverside* too. I have to admit, Nate and Vivien looked good together, almost filmstar-like. Nate had tidied up his appearance and Viv continued looking either glamorous or typically sixties.

'Shame they're not as sensible as they're good-looking,' Bert commented to me at *Riverside* one weekend when he'd seen Viv talking to Nate over at Tom's place.

*What can I say?* 'Viv's happy. She'd be bored with a sensible man.'

Bert sighed. 'Well, there's that, certainly. My girl likes a lot of fun.' He frowned. 'I'd like to see her settle down.' His forehead creased more. 'Is Vivien still going to church in Brisbane, Claire? I sometimes wonder if she comes along with us here, just to keep the peace.'

May looked dubious.

'Yes. She goes regularly.' To my surprise she had continued her Christian involvements. I had no idea how Nate felt about it.

May pursed her lips. 'Well, if she and Nate stay together, I hope they can work out the important things.' I realised she had no idea I was not religious.

I said, 'Mmm,' and hoped they would change the subject. Luckily, Viv walked in then. I should say, she bounced in. She began talking about a tree Bert had pruned, to her disappointment. She'd preferred it bushy.

The following day, Viv and I drove back to Brisbane. I took a deep breath and glanced at her now-shortish hair flying in the breeze with the open window. 'Viv?'

'Mmm.'

'How do you reconcile going to church like a good Christian and yet going steady with a guy like Nate?'

'Claire! Nate isn't *a guy like Nate*. He's *Nate*, the one and only. In the eyes of God too. And I believe in going to church. I enjoy it. I pray for Nate, that he'll come to find the happiness I've found with God. He so needs it.' Tears began to seep from under her sunglasses and trickle down her cheeks. She brushed them away. 'I pray for him a lot, actually. He needs prayer. If you believed, I'd ask you to pray too.'

'Well, don't write me off totally like that. It's just that I haven't decided yet.'

Viv sighed and wiped her eyes again. 'He's still on parole, you know. But he's been very careful. And I don't *think* he's taking drugs.'

A few days later I came upstairs after teaching a talented fourteen-year-old girl Speech and Drama, only to hear stifled sobs coming from Viv's bedroom. *Oh no, what now?* I had a fifteen minute break to get a cuppa and snack before my next pupil, so I put on the jug and then knocked at Viv's door.

'That you, Claire?'

'It's me, yes. I've only got a minute. Are you okay?'

The door opened and there was Viv with messy mascara around her eyes and her hair in a tangle. She sniffed and blew her nose. 'Claire, Nate told me he hates Christians, except my parents. He's anti-Christian. He's glad I'm not a Christian.'

'But you *are* a Christian.'

She sniffed again. 'I know. I haven't been game to tell him yet.'

'What? All this time you've been going together, you haven't told him that?' Anger welled up inside me, but I stuck to my resolution to feel my emotions but not always express them. So I just sympathised with her. 'So what are you going to do? At the rate you two have been going, he'll propose to you soon—if he's into marriage. Is he?'

'I think he'd marry me just to be sure he kept me.'

It was too late. I was angry and couldn't hold it in. 'Heck Viv, you shouldn't marry him at all if he does it to "keep" you. That's like *abuse*. And I honestly think you need to tell him you're a Christian. It's changed you. You have different values now. He needs to know that before you commit yourself to him.'

'Well, there's no need to get angry about it.'

'I just can't stand by and see you both ruin your lives because of your gutlessness. You used to be so brave.'

She sniffed again. 'I suppose you're right. Okay, I'll tell him as soon as I can.'

'Well, when are you seeing him next?'

'Tonight. He's picking me up to go out for tea and a movie.'

'Okay, well, honestly Viv, you need to tell him tonight.'

She sighed. 'I'll try.'

'You need to, Viv.'

I'd always considered Viv a strong girl. And she was—except when it came to Nate.

So several hours later Viv and Nate arrived home after the movie. I was up, preparing lesson plans. After we'd all had a cup of coffee and I'd left them to say their goodnights in the lounge, I came back out when I heard the front door slam.

I took a deep breath. 'So did you tell him?'

'Yes, I did. He said he didn't care what I believed as long as I didn't expect him to be part of anything Christian and didn't become too holy. He said, "Just don't let it take the fun out of life."'

I didn't think there was much danger of Viv's becoming too holy the way she was going, but she was sincere in her own way. What did he mean about 'take the fun out of life', though? Drugs? Sex? Was Viv keeping Christian boundaries? I had no idea. For myself, I felt the Christian values were a good idea and, after a few tentative flings, I'd reneged and decided I was keen to keep myself for my husband. Who'd want to end up sleeping around like Sally or Ophelia? I wondered, too, if Mark would see any reason *ever* to get legally married if we were already sleeping together. Still, perhaps I did him an injustice.

As for me and religion, I was still undecided. I'd been hoping Viv would be an example so I could see what being a Christian really did for you, but she'd been just as influenced by Nate as by God, I'd say.

'Oh well, good luck with him.' I said goodnight and went back to my room.

A week later Viv arrived home from an afternoon session of *The Warning* with Nate, looking elated.

'Where's that film on?' I asked. 'I thought it was over.'

'In the city. One of those big cinemas. It was a special showing. Nate hated it and I thought it was well done but it left a funny feeling inside me. Sort of jittery.' She held out her hand. 'But look!' There, glittering on her finger in the evening lamplight, was a small diamond ring. 'We're engaged! We'll have a dinner to celebrate but because of his situation, we won't have a big party. At least my parents will be part of it now. And you and I will see them tomorrow.'

So it appeared Nate was serious about his commitment to Viv.

# CHAPTER 27

THAT NIGHT VIV PULLED OUT a bottle of wine from the fridge as I fried some fish and steamed some veggies.

'Bit of a celebration again before we head off into the fray.' Viv's voice was nervous. 'Are you right for that, Claire? Nate can't come tonight but we'll celebrate with him soon. But I feel like I need to celebrate a bit anyway.'

'Sure. As long as we don't drink too much. We have to be up early to do the drive.'

The wine was delicious. The bottle was left over from a dinner party a few nights ago. So we sipped our way through it all. I was still a bit unused to drinking wine with meals and Viv's family never served it, so we were both giggling by dessert time.

'Are you a head or a heart person?' Viv asked as she spooned chocolate sauce onto her ice-cream and nuts. 'I've been discussing it with a few of the girls at uni. I'm definitely a heart person. I guess that's why I love Nate and have put my lot in with him.'

This was the first time I'd heard her imply Nate was an unusual choice. But me ...?

'I suppose I'm a head person. But if I were totally that, I'd break it off completely with Mark and choose a guy who wants to get married soon.' I grimaced as Viv smiled knowingly. 'So I suppose I'm a heart person too. A mixture.'

'Definitely a mixture,' Viv said with a burst of laughter. 'Mark doesn't know the half of it.'

I frowned, then saw her laughing and smiled.

'You know, Claire, I still often think I'd be so much better off with a different kind of man to marry, and yet there's this thing inside me that's sort of attached to him. It feels like my destiny to marry Nate. I always come back to knowing I love him, when I get to weighing up the good and bad points. If I broke it off, I reckon I'd come running back the next day.'

A crash of thunder suddenly made us jump. I looked at Viv.

'Harbinger of I-wonder-what,' she laughed.

'Of a storm,' I said.

'Head.' Viv raised her eyebrows.

We discussed several of the girls at uni and agreed that the guys were nearly all head and body, with only a bit of heart kicking in after they got to know you.

'Time to wash up and get packed,' I said after the storm had passed. 'We can't leave dirty dishes in the sink for the whole weekend.'

So half an hour later we were both in bed and looking forward to the next day. I realised Viv might be dreading it, though. As I began to drift towards sleep, I suddenly realised: Viv must be aware she was not doing the best thing in marrying Nate. She claimed she'd choose differently if she were a head person. And what was the bond that she referred to? Was it the power of his thoughts? Or her own attraction? It sounded more like bondage than a good bond to me but I wasn't exactly an experienced woman of the world.

# CHAPTER 28

Poor Viv! She was missing out on some of the frills of being engaged, with Nate still on parole and Bert and May not accepting him as Viv's husband-to-be. But she was still convinced he was right for her. 'I love him,' she asserted when anyone queried her. She agonised over his lack of Christian belief but most of the time she was ecstatic.

'When are you getting married?' I asked as we finished packing for *Riverside* the next morning, thankful for the sunny day after last night's storm.

Viv gave her typical shrug. 'Who knows? Neither of us is a planner.'

My stomach felt tense. Would Viv ever actually get married? Marriage and being a mother were the things she wanted most. She was not a career girl at all.

I was hesitant about this trip. Normally I'd jump at any chance to go to *Riverside* but my three-month break with Mark was up. He'd appeared quite casually on the doorstep to announce it—at least he'd remembered!—and had taken me out to an elaborate dinner that night. To my disappointment, everything seemed much the same as before our break. But I didn't want to go away without him so soon. 'Can Mark come too?' I asked Viv.

She looked uncertain. 'I guess so. He's welcome but I may need your support if Mum and Dad make it hard about me and Nate.'

'He's fine to go walking by himself if I'm with you all. Can we go together in your car?'

Viv still looked uncertain. 'I don't feel comfortable driving Mark. He laughs at me when I make a mistake. You can go with him if you like.'

In the end, we all went in the Ford. Mark was a bit impatient with Viv's driving but on the whole the trip went well. Not surprisingly, Bert was furious. He stood up and glowered at us both. 'How can you be so irresponsible, Vivien? He's a drug addict, a dealer, I hear, someone who's led younger teens away from a normal lifestyle. And he's not even a Christian. The Bible says you shouldn't be yoked together with unbelievers.'

'Dad!' Vivien had regained her courage. 'He's a good man at heart. He's just lost his way. I'm helping him find it and I'm praying for him. Where's your faith, Dad? You could join me in praying for him.'

'Well, if that's the case, you've jumped the gun. You should have prayed before and waited until this faith of yours sees results.'

'Dad, I thought you'd stick by me, at least.' She burst into tears and ran to her bedroom.

May, who had sat silently all this time, slipped out after Viv. I heard the faint sound of sobbing.

'Mum was great,' Viv told me later.

But I could tell May was concerned.

The next day Mark and I went for a walk along the riverbank. I was hoping he'd tell me he'd missed me during our three-month break but I could tell something was bothering him.

'What's wrong?'

He sighed eloquently. 'For goodness sake, I reckon her parents are more right than Vivien is. She must be a bit of a drip to plan to have her whole future with a guy like Nate. He's a dealer. He's often really high. How the hell could she ever trust him?'

'She loves him! She always has, ever since they first met in her teens when he was at Tom's farm. Tom's a good guy. He takes in young people to teach them farming and it works both ways. He gets help on his farm. Viv says when she first met Nate it was love at first sight. Well let's say, "attraction at first sight."'

I gazed down at the river, a silver thread like a gleaming vein running through the land, feeding it. Mark put his hand on my shoulder. 'Ah well. We'd better get on with our own lives and let Viv work it out. I just hate to see a nice chick like that get sucked in.'

'I don't know.' I really didn't. 'Um, by the way, how did you enjoy having the three-month break from our relationship?'

'Mixed.' Mark took a deep-sounding breath. 'I actually missed you much more than I'd expected but I had a lot of fun.'

'Fun?'

He cleared his throat. 'Well, I took out a lot of different chicks. Mainly just good time girls like Sally and Ophelia.

Might as well have fun while I'm free, you know. I'm not thirty yet.'

Did he think of marriage as a sort of prison? I didn't have the courage to ask him. 'Oh. Okay. I guess that's fair enough if you feel that way.'

'Yeah. You know how Viv sort of flows with the wind. I'm not like that and you're *certainly* not, but we could loosen up a little bit, I think.'

'Mmm. I'll try, I suppose.' I gave him a weak smile. 'I think you're mainly just seeing Viv's whimsical streak. It doesn't mean she'll be happy however things turn out but she's tougher than she looks. I don't know what it would take to get her seriously long-term upset.'

I hoped I'd never find out.

## Part Eight: Claire

1967

## CHAPTER 29

1967 IN BRISBANE was a year of radical social change. Political protests and wild, sometimes drug-inspired music filled many popular venues. Traditional values were upended. Many young people wanted to experiment with moral values and 'free love' while some even tried hallucinogenic drugs. 'Find out who you really are' was the misleading catch-cry of people selling LSD and similar drugs. Everywhere there were colourful variations on the hippy lifestyle both in the country and in the arty city scene. At many parties, the air was scented with marijuana or incense.

Most of the girls had grown out their short trendy haircuts and had the beginnings of long hair. So at least my own look was in fashion. The girl we called Ophelia floated around the uni campus in long semitransparent dresses. She got away with it at uni by wearing a bra and undies under her dress. The bra was shed for parties. To my annoyance, Mark still seemed to find her attractive. Viv and I giggled about her but there was a sting in it for me.

At a few of the smaller parties, Nate brought his flute and filled the air with surprisingly lovely melodies. He was definitely gifted and expressed real beauty—and sorrow—in his tunes. He had a chameleon quality with his wildly varying moods. No wonder Viv was all over the place.

Many young people were influenced by the Beatles whose music blared out in the shops, occasionally at uni, and, of course, parties. Others had adopted the hippy trend, both in the country and in the city where girls appeared like hippies or beatniks and men wore long scruffy hair and untidy, bleach-stained jeans.

By the end of May, *San Francisco* seemed to be playing everywhere we went. Inspired by the song, Sally often had a hibiscus or frangipani poked behind her ear. I caught Viv experimenting with flowers one morning. She stood in front of the bathroom mirror, a little posy of garden blossoms on the bench as she tried different flowers behind her ear or in her short ponytail.

She laughed when I caught her eye. 'Maybe I'll leave it for parties. I don't want to feel like I'm trying to be another Ophelia. I think her name's actually Mary, by the way. I found out. And Sally's following the flower trend too.'

I cringed inwardly. Sally was very attractive to men, including Mark. And Nate.

Viv's parents were anxious about the changes in society. 'What's the world coming to?' May sighed, as she carefully placed mugs of milo on the grate around the fire when we were at *Riverside* one weekend. 'Not only the Vietnam war, although that's a real concern, but all you young ones seem to have gone a bit mad. A group of young people in the town were calling out "flower power". It's silly!'

'Mum! What do you mean?' Viv sounded quite annoyed. She was enjoying the so-called Cultural Revolution and often played Beatles' music, poked flowers in her hair and hinted at more dangerous ventures.

Bert interrupted. 'I don't know where you get your strange ideas, Vivien. We brought you up to be a Christian and to live with Godly values. The dress you arrived in was so short I was embarrassed. My daughter showing off her legs to the world. It's different if you're swimming but you girls need to live carefully. I don't know how you can consider Nate a potential husband. And Claire, you've still got your heart set on this Mark and I don't know if he's much better than Nate.'

'Dad, we're young still. I love Nate. You'll be surprised— I'll pray him free of drugs.'

I winced. Bert's grim streak intimidated me a bit.

We made an effort after that to dress modestly when we went to *Riverside*. Not that my own clothes were ever as revealing as Viv's.

One spring day, later in 1967, the cottage doorbell rang. Viv was out shopping. I ran to the mirror and tidied my hair, then opened the door.

Mark stood there in his old jeans and a new blue t-shirt. For a moment I forgot we were only *sort of* going together— sadly, I'd never managed to discuss our future with him since our three-month break. Forgetting myself, I nearly hugged him. He'd lost the slightly distant expression he'd worn for the past months and looked like his dear old self, friendly, loving, and lots of fun. I took a deep breath and pulled my thoughts into submission. 'Mark! How are you? Come in.'

He looked almost shy—and Mark was never shy.

I was wearing my friendship ring. I hadn't been sure about that after our break, but he hadn't commented. The conversation always ended up going somewhere else. I was afraid to broach the subject again in case it brought more stress into the relationship.

'Claire, you look lovely!'

As I was wearing my house-cleaning clothes—jeans and an old red t-shirt, I was amazed. And the fact that he'd commented. He rarely noticed what I wore.

'You've lost weight. It suits you. You're eating properly, are you?' Was this *Mark*? He hardly ever asked about me at all, let alone if I were eating well enough.

We sat in the lounge. I went to sit on a separate chair but he grabbed me and pulled me over to sit with him on the sofa. It felt cosy. And right. My heart began to speed up.

'Can I get you a drink? Cuppa?' I asked.

'Soon. I want to ask you something first.'

My heart was hammering now. 'Sure.'

'Claire, I want us to be serious. I'm still sweating through the issues of marriage and being tied down but I love you and I want to be with you as often as we can manage it. How do you feel about that now, but still without any long-term commitment?'

I half-sighed, half-sobbed. 'Mark, I love you too. Yes. I'd like us to be serious.'

He engulfed me in a hug and kissed me. And kept on kissing me. 'I'm sorry I'm so slow about the Big Thing. Marriage. But I've seen too much pain in my own family to risk buying into that myself.'

'It's okay, Mark. I understand. We'll just take our time and ignore anyone who says we should be engaged or something. I'm okay with that now. I miss you whenever you're not there.'

Mark stayed for a few hours and we talked about everything and nothing.

'What about all those sexy chicks like Sally?' I asked. 'Won't you miss them if you're serious with me?'

Mark laughed. 'Hell, no. Sally and those girls are just good-time girls. Nothing much between their ears. I'd be bored out of my brain.'

I sighed with relief.

Viv arrived home. She bounced into the lounge and stared at us. I suppose she tried to hide her surprise. 'Hi, Mark. Great to see you,' was all she said.

Later, needless to say, she grabbed me and asked if we were engaged at last. I just laughed and said, 'Not exactly.'

Bill, one of the guys in our tute group, arrived soon after Mark had reluctantly left. 'Party at Jacko's place tonight,' he told us. 'Should be fantastic. It's his twenty-fifth birthday and they've hired lighting and all that stuff. Hey Claire, you looked nice in that dress, the short one. Nice legs. Dress up a bit again, eh?'

I was irritated. How dare he tell people how to dress! It wasn't his party. But a niggle inside me made me decide to wear yet another new dress. I'd bought one in a nice shade of bright green, shorter than my usual and cut a teeny bit low, with a fashionable low waist. I scrutinised myself in the mirror. I *had* lost weight! Not a lot, but enough to look better.

Viv was going too, with Ian, one of her admirers. She was angry with Nate who had taken out a few of the wilder girls. 'Nate, you've made a commitment to me. We're engaged!' she'd told him angrily.

'Well, it's not like being married. We're only engaged.'

She was furious and I was puzzled. Gosh, if ever I managed to get engaged—hopefully to Mark—there'd be no 'only' about it. I told Viv how I felt.

'Yes, I know. I'm disappointed in him. But if he has to get it out of his system, better now than when we're married. I'd always thought of engagement as a special time of preparation but maybe it's not for everyone.'

'Well, I think it's meant to be. If I get engaged, it'll definitely be like that. No going out with other blokes for me. Or for Mark, if he's the one. It's an important time.'

Viv burst into tears again. 'Nate doesn't like doing traditional things. Which is great—sometimes. At the moment I don't feel so great about it.'

'Well, personally I think it's making a farce of being engaged.' Viv looked as if I'd slapped her on the face, and I almost regretted saying that. Almost but not quite.

It bothered me though. I'd gone with expressing my feelings and had not given a polite, caring answer. Would the mask have been more appropriate at that point? But I decided it was good I'd voiced my opinion. Perhaps Viv needed to think about her relationship with Nate. She was quite capable of getting herself in a mess, with her impulsive nature.

Anyway, that's why Viv was going to the party with Ian and not Nate.

'Ellie's coming down for that party too. She should be here already. Would you be okay if she stayed overnight after it? She'll sleep on the sofa,' Viv called from her room as she dressed.

'Course! It'll be nice to see her.'

*But what if Mark falls for her? Ellie really is beautiful. Stunning.*

So I welcomed her when she arrived but fought a slight trepidation as she pulled out a glowing blue silky dress and ran to the bathroom to change. Twenty minutes later she emerged. She looked terrific. Surely no man—like Mark— could resist her? She sat in the lounge, waiting to go with Viv and her partner.

Viv emerged from her bedroom and I blinked. She wore a psychedelic-patterned ankle-length dress in a soft material. She looked quite lovely in its light-bright colours that suited her so well—primrose, peach, blue, mauve, green. Only Viv— or perhaps Ophelia or Sally—would have the courage to wear something like that. She seemed relaxed. As she turned around, I noticed she had a flower, a red hibiscus, in her hair. At least all this religion hadn't cramped her style in clothes.

The doorbell rang.

We both hurried to get it. Ian stood there, so as Viv called out, 'See you there,' I ran to my room to get ready.

'Wow!' I heard Ian say when Ellie emerged as well as Viv. 'I get two for the price of one tonight?'

Ellie laughed. 'I'm meeting a friend there. Bruce.' I breathed a sigh of relief. She'd be 'taken' for tonight.

I hurried to the bathroom and put a few extra touches to my makeup and my hair.

The doorbell rang again.

'Hi, Mark.' He was in a t-shirt and his usual jeans, with whitish patches on the jeans here and there where he'd deliberately bleached them as part of the trend.

'Wow, you're looking great.' He greeted me with a hug.

'Thanks.'

He was driving the car tonight, not the bike. He had the top closed—'in case it rains again later and wrecks the seats.' We wove in and out of the little streets, then zoomed over the big old Indooroopilly Bridge until we reached a lovely Queenslander in Graceville. The garden was lit with small coloured lights and music blared out from the house.

Soon we'd joined the group inside and were dancing to loud music. The Beatles' recent release, *Lucy in the Sky with Diamonds*, was on repeat so we danced and danced to it. The room was soon filled with overheated, scantily-clad bodies swaying and gyrating to the music. Strange-smelling smoke drifted from a vase on the mantel piece. Marijuana or hash, I supposed. I could smell incense too.

When Viv and Ellie entered, several of the boys whistled loudly. Viv smiled, then giggled, enjoying the attention.

*Oh no!* I noticed Nate over in a corner wrapped around a woman. Sally, probably, considering the lack of clothing visible.

Sure enough, after a few minutes, the whistling and general noise drew Nate's attention and he saw Viv. He let

Sally go into the eager arms of another man, and he sauntered over to Viv, who was waiting while Ian fetched their drinks. Nate grabbed her arm and began to dance with her. *Poor Viv. Her emotions must be all over the place.*

For a few minutes Mark whirled me around. 'Come on. You're a bit slow tonight'. Then: 'Sorry. You can go slowly if you want to, Claire.' I relaxed into his arms and let the music lead me. I had a headache now as the strobe light was irritating my eyes. On off on off. Dark light dark light. Insistent, demanding rhythm.

'Have you ever known a girl with kaleidoscope eyes?' Mark asked me, as he listened to the words of the song. 'It sounds beautiful but I haven't actually encountered that. Closest would be a girl in one of my tutes. She has bluey-green eyes with little golden flecks in them.'

He must have been close to her to notice all that. 'Sounds cosy,' I said crankily.

He laughed. 'Everyone notices her eyes and looks at them. They're lovely eyes but she doesn't have the temperament to match. I must say kaleidoscope eyes sound very romantic.'

I was suddenly conscious of my own plain brown eyes.

He pulled me closer. 'Your eyes are beautiful. They shine. And I can usually tell more or less what you're thinking by looking into your eyes. I like that.'

'Did you notice Ellie's here tonight?' I just had to know how he'd reacted to her stunning appearance.

Mark grinned and nodded. 'Those Barlow girls are good lookers, that's for sure. Not my type, actually, but they're nice enough.'

I breathed a sigh of relief.

Tom from Kenilworth was there, looking very handsome. There were many of my friends, and many of their friends as well. 'Hi Claire!' Tom called.

'Hi Tom.' For me, Tom embodied *Riverside*. For just a moment I imagined I was there and could hear the river song—its murmuring and gurgling, the twitter of tiny birds, the song of a magpie. I pulled myself back to the present, to find Tom smiling at me.

I could see Mark getting That Look. Which meant: you're with *me*, not *him*. Mark was a bit possessive and sometimes quite jealous. I found this quite hard to handle, considering his own inability to commit to marriage.

Tom grasped my arm and whirled me around the room a few times in time to the music. 'How's it going, Claire?'

'Good,' I replied. 'Great, actually.'

Tom cleared his throat. 'Doesn't Ellie look beautiful tonight?'

I smiled and nodded. She did. I noticed with interest, Tom's whole face lit up when he looked at Ellie. And she blushed when he caught her eye.

'I guess you came with Mark?' Tom asked.

I nodded. 'We're going together properly now.'

'Oh, congratulations! I suppose he'll propose soon. He's got a great girl. I'd better return you. He's looking a bit fierce.'

It flickered through my mind again: Mark rarely used to ask me how I was, but that had changed. Mark had changed. He had become a caring bloke—one of the main things I wanted in a man.

Later as Mark and I were leaving, I noticed Viv standing with two guys who were arguing. Ian and Nate. 'I'm going home with Nate. I'm sorry, Ian, but I owe him an explanation about something,' she said. Needless to say, Ian looked annoyed.

When we reached the cottage, I asked Mark in for coffee, but made it clear I'd only last for half an hour or so. I was tired and my head ached. He looked disappointed when I told him. 'I've got my violin in the car. Are you okay if I bring it in and play a bit?'

'Sure, but not too late. I'd love it.' I hoped my headache wouldn't get worse but Mark so rarely offered to play his violin in front of us ...

He ran down and clomped back up the steps with his violin. I gave him the big three-seater chair so he could spread out to play. He began slowly, gently, then increased his volume and pace until the music was loud and filled with something like turmoil. I loved the music but felt tense. What inner torment was he expressing? What did he actually feel when he played like that? The music was beautiful, though. His own composition and a lovely melody.

He was perspiring when he'd finished and sat back, wiping his forehead.

'That was wonderful, Mark,' I said. 'But what actual feelings were motivating it?'

He groaned. 'Hell, Claire. A mix of everything on my plate, I suppose. You and me and where we're at, Mum and Dad and where that leaves me, life now, the darned Vietnam War, you name it. Life's a mess at the moment.'

'Well, the war certainly is but I don't feel too bad about life in general. Although the society we live in now is very experimental in lots of ways. I sometimes find that intimidating.'

'Oh, Claire. Often you're like a glass of cool water on a hot day. And other times you're just too good to be true. Do you realise we're mixing with the In Crowd? There are still quite a few people our age who are living relatively conservative lives. But you've landed on your feet with Viv and this whole crowd. We're setting the trend for the future and it's fun and exciting.'

'What on earth did I say to make you think about cool water?' I asked.

'Don't worry about it. Just keep on being you.'

*Am I? Am I at last just being myself?*

Mark played one of my favourites, *Stranger on the Shore*, then heaved himself out of the chair and helped himself to another drink.

Ellie had already come home and was in Viv's room getting changed, so I took her a cup of coffee and suggested she lie on Viv's bed until Mark had gone. 'It won't be long,' I assured her.

My head throbbed as I sipped my coffee and I wondered how soon Mark would leave. Usually I'd be hoping he'd stay longer but this was a shocker of a headache. Then the front door opened with a clatter and Viv's giggle. She led Nate into the lounge where we sat, then went to her room, lent Ellie a dress and brought her out to join us.

I noticed Viv had been crying and was flushed. She looked radiantly happy, though. 'Well, you three will be the first to know,' she announced. 'We're really celebrating our engagement now. We're *properly* engaged.' And a few tears slid down her flushed cheeks.

Nate wrapped her in an embrace. Mark clapped and whistled. Ellie looked worried. And I wondered how on earth it could all work out. Would Nate take it seriously now? I wondered again about Viv's Christian faith. Nate seemed an unusual choice for a Christian girl. Had she given up on Christianity? And those kind parents of hers were Christians too.

After a short time Mark left and I told Viv, Ellie and Nate I needed to go and get some sleep.

'Not yet!' Viv cried. 'Look!' She nudged Nate and he produced a bottle of champagne. Inwardly, I groaned.

'Just a little for me but, yes, we must celebrate,' I said.

Ellie had a small glass of champagne but she still looked worried. 'Engaged *again*! Or didn't you celebrate last time around? Mum and Dad'll think you're silly.'

Typically, Viv shrugged. 'They'll cope.'

Not long after we'd drunk to their happiness, I took two Panadol and went to bed. As I drifted off to sleep, I thought, *Viv and I and these guys and our on-off relationships. Now we're engaged* ... Sleep engulfed me.

# Chapter 30

THE LAST FEW MONTHS of the uni year passed quickly with a lot of study to do. We planned to take a break, perhaps picking up more study in a few years' time and getting our Master's Degrees.

While I was studying one evening, the phone rang. 'For you, Claire,' Viv called.

'Darling,' Mum said, 'I have to spend a day or two in hospital for a very minor procedure next Friday evening. Nothing serious. But both the other girls are busy then and I wondered if you could bring your study over here for a few days and just keep a bit of an eye on Dad.'

'Sure. No problem. Are you okay, Mum?'

'I'm fine, love. Just routine things. See you next Friday after your teaching. Or if I've left, I'll leave you a note.'

The weekend went quickly and I enjoyed chatting to Dad. When Mum came home from hospital on the Sunday, I was shocked to see her looking quite tired and drained. But she seemed to gather energy and colour as the day progressed. Perhaps she was, in her own way, in her element, so I returned to the cottage, feeling a little concerned but knowing Mum would bounce back.

When Viv came in, I was surprised. She looked worried, and yet had a curious glow about her. Her eyes shone as usual but she often looked away, barely meeting my gaze. Perhaps she was concerned about these exams, although she always sailed through.

We both still enjoyed our routine teaching—but our focus now was on our university exams. In October the jacarandas in the backyard with their beautiful but scary symbolism joined the smudgy mauve mist of trees all over Brisbane. 'Exam flowers' we called them as they heralded test time every year. Viv and I were both studying hard and, in addition, I was preparing my pupils for Drama exams and auditions.

Viv and I took a weekend's break at *Riverside* just before two of our main exams. 'Fresh air and a day off will freshen up our brains, Claire,' she insisted. The jacarandas were still out at *Riverside*, with the cooler nights there. As we approached the entrance it was like seeing an ethereal cloud—first a golden silky oak haze and then a soft mauve mist of jacarandas. A reminder, not so ethereal, of what lay ahead at uni.

I still felt Viv had something on her mind. In some inexplicable way, she was different.

Late on Saturday afternoon, as the sun sank behind the row of black silhouetted hills huddling on the horizon, we went for a walk along the riverbank. A white thread of water shone below us, so different from the brown surging mass that had gouged out chunks of the muddy bank last year.

Viv seemed unusually serious.

'Anything wrong, Viv?'

She sighed. 'Yes and no. But you know I'm wondering—again—if I'm doing the wrong thing. Nate's so selfish at times. And then he's all love and kindness to me. So affectionate. I guess I still sometimes wonder if I'd be better off marrying a good, kind, sensible man. Someone who'd look after me and my feelings and not just himself. I always come back to Mum and Dad's marriage. They're so happy. Dad does so much to make Mum feel appreciated and loved. She's told me bits and pieces for years. I don't get that from Nate except when he's trying to get his own way with me. But Claire, I love him, I really do. So that's that.' She gave a deep sigh. 'And I'll marry him. I definitely will.'

'I think you should take your doubts seriously,' I said. 'Even wait longer before you get married. It's so permanent. Well, it's meant to be.'

She sniffed and blew her nose with a crumpled tissue. 'I don't know. Thanks for listening, Claire. Please don't get me wrong. I love Nate and I want to marry him.'

She paused and cleared her throat. 'Claire, even Mark doesn't take our engagement seriously.'

'Yes, he does.'

'Well, he's one of the guys who greets me and Nate with a sarcastic, "Here comes the happy couple, da da!"'

I cringed. Mark could be like that at times. Perhaps he spoke out of his own conflict about marriage. And obviously some people weren't taking the relationship seriously. Perhaps not everyone knew they were actually engaged, with all the ups and downs they'd had. Mark did know, though, and I'd have hoped he'd take it more seriously. Perhaps his own indecisiveness was bugging him.

All I felt later, when I sat by myself in my favourite place by the river, was an inexplicable sense of sorrow. It seemed to relate to Viv—but Viv was happy. Bubbly! So I filed it away in the back of my mind, hoping this wasn't an omen, a sort of warning.

We went back to the cottage on Sunday night and resumed our rigorous study routine. Even Viv took it seriously now. This made Nate irritable. I think he missed being the centre of Viv's life as she immersed herself in study.

'I'll have to work hard, Claire,' she told me, 'I'm behind with my studies this year with all the emotional turmoil.' She seemed unusually stressed and worked hard, rarely seeing Nate. He tried hanging around our cottage but Viv was tense and nervy, telling me she feared for once she'd fail her exams.

Nate appeared in the doorway late one evening, hoping to spend time with her. 'I may as well be out living it up,' he retorted when she had greeted him perfunctorily, made him a cup of coffee, and then disappeared to her room to study.

'It's only for a few weeks,' I reminded him.

'Huh!'

But he still crept in often and tried to get time with Vivien. 'It all seems flat out there,' he pointed to the other houses and towards the university. 'Viv's got more life in her than most people I know.'

I knew what he meant.

The next day Suzanne turned up. Her exams were nearly over. 'You'll never guess,' she began. I wondered if she were mimicking Viv with 'you'll never guess'.

'What?' I asked.

'My cousin is holidaying in America and he's just seen the preview of a movie called *Bonnie and Clyde*. Fantastic, he reckons. It's about a pretty girl who gets together with a robber and they rob banks together. Something like that anyway. With Viv planning to marry Nate, who's still on parole I think, they'll be like Bonnie and Clyde.'

I stared at her. 'What on earth do you mean? Viv won't be robbing banks.'

'Don't kid yourselves that Nate will go straight. He's a druggie to the core. He thrives on the life. And Viv will be part of it. Like in the film. There's no way she'll avoid being dragged into it all with Nate at the helm.'

'Rubbish,' I said angrily. 'You underestimate Viv.'

It was complex. I suppose only her family and I and one or two others knew the soft, vulnerable side of Vivien beneath her resilience. Or recognised her strength of character. She presented as fairly strong, vibrant, even a bit wild. Erratic. I suppose that's the way she wanted it.

## CHAPTER 31

'WHAT'S WRONG, LOVE?' Bert asked.

May turned away from the dishes in the sink and pulled a wry face. 'Nothing, Bert. You know me. I just feel uneasy. Can't stop thinking about Vivvie. I'm a bit worried about her.'

Bert sighed and then laughed. 'Well, she'll be home in a few days, so you'll be able to see her then. I'm sure she'll be her usual bright, healthy self. Only thing is I hope she's not getting up to any mischief.' He caught May's frown and said, 'Yes, I know. She's an adult now, well and truly. It's up to her what she does. But she's still my daughter and I care about the choices she makes. She's a Christian too so she's not likely to do anything too bad. Don't worry, love.'

May gave a rueful smile. 'You know, love, I always expected she and Tom would get together. It just seemed so right. He's what I'd call real husband material. Such a fine young man. A gentleman. But I realise now she won't. Even if she and Nate end up breaking it off, I do know Vivvie's looking for someone livelier than Tom. Someone like Nate, I suppose.' She wiped an errant tear from her cheek.

Bert hugged her. 'Vivien will find happiness, I'm sure. With or without Nate.' He squeezed May's tense shoulders, then hurried up to the dairy.

May gazed out the window and thought about Vivien and Nate. What did Vivvie see in him? He seemed to go from one lot of trouble to another. Cheeky fellow at times, too. *Respect. Does he know what that means?* The nervous niggle was there again in her stomach. She would finish these dishes and go for a walk along the riverbank. Perhaps God would settle her emotions. The murmur of the breeze rustling the river oaks, the gurgle of the water, the birdsong—it all helped calm her and release joy inside her again. And she would pray. The riverbank was such a peaceful place.

Soon she headed off and wandered along the familiar, well-loved parts near the river. Some of her favourite Scriptures ran through her mind as she walked and she began to sing some of them aloud. But Vivvie was still there in all her thoughts, even more than before. May sighed and began to pray for her—for her safety, her health, her relationships, her relationship with Nate, and on it went. She barely mentioned Claire. Claire seemed a good influence even though she possibly wasn't a Christian. A sensible girl and loving as well. In a few days she would see Vivvie and probably Claire too. May missed them a lot.

## CHAPTER 32

VIVIEN AND I used to have breakfast together most mornings. We'd chat about the coming day's activities. The last week or two, Viv seemed to avoid me at breakfast time. *Or am I being silly?* Surely she wouldn't. It must be coincidence.

One morning Viv had a cup of coffee and a small piece of toast, then disappeared to the bathroom. 'Don't you need to eat more than that with this intense time at uni?' I asked her when she emerged. 'Are you sick?'

Tears shone in her eyes for just a moment. 'No. I'm just not hungry with all this stress.'

*All what stress?* Admittedly there'd been the Nate ups and downs and the whole Barlow family was still hurting. The exams were a breeze after some we'd done in the past.

Seeing my puzzled face, Viv said, 'Well, this is it. Our final exams for these post grad units. So much hinges on our results. You seem to be taking it very lightly.'

I shrugged, still mystified by the change in the usually light-hearted Vivien.

'I guess I'm finding them quite easy. I thought you were too.'

Vivien watched me sipping coffee and suddenly ran from the room. I heard her being sick in the bathroom. After a few minutes she gargled loudly and emerged. 'Viv, you *are* sick. Or are you just super-stressed?'

Vivien sighed. 'Claire, haven't you guessed?' She broke down, sobbing.

A vague thought nudged my brain.

'Viv, you're not ... you *couldn't* be ... pregnant?'

She began to cry in earnest and nodded.

My world teetered on its axis.

'Does Nate know?'

She shook her head and her sobs grew more intense. After a few minutes, she calmed down and I said, 'Viv, if you don't want it, if Nate doesn't want it or something, Suze told me about a place ...'

'Claire! How could you? This is a baby, not a thing. I'll be keeping her.'

'Would you go to one of those places like Boothville and have the baby and adopt it out? It would bless a couple who want kids.'

Vivien went white and then flushed again.

'Claire, I'll be keeping the baby. This is *my child*. And she's not an "it". Mum doesn't know about the baby yet but she's an experienced matron and midwife so I'll have her at home if possible and take a few years off before resuming teaching. I'll just be a mum for a while.'

My world reeled some more.

'Why don't you marry Nate? Aren't you still engaged to him?'

Vivien began to cry again. 'I haven't felt ready to tell him. It's his baby, of course.'

I groaned inwardly. 'But he's still going out with floozies like Sally sometimes. Or is it back to just you and him? You told me you weren't going to sleep with him until you were married. So I suppose he forced you.'

'No. Not really. I wanted to.' She ran her hands through her hair. 'No, that's not true. I didn't actually want to. I wanted to do it God's way. But I did it anyway.'

'Do you want to tell me more about it or would you rather I stayed out of it?'

Vivien sighed. 'It'd be easier to have you knowing, I think. It'll be obvious before long anyway, I suppose, and I'll have people's opinions to cope with. So make yourself another cuppa if you want one and I might have just a little cup too. And perhaps a little bit of toast and vegemite. I'll ring the school and tell them I'll be late.'

So while I boiled the jug and made some toast, Viv rang the school, then began her story, sniffing as she talked. 'Well,' she half-sobbed, 'to begin at the end, I've told God I'm sorry, incredibly sorry—and I do regret it. I've failed. But I sense God's peace about it now I've repented, so I'll be okay. I mean, well, I wouldn't do it again. Not while I'm single.' She coughed. 'Actually, when the doctor confirmed it, I spent most of the night awake, wondering and praying about what on earth to do. I thought I'd have to adopt the baby out but I couldn't face the idea. Then I thought about Mum being a midwife and all that, and how I could just go and live at *Riverside* for a few years while I was pregnant and then when the baby was small.'

'You didn't consider aborting it?'

'No way.' Viv looked shocked. Perhaps I would have to think more carefully about this issue. I'd never been pregnant so the situation had never confronted me personally. Suzanne and her ilk were hardly girls I'd emulate.

Viv was still upset. 'I told you, the baby isn't an "it". He-or-she's a real human being. A tiny one.'

I definitely would have to think more about this. *When does life actually begin? If it begins with the first impregnated cell, it would be unthinkable to abort.*

I stared and sighed. 'So how did it happen? You've always had such high standards.'

'Yes. I've always really, really wanted to do it God's way. But I was home by myself. You were over at your parents' place—yes, about six weeks ago. I was feeling lonely and still upset about Nate's drug trouble; I was craving company and there was a knock at the door. It was him. I was surprised to see him—I'd thought he was out on Tom's farm. So I asked him in.' She sighed. 'He soon picked up I was feeling flat. We talked for a short time and then ... well I've always been intensely attracted to him, as you know, but we just couldn't make a go of a stable relationship, even being engaged. So anyway, he was feeling a bit down too after jail and being on parole, so he ended up giving me a big hug and I just didn't have the resistance I'd had the other times we'd been out together. He'd been wanting it, of course, but I'd managed to resist him. Until then. There were emotions everywhere which didn't help.

'We'd never properly discussed his drug involvements. He'd always fobbed me off. So I was still devastated about all that and I burst into tears and said, "How could you do it?" and I started to cry. His arms were around me and I couldn't stop crying. "I trusted you," I told him. He swore and hugged me more. Well, it just went from there.' She sighed again. 'He left before dawn. About a month later I went to the doctor with some yucky symptoms and he told me I was pregnant.'

'So what about your family?' I asked. 'I guess you feel guilty towards all of them?'

Viv began to cry again. 'I haven't decided whether to tell any of my family who the father is but of course they'll guess. I'll pray about all that. It's a mess—but I like being pregnant with Nate's child. I guess I've never stopped being attracted to him.' She gasped and burst into a fresh round of tears. 'But yeah—Ellie and Annie look to me as a role model. Even Lydia already, I guess. Oh shivers. I've let them down badly.'

'Phew!' I said. 'So that's why you looked so radiant when I came back from looking after Dad?'

She blushed. 'No. It would have been part of it, but I'd already told God I was sorry about the time with Nate—even before I knew I was pregnant—and He'd given me so much comfort with His presence. I was actually feeling very close to Him. Sounds funny, I know. I was a bit scared because I realised I might be pregnant. And after seeing the doctor, I still didn't tell Nate. I certainly had no intention of sleeping with him again. He wants to, of course.'

'You're a complicated lady. Nate's the father so he should know, I suppose.'

She smiled sadly.

I frowned at the jacarandas' last few flowers down in the park and the lavender carpet on the grass. 'So it's a settled thing about marrying Nate once he knows about it?'

Viv sighed. 'Well, I guess I'll have to marry him if he loves me, anyway. But I often suspect it's mainly attraction. Love, yes, but … oh, I don't know. He's certainly an appealing bloke. I reckon he could have any girl he wants. Oh, sorry, except you! I love him but he'd be a pain to live with, if he ever does settle down. He's so incredibly complex. That's why it's been so on and off. Anyway, I've told God I'm sorry. That's the good thing about being a Christian, you don't have to live with ongoing guilt. But there sure are consequences.' She patted her stomach and pulled a wry face. 'But it's all forgiven with God if you really repent. I feel awfully disappointed though. Don't get me wrong—I don't mean I'd run out and do it again. That'd be different. I was just feeling incredibly fragile, needing comfort.' She gave a half-laugh, half-sob. 'Something more than chocolate. But that's definitely not the way to fix things.'

She took a deep breath. 'And I'm awfully disappointed I didn't wait until I was married. It would have been so much more special. As well as being what God wants.'

'You know all those times you disappeared for a drive?' I asked.

'Mmm?'

'Were you seeing Nate?'

'Once or twice. Just as a friend. Not exactly anything romantic, although you know what Nate's like. But usually I'd just go to the shop or somewhere. That's just me. I get these whims to get up and about.' She looked away, then cleared her throat. 'Actually he did take me to a nightclub once. He was disappointed because I didn't like it.'

A nightclub! I hadn't even realised we had one in Brisbane.

Vivien paused. 'You know, I'm looking forward to being a mother. I'll love it. It's one of the main things I've wanted all along.'

'Viv,' I approached this cautiously, 'I reckon it'll take a lot of courage to face everyone being pregnant and single if you don't end up marrying Nate.'

Her eyes shone with tears for a moment. 'I know. It will. I do realise this is not God's best way, believe me.'

I ignored the God bit.

I went to my room to study but my mind was focused on Vivien and her situation. I gazed at the honeysuckle budding at the gate. A waft of breeze cooled my face. After a minute or two I knew Vivien would manage; she had grit. She'd even enjoy having her very own baby.

Later that night, after I'd turned my light off, I heard it again. The sound of muffled sobbing. *Vivien. Should I leave her alone?*

I tiptoed to her doorway and whispered, 'Viv, are you all right?'

She switched her lamp on. She looked golden but frail in its circle of light. 'I *have* blown it, haven't it? I just wanted to do it God's way—to get married and then sleep together. But I failed. I suppose I'm still coming to terms with that. I'm disappointed in myself. It's too late to do it the right way now. And my family will be incredibly disappointed in me too.' She sniffed and blew her nose.

'Viv, I think you should tell Nate. When you feel ready, anyway.'

She sniffed again. 'Not yet, but I will. I'll get there. Thanks, Claire. I'm sorry to put you through all this.'

'Heck, Viv, what are friends for?' I said goodnight and went back to try to sleep. As I settled in to the night-time silence, I was blown away by the thought that there were now not two but three lives in this house.

# Chapter 33

At last our exams were over. My pupils had done well in their Speech and Drama exams. Viv felt she had at least passed but she still hadn't told Nate about the baby.

'Jake's having a party on Friday night,' I told her.

'Oh, is he? Well, I want to go home for the weekend. I miss *Riverside* terribly. I want to spend quality time with Nate too. I feel guilty about not telling him yet. Poor darling, I've pushed him out of the way so often while we were studying. I might even ask Dad if he can come home this time.'

'How about going to the party and then getting up early Saturday morning and driving up? Better not drink too much!'

'I guess that'd work. I'll ring Nate and see if he's coming to the party for starters. He probably isn't. He hasn't mentioned it. But Claire, you'll come home with me on the Saturday, won't you? Stay for the first week or more of the holidays. The river will be wonderful at the moment.' She wiped some imaginary perspiration from her forehead and grinned as we both felt the heaviness of the hot, humid air. 'Lovely cool silky water.'

She dialled Nate's number and I couldn't help hearing them as they talked. The phone was on the bench where I was up to my elbows preparing spaghetti bolognaise.

'Hi Nate, do you want to go to the party at Jake's on Friday night?' Her face crumpled. 'Why on earth not?'

Nate's voice, a bit tense but teasing. 'You always said you wanted me to take you to the beach for a day. Well, Friday's when we're going. Before you go home. I'll pick you up about nine in the morning.'

She shrugged and her mouth drooped. 'Well, I'll have to get back here in time to pack for going home and then get ready for the party. I always look a mess after swimming outings. So we'd have to be home by, say, six.'

'I wouldn't worry too much about the party,' Nate continued. 'I reckon it'll be a fizzer. Everyone's already gone home for the holidays or will be on their way this week.'

'But you'll come, won't you?' Viv persisted.

'Not keen. I'll be wrecked after a day out. So will you, for that matter.'

'Well, if you didn't take anything or drink so much, you wouldn't feel so bad.'

'Look Viv, I just don't feel in a party mood at the moment, all right? And you'd be better off having an early night before you tackle the highway home.'

'Oh, please come, Nate. Even if it's just for an hour or two. I'd love to go and see everyone and for you to be with me. It'll be special.'

'Well ... I suppose I might turn up if I feel like it. I'll see where I'm at after Friday. Assume we're not going to the party.'

'You *might turn up if you feel like it*?' Disgust clouded her face. 'Okay, if that's the way you want it, I'll go with Claire. She won't have any ifs or buts. I'm definitely going. Well, what's wrong with that? You think I should stay away? What on earth for?'

'I'm asking you, as my fiancée, to stay home. You'll be too tired.'

She hung up abruptly with a clunk. 'I don't know where he's coming from tonight. Maybe he's on drugs again. Oh gosh, I hung up on him.'

I felt uneasy. Clouds of foreboding nudged my mind.

That night I heard Viv crying again.

'I need to talk to Suzanne before we go on Saturday,' Viv told me. 'I want my bracelet back.'

'Oh. Okay.' I was apprehensive.

So Viv managed to get herself invited to a formal dinner party she knew Suze would be at, and would probably be dressed up as well. It was the night before Jake's party and Viv's day out with Nate. She arrived home late-ish and slammed the door after her. *Oh no, it must have gone badly.*

I hauled myself out of bed and went out to have a hot drink with her. 'So ... how did it go?'

Viv scowled. 'Awful. She still won't admit it and she *wore* it, would you believe? To the dinner party. I saw my special charm I'd had made. She said the Nate-and-Viv charm was already on the bracelet when she bought it. Bought it! Huh! Not that I told her what the N and V stood for. She's totally dishonest. Like that husband of hers. I think he's been a bad influence on Nate.'

'She actually had the bracelet on?'

'Yeah. The nerve.'

Who could know who influenced whom with Nate and Jeff? I grimaced. 'So what can you do about it?'

'Nothing, I guess, but I don't plan to speak well of her.'

Not that she did at the best of times. I decided to keep my distance from Suze too, when possible, at least until this was sorted out.

I packed a small bag of clothes for about ten days at *Riverside*. My thoughts slipped to the boys as I stowed each item. Would they like my new swimsuit if they saw me? I'd lost a few kilos and Mark had told me I looked 'pretty good' when we went swimming a few days ago. Should I take my long dress? A new blue blouse? So I'd soon packed everything except last minute toiletries.

On the Friday night Viv and I prepared for Jake's party. Mark was taking us. At the last minute, he rang and told me he'd been held up and asked if Viv could drive us to the party and meet him there. Viv had arrived home from the Coast exhausted after a strenuous day with Nate on the beach. They'd walked up and down a fairly long track after swimming.

'Nate's had it,' Viv had informed me. 'I can't imagine he'll turn up tonight. I'm almost too tired to go myself. He bought fish and chips so we ended up having dinner on Burleigh Headland and watching the sun set behind the ranges. It was gorgeous but heck, Claire, I'm too tired to go out now. Let alone having to drive.'

My disappointment must have shown. Viv said, 'Oh, look I'll lie down for half an hour and then have a good strong coffee and I'll be right. Like you said, it's the last time this group of us will be together, assuming most of the old crowd turn up. I can't see Nate going. He never was keen about it. Only if he takes something and gets high, I guess he might be there. Gosh, he is my fiancé, though—as he so high-handedly reminded me.

'But he was even more wrecked than I was this afternoon. I don't know why he overdid it so badly. He's not all that fit now and he knew I wanted to go to the party. Stubborn man. He doesn't know the big news yet, though. I kept planning to tell him and then chickening out. Honestly Claire, I nearly threw up a few times walking around that hill when I was already tired. And then to have to eat fish and chips! It was touch and go.

'Oh gosh, look at the time. It's eight o'clock already and I have to pack a few last things before we go out. I wish Nate was more sensible at times.' She laughed. 'I suppose I'd be bored with him, if he was. And if he's planning to be one of those domineering husbands, he's in for a shock.'

She went to her room and had a rest. After half an hour, I knocked on her door. Sure enough, she'd fallen asleep. 'Oh,' she groaned. 'I'm so tired. But I said I'd go and I will.' She swung her legs off the bed and finished packing for *Riverside*. She began to sing *Lucy in the Sky with Diamonds* as she packed. *Getting herself into party mood*, I thought.

'Let's dress up a bit.' Viv had snapped out of her disappointment about Nate. 'It's our last proper uni party— well, with all the crowd there this time anyway.'

I guessed she wanted an occasion to wear May's latest creation—an exotic aqua and blue dress. She looked stunning in it—as always. I wore my favourite multi-coloured mini-dress again. It was one Mark had liked.

Viv looked at her reflection in the tall mirror in the hallway. 'I love the dress. I wish to goodness Nate was going to be there to see me in it.'

'There'll be other times,' I told her. 'And he could show up.'

'Yeah. I guess so.' She swivelled around and the dress floated in a cloud of ocean-coloured silk. 'Well, this is goodbye, for now at least, university.' She giggled. 'And Mark and Ian and Sally and Ophelia and Suzanne and Jeff and all the others. I wonder if they'll like my dress.'

'Viv! You look gorgeous. People always think you look great.'

She was flushed with enthusiasm. I felt peculiarly disconnected. I'd been looking forward to the party but now something inside me felt uncertain. Perhaps it was the combination of emotions at the end of the year so I ignored the feelings.

We arrived late, about midnight. The party was in full swing and lots of our friends were there. I felt quite glamorous and was enjoying it. Viv was giggling as we made our way through the crush of hot bodies. We expected to have fun. Mark grabbed me and kissed me in front of everyone.

One of the guys handed us each a glass of wine. I sipped away happily for a short time while Mark went off to get more to drink. I was surprised to notice the nice psychology lecturer, Pete, who had taken Viv out, in a corner with several attractive-looking girls around him. I rarely saw him at parties and remembered Viv's comment that he wanted only a serious relationship leading to marriage. For now, though, he looked relaxed and interesting. If it hadn't been for Mark … then I realised Pete's gaze was fixed on Vivien. There was no mistaking it. He admired her. And as far as I could tell, he didn't have any particular girl with him. Viv looked beautiful in her new dress, her face glowing and eager. Perhaps he would get to know her a bit better tonight.

Then I remembered Viv was pregnant. To Nate.

Only minutes later, Vivien grabbed my arm hard, with a loud gasp. I turned to her and my stomach clenched.

She stood there shaking and wide-eyed. I watched the blood drain quickly from her face until she was deathly white. Her mouth opened and shut as if she were trying unsuccessfully to speak. Perhaps without realising it, she had one hand protectively over her abdomen.

'What is it?'

She made a choking noise. 'Nate's here. After all his grand performance today. *He's with Sally. That woman! She's half-naked.*' Viv's voice was now a fierce whisper. She nudged her chin angrily in his direction and I looked.

Sally wore her lace dress with a pair of tiny undies and nothing else under it. Nate looked tired and bedraggled but was draped all over Sally. I could hardly believe it. He was not only Viv's fiancé but the father of her baby. Not that he knew about that.

I took a deep breath and went over to talk to him, hoping to break the ice and ask how he was. My throat tightened as I neared him.

He looked at me and raised an eyebrow. 'Don't ask. Full stop.' He swore.

That was a slap in the face after all our times together. Had it all been an act for him? Even his engagement to Vivien? Just another adventure? What if someone had dared him to get engaged?

As I returned to Viv, I saw Nate and Sally slip out the side door. Vivien looked sick. 'Claire, I can't cope with this.' She was trembling.

'Should we go home? You don't look too good.' I buried my disappointment.

She nodded and said in a strained, wooden voice, 'Well, there's no point in pretending to have fun. Do you mind? You could come back here after dropping me. You can take the car.'

I shook my head and pushed my way through the jostling dancers to Mark. 'Darl, Viv's feeling awful. I'll have to go home with her. We might even be leaving for *Riverside* tomorrow very early. So it's farewell for now.'

He begged me to stay but I was adamant. That funny gut feeling had been right. We shouldn't be there.

He looked disappointed and kissed me again. 'Stay in touch. Maybe I'll see you soon. Hope so.' Then I had to leave. Viv looked terrible. I glanced around and waved to a few people as we left. Goodness knows when I'd see them again. Pete's face stood out, gazing intently at us as we hurried towards the door and out into the night.

I drove, at Viv's insistence. When we arrived home, she sobbed, 'How *could* he? He lied to me. He didn't want me there, Claire. He tried to stop me going. That's why he made us both so tired today. And he's high on his stupid dope now too.' She gave a vicious kick at a cushion on the floor to get it out of the way. 'That night when he proposed, he told me he loved me and always had. I believed him. We've been close for so long.' She cried noisily for a few minutes and then took a deep breath. 'Has he forgotten that night here while you were away? I can't believe it.' She swore angrily and I tried not to wince. 'He's just treating me like one of his women. And he's a father. I'm not telling him now. She's MY baby.' She patted her stomach. 'I can't bear it, Claire, I really can't. I'm not staying here even one more night.' Her voice was rising, louder and higher, almost to a scream. I glanced nervously at the open window with neighbours close by. 'I *need* to get away. Are you awake enough to go right home—to *Riverside*—now, instead of waiting until the morning?'

A yawn nearly escaped me before I stifled it. I was tired despite my hype.

Vivien saw my uncertainty and went berserk. 'Claire, I *have* to get home. I can't bear it here. Nate was all over that woman ... he had his hands everywhere. Claire, come on, we have to go home.' Her words tumbled out and she began to sob violently. Hysterically. 'How dare he?' she half-sobbed, half-screamed. 'And he said he loved me. He must have known all along he was going to that party with Sally. No wonder he had us just about walking our legs off. Serve him right if he gets sick from overdoing it on top of all his dope.'

Panic erupted inside me. Here was Vivien, light-hearted Vivien, falling apart. Going half-crazy. I looked at my watch. Two-thirty. I remembered all my old ways of dealing with inappropriate emotions and pushed my own panic way down inside myself. I took a deep breath and looked at her as calmly as I could. 'Well, you're in no fit state to drive,' I said. 'If we *do* go, I'd have to drive.'

She shrugged but looked dubious. 'So? You're fine with the car.'

I thought about it. 'I guess I can do it. I only had a few sips of wine and that was before I saw Nate. Perhaps ten minutes rest and a cup of coffee before we go?'

'Are you packed?' she asked.

'Nearly. It'll only take a few minutes.' My brain was crystal clear now, on overdrive if anything. My clothes and bits were mostly packed. It would be terrific to drive up now as long as Viv settled down.

'It'll be sunrise in two or three hours, so if we relax over a cup of coffee and perhaps rest for a little while now, we'll be fine to do it. It'll be wonderful driving into the sunrise. Perhaps you can even grab a few minutes' sleep.'

Viv tore off her dress and pulled on a pair of shorts and a blouse. She threw her dress out of her room into a corner, where it lay in a colourful, crumpled heap like a huge broken butterfly.

I changed into jeans and a t-shirt. After a cup of strong coffee and the remains of a cake between us, we had a short rest and packed our things into the car. Viv was subdued now and looked pale. She yawned as we locked the house. 'I'm glad you're driving. I'm tired. You seem full of life still. Do you honestly feel up to it?'

'I'm fine. It's a great idea.'

As we packed the car, Viv said angrily, 'The nerve of him, flaunting Sally like that when everyone knows about his relationship with me. I don't suppose most people know we're engaged, though. I'm not sure who'd know. I had to have the engagement ring altered. It was too tight. So I haven't worn it around yet. Huh! I'll bet he didn't expect to see me there after walking me up hill and down dale.' Her face shone with tears in the yellow electric light in the garage.

'Perhaps it wasn't such a good idea to be okay about him going out with other people while you were "just" engaged,' I said. 'Although I was never sure when it was on and when it was off. I'd thought this was "the real thing" now.'

Viv burst into a fresh flood of tears. 'You know—we had champagne to celebrate being serious as an engaged couple. That was supposed to mean not going out with anyone else. But now I don't know if we're still supposed to be engaged at all. What am I meant to think? I'll have to discuss it with him when I feel ready. And I'm not telling anyone at all—except you—and of course Ellie and Mark know, and my parents definitely do—that we're engaged. *If* we still are. Claire, I don't know if I could trust him after this. I still love him, you know, but I don't know what to do.' She frowned and yawned.

I knew what I'd be doing, but Viv was Viv.

'Oh dear, it's such a mess. What will Mum and Dad say?' She sighed.

So off we went into the pre-dawn darkness.

# Chapter 34

Soon we were on the highway in the dark grey light that cloaks the land just before sunrise. I was feeling quite alert and for a while we talked.

At first Viv chattered a lot, seeming agitated and angry, but soon she wept again and then began to doze. After a couple of futile attempts to get her talking, I left her to sleep.

She woke just as we passed the Glass House Mountains. They loomed black and hulking like dark ships coming towards us on a foggy ocean. I glanced at them through the smudgy mist while we whizzed along. A faint streak of light tinged the top of Mt Tibrogargan with a pink glow. Dawn!

'Even in the middle of all this, it's terrific at this time of day,' Viv said. 'I love the mist too.'

'Gorgeous. There's a bit of traffic already, though. I was hoping we'd beat it. That car behind us is on my tail.'

'Mmm. It's not too bad, though.' Viv sighed and blew her nose, then gazed out the window.

The light grew stronger until it was almost daylight.

Suddenly I saw it.

A white car appeared from a lane through the cane fields and crossed the road so it crawled straight towards us, in the wrong lane. Our lane. Perhaps the driver was drunk. I blasted the horn as loudly as I could, hoping he'd somehow move out of the way. And again, trying not to panic, I pressed hard on the horn. 'Help! Viv, what's he doing?'

'God! Jesus!' called Vivien.

I couldn't stop; that other car was still on my tail. There was no extra lane to move into here. I beeped frantically. Then, as the white car continued to move inexorably towards us, I pressed the horn with all my might and kept my hand there.

He just kept on coming.

'Must be drunk or on dope,' Viv shrieked.

*God*, I thought, *make him stop.*

But he didn't.

I had no choice.

There was a lot of traffic on the other side, coming towards us.

I swerved hard to miss him and our car skidded off the road and rolled over and over down an embankment, finally wrapping itself around a gum tree.

I heard a scream; a scream I will never forget.

A hideous metallic crunch grated on my ears; then everything was black. As I groped my way to consciousness, a man was helping me out of the wreckage of Vivien's car, which was crumpled in an ugly mess.

I could barely move. My legs weren't working. The pain in them was crippling. Someone produced a rug and carefully put me on it. I couldn't even sit up and lay back awkwardly. Pain raged through me.

'Viv?' I croaked, in sudden terror. 'Vivien?'

I craned my neck painfully to try to see her. She'd worn her seatbelt—her father was adamant about it—but the car was dented and crushed there. Her head lolled to the side and blood was smeared all over her face and through her fair hair.

I stretched out my hand but couldn't reach her from where I lay on the ground. 'Viv?' I asked. I was gasping for breath. 'Are you okay?'

Silence.

Another man released her from her seatbelt and lifted her onto the grass near me. She lay there unconscious, deathly pale, her blonde waves spread out around her in sticky-looking blood-smeared clumps.

The man did what he could to make her as comfortable as possible, for what seemed ages.

She didn't move. She barely breathed.

The man looked up at me. 'I'm sorry. Your friend's unconscious. We've rung the ambulance from the fruit shop over there, though. They should be able to bring her around.' He wiped perspiration from his forehead. 'I'm sorry,' he said again.

I looked in vague horror at Vivien. Nothing seemed real. I felt detached as if looking through a thick pane of glass at someone else's world. I suppose I was in shock. I could feel nothing except the physical pain and the weight of the terrible thought, *What if Viv ... dies?*

It would be my fault. I should have stayed home and slept last night and then we'd have missed the collision. Viv would have been driving by then too.

My mind felt foggy. 'I've done something terrible,' I said to a bystander. People had gathered to look at us. Perhaps they hoped they could help. Quite a crowd had gathered and stood there looking awkward in the early morning light.

'Wasn't your fault, love,' a man said. 'I saw the whole thing. Darned ole fella in the white car, hit the bloke behind you but then somehow 'e got away all right in a smashed-up bomb of a car, but 'e musta been as drunk as a skunk. Drivin' a wreck after that. Both the other cars took a beatin'. Served 'em right. Helluva thing to happen. Nothin' more ya coulda done except take the white car out on the road. Let 'im wear it. But that woulda been worse. The car behind ya woulda crashed into you. Then there'd 'ave been three cars in the one wreck.' He pointed to where the car was dented right in, where I'd been sitting. 'Blow me down, look! Reckon Someone musta bin lookin afta ya.'

I looked and shivered, but felt nothing. My head swam and still I was aware of nothing except pain. The thought wandered through my mind, *It will be good if he's right and it really isn't my fault. Especially if Vivien is* ... I couldn't go there. The ambulance people would bring her through.

Vivacious people like Vivien didn't die young.

A siren's terrible scream rent the morning. The next thing I knew, ambulance workers lifted me carefully onto a stretcher and we were off to Nambour Hospital, the siren still blaring. The pain in my back and legs seared through me like hot knives. The nurse beside me gave me an injection, and my thoughts began to fade into oblivion.

*Someone musta bin lookin afta ya, someone musta bin lookin afta ya* ...

The words swam through my head as I groped my way through the haze in my brain, trying to regain consciousness. *Someone* ... who? Maybe he meant God. Maybe he was right. And maybe ... my thoughts dissolved mid-stream. I gave up and let the drugs take me back into darkness.

# Part Nine: Claire

## CHAPTER 35

I GROPED MY WAY through blinding pain to consciousness. My legs hurt. My back ached. A dim blue and white clad figure adjusted a tube beside my bed. There seemed to be a few other tubes attached to me too.

'Well, you're awake,' the dim figure said. A woman, I gathered. I tried to see her properly. Her face was swimming in and out of focus.

'My legs are hurting,' I said. My voice sounded strange and croaky. 'And my back.'

'You've got a pain-killer drip in your arm. You'll have to wait a while before we can give you any more.'

I tried not to groan. The room was swirling. Where was I? And what was I doing here? Fragments of memory began to form a picture. *Vivien screaming that she has to go home. Me driving the big car along the highway in the hazy grey pre-dawn. A white car coming towards us and Viv shrieking. Viv praying. The other car not stopping as I jam my hand on the horn. A terrifying metallic crash. Pain. Then darkness.*

My heart was trying to speed up as I lay on the bed, remembering. I felt woozy though. Everything seemed unreal.

Why had we been driving like that? It seemed crazy. And me driving—why wasn't Viv driving?

'Nurse?' I asked.

She kept fiddling with the tubes as she answered. 'What, love?'

'Where's Vivien? She's probably in here too.'

My eyes were in focus now. The nurse had a name tag. *Carol.* So Carol stood up straight, stretched her shoulders and gazed at me. She was frowning. 'Your friend's very sick. She was badly hurt in that accident you girls were in. You must've been driving like crazy.'

My eyes filled with tears that began to trickle down my cheeks. *Have I done something terrible?* I searched my hazy brain, trying to remember what had happened in the lead up. And bit by bit, it clarified. Viv's horrible drama over Nate. Driving Viv's car when she insisted on going home but was too hysterical to drive, and then that other car—*oh heck*, the driver must have been drunk or high.

'Is there someone I can talk to?' I asked. 'Someone who knows what happened? Oh—and where are we?'

'Nambour Hospital, love. There's a policeman who wants to talk to you as soon as you're well enough. If you're feeling up to it, you might like to talk to him before I give you any more pethidine.'

I nodded. 'I think I'm okay to talk.'

A navy-clad figure was soon hovering over my bed. I was propped up on pillows so I could see him as clearly as my fuzzy brain would allow. I gave him a rueful smile.

'Well, you're in the wars after that accident, aren't you?' he said.

I tried to smile again. My face felt funny.

'It wasn't your fault, you know,' he told me.

I had only hazy memories of the accident. I'd been driving Vivien's car—that memory was fixed in my tortured mind. I remembered the white car coming straight at us. Then it all seemed like a nightmare. 'Are you sure it wasn't my fault?' My voice wobbled.

'Got a clear report from the shopkeepers from the nearby fruit store and some of the people who stopped at the scene to try and help you. They were mainly local people and one fellow actually knew Vivien's car. Must've been a friend of the Barlow family. On his way home to near Vivien's property. He said the bloke in the white car must have been drunk or even on drugs. We'll get him. One bystander had the wherewithal to get his number plate. Hell, he got off easily—regarding the accident anyway. Had a prang with the bloke who was tailing you, though. Nothing like your accident. He kept driving a beat-up car. The bloke behind you was smashed up too but he ran for it, so to speak. You took it all, the way you swerved off the road. I'm just sorry to see you in so much pain and I hear your friend's seriously ill.'

'Viv! Please tell me, is she okay?'

'You'll have to ask the nurses that. But I know she was badly impacted by the crash. I've got her parents' number and I'm about to ring them. She had her licence and other bits in her handbag. We managed to get their number.'

He proceeded to ask me about my parents, my home phone number, and other details. *Oh dear! My parents!* He'd probably contact them. Poor Mum. As if she didn't have enough on her plate already. I tensed up, under the white blankets.

Soon after he left, the nurse came back. She asked me my date of birth, for some reason, then added more pethidine to my drip. The room swirled and faded, then I fell asleep again. I must have slept for ages because the next thing I knew, my parents were there.

'Darling!' It was Mum's voice, full of anxiety. 'Darling, how on earth did this happen?'

I groaned. 'Sorry, Mum, I'll tell you another time. I had to drive Viv's car. There was a car coming straight for us, on the wrong side of the road, so I swerved.' To my dismay, tears began to trickle down my face.

'Apparently they don't know the extent of your injuries yet,' Mum continued. 'But I brought you some things you might need.' She picked up an overnight bag and unzipped it, then lifted out a pretty nightie, some sets of underwear, and all sorts of bits—soap, shampoo, face cream, the works. Even makeup, which I had no intention of wearing in hospital. They were all feminine, though, and I smiled my thanks at Mum.

She gave me a careful half-hug, afraid she'd hurt me. 'So was Vivien with you?'

Tears started pricking my eyes again and Mum handed me a tissue from a box beside the bed. Dad was hovering behind Mum. I could see he was worried. Not surprisingly. Poor Dad. He'd had so much to cope with. I gave a wobbly smile then told them, 'I don't know how Viv is yet. But I hear she was badly hurt. My mind's still a bit vague about it all.'

'Of course, darling. We'd better not stress you. Is there anything you'd like us to buy for you?'

'Not at the moment, thanks Mum. I might fancy some fruit or something after a while.'

'We'll stay with Auntie Dorrie in Nambour overnight and come and see you again tomorrow. The girls are fine at home for a night or two. It's high time they were out of the nest anyway. But these days you never know how long they'll stay at home.'

The pain was kicking in again. I realised I'd slept for hours. Soon Mum and Dad left and the nurse gave me more pethidine. I was back floating in no-man's-land.

Again I pushed through to consciousness. The nurses nearby were talking quietly. 'Her friend's still unconscious,' Carol's voice said. 'I don't know if she'll make it. She's badly concussed.'

'Yeah. This one was driving, wasn't she?' That was the shrill voice of the dark-haired nurse. 'That'll be hard for her.'

I tensed up. *Viv really might die.* The well of trauma inside me sank deeper. Painfully. No matter what the policeman said, it definitely would be my fault. I could view it clearly now. We should never have been driving at all then. We should have stayed home until daylight and taken time for Viv to settle down so she could drive. It was her car.

If Viv was *dying*, I needed to see her. 'Carol?' I asked. My voice sounded croaky.

'What is it, love?'

'Can I see Vivien? I know I'm all hooked up here, but there must be some way I could get to wherever she is.'

Carol sighed. 'I'll ask the doctor. But your friend's unconscious so it's a waste of time, you know.'

'No, it's not! I need to see her. To see how she is for myself. I'm worried.'

'Yeah, well, she's in Intensive Care now. They might let you have a quick peep but you couldn't stay long. It's meant to be family only.'

A few minutes later, she arrived back with a doctor. He peered at me and frowned. 'You want to see your friend?'

'Yes, I need to see her.'

'She's a very, very sick girl. You'd have to be quiet and just whisper hello or something, then go back.'

My stomach felt tied in knots. But anything would be better than nothing. 'Yes, I will. Please let me.'

The doctor nodded at Carol, who began to adjust my tubes so they were attached to a pole on wheels. She went and found a wheelchair and brought it in. She and the dark-headed nurse helped me onto the chair. The pain pierced my right leg and nearly made me sick.

They wheeled me along a corridor and down another one. 'Here's Intensive Care,' Carol told me. 'I'll wheel you very quietly and you'll have to be quick.'

They pulled aside a curtain and there, lying on a bed, was Vivien. They wheeled my chair up close to her so I could see her properly. She was dead white and lay perfectly still. For just a moment I wondered ... then I pushed the thought aside. She was alive. There was hope. Then the memory clattered into my mind. She was pregnant. But was she, still? Or had the accident made her lose the baby? To my way of thinking, that would be a mercy.

'Viv,' I whispered. 'Can you hear me?'

Silence.

'Viv, if you can hear me, I'm sorry I drove the car and we had the accident. I'm so sorry. Please get better. Soon.'

She lay there, white and still. Tears were streaming down my face and the nurse turned my chair around and wheeled me away back to my own bed.

An hour later I was still weepy but awake when Carol called out, 'Visitor for you, Claire. Are you feeling up to seeing a friend?'

It was Mark. He was flushed and flustered, unlike himself.

'Claire!' He sounded almost distraught. 'Are you okay?'

'Well, apparently I've got a broken ankle and the other knee's sprained or something like that. And my back's sore. I think it's okay but it's twisted or something.'

Mark pulled a huge bunch of flowers from behind his back—bright gerberas, fragrant roses and various other pretty flowers. 'Claire, I don't want to think how I might have lost you. I'm not risking really losing you. So—will you marry me?'

I was laughing and crying all at once. 'Oh, Mark, of course I will. As long as you're sure.'

'Hell, Claire, I'm certain. I was devastated when I heard about the accident. I was so scared I'd lost you and realised my life would be a mess without you. I need you, Claire. You're my anchor. And I find you very, very attractive.'

'Even like this?' I asked with an attempt at a smile.

'Even like that.' He swore. 'You're beautiful. But I apologise, I didn't stop to buy you a ring. I didn't have time because I wanted to see for myself you were okay. We'll go shopping together straight away when you're well enough. And let's get married as soon as possible. We've been going together for donkeys' years.'

Tears were running down my face and I was smiling. He leant over and kissed me gently.

'How did you know I'd had an accident? And where to find me?'

'Your mother rang me. You must have given her my number for some reason.'

*Dear Mum.* She'd be thrilled at the outcome once she got over my injuries. I had to have surgery on my ankle so she was staying with Auntie Dorrie for a while yet.

'I'll drop Dad home after a day or so,' she'd said. 'He'll be all right on his own for a few days, now, and the girls can help if necessary. Julie's mature now. She can let the boyfriends have a few days without her. Lee's at work at the hospital a lot of the time.'

Mark cleared his throat. 'I'm sorry I took all these years to be sure about marriage. But there were actually two things holding me back.'

'What? Oh, your parents.'

'That's number one, well and truly. But I sometimes wondered if you were a bit too phlegmatic for me. You know, you hardly ever showed any emotions in those first few years. But wow!—I know you're a loving, caring woman with plenty of emotions. You've changed over the years, actually.'

'Well, there's a story behind that, Mark. I'll tell you one day.'

Mark was concerned that I was still in pain. 'Nurse!' he called to Carol. 'Claire needs a bit more of that painkiller.'

Carol looked grim. 'It's too early. She'll be getting more in an hour.'

Mark looked strained. He seemed to find my pain harder to handle than I did. He sat beside my bed for ages until, to my slight embarrassment later, I drifted off to sleep after the nurse put more pethidine in my drip.

I woke to find myself crying. Sobs welled up from deep inside me. I was going to marry Mark! He had proposed at last! All the tears I'd bottled over the years welled up in great sobs.

After a few minutes, I realised they'd become happy tears. *Dear Mark.* He'd always been the man for me. And at last we'd be marrying. I drifted again into a happy doze. I'd been half-asleep for perhaps an hour when a nurse woke me, gently stroking my arm. I made my eyes focus on her. Big green eyes, dark hair. A friendly face.

'I've been asleep again and Mark's gone,' I said stupidly. I began to tell her my news. I had a vague memory of Viv saying Mark needed a fright to shake him into proposing to me. Seems she'd been right—but never imagined anything this terrible. But he would have come to it one way or another, I believed.

The nurse nodded. 'That's wonderful. I put your flowers in a big vase. Look!' She pointed to a large glass vase sitting on top of my dresser. 'But Claire, there's a young fellow here who says he's Vivien's fiancé. He's insisting on seeing her, even though it's family only and you, I suppose. I assume if they're engaged, it's like family, isn't it? Is she really engaged?'

My heart thudded. Nate. 'She's sort of engaged but he's given her a lot of trouble and I think she'd be much better off not seeing him yet. Not that she knows who's there. She's unconscious.'

'You'd be surprised,' said the nurse. *Steph*, this one had on her nametag. 'People say stuff to an unconscious person, thinking she doesn't hear, and she tells you afterwards what was said. It's spooky.'

'Well, I seriously don't think you should let Nate see her at this point.' My voice was shaking. Nate! After that awful night. Nate and his drugs and never-ending trouble. Nate with Sally.

Steph walked away and a minute later returned. 'Could Nate talk to you instead? Do you feel up to it?'

'As much as I ever will.'

Soon after, Nate came in, holding a big bunch of pink roses. 'Hi Claire. These are for Viv when she wakes up.'

I pointed to another vase on the dresser and a sink with a tap. 'Would you put them in water for now, please, Nate?'

He plonked them in the vase and turned to me. 'Hey Claire, this accident, it wasn't anything to do with me, was it? I mean, Viv might have got a bit upset seeing me at that party.

I'd told her I wasn't going so it would have been a bit of a, hell, a bit of a surprise, I gather.'

'Nate! Of course she was upset. You're meant to be engaged to her. Viv said you'd agreed not to take out other girls now, hadn't you? And Nate, for goodness sake, everyone knows Sally's reputation. No criticism intended but ... where's your commitment to Viv?' I nearly choked on the words that wanted to pour out of me. Words like: *do you know you're a father now? Are you going to look after Viv and the child?* And a lot of ugly words I'd been brought up to avoid saying.

'Hell, Claire. Sally was only for one night that time. I'd arranged it days ago. A sort of a last fling before I settled down to being serious with Viv. There was nothing in it. Sal's a good-time girl.'

I bit back everything I felt like saying. Burning inside me was the thing I most longed to tell him: to get right out of Viv's life and leave her to find a decent man and settle down.

'I'm sorry, Nate. It backfired badly. I think you've got some serious thinking to do or you'll hurt Viv again.'

'Treating me like the big bad wolf, eh? And when *can* I see her? Hell, I dunno, Claire. Well, I hope you get better soon. You were hurt too, were you?'

'Yes, a broken ankle and a few other bits and pieces. Nothing as bad as Viv.'

'Well, get well soon.' He disappeared out into the corridor.

My head was aching after the encounter, in spite of the pethidine. Would Viv still forgive him and marry him? I found the idea appalling but ... Viv was Viv.

# Chapter 36

'Oh, darling!' May's voice woke me as I dozed the next day. I'd just come out of the anaesthetic after surgery on my ankle and, according to Carol's chat beforehand, they'd planned to put several metal pieces in my ankle to shape it in the right position as it healed. So—I shuddered at the idea—I now had metal in my ankle. I pushed my way through the post-operative sedative to see May arranging beautiful flowers from their front garden in another vase she'd found.

'Darling, you're awake! How are you feeling?'

I groaned and then gave an attempt at a laugh. 'Sore.'

'What a terrible thing to happen to you dear girls. When you're feeling a bit better, you can tell me more about how it all happened but for now we just need to get you both well and up and walking again.' She half-choked on a sob. 'Oh dear, I was so upset when the police rang us. I just couldn't believe it. Vivvie's such a good driver. Whatever other silly things she might do, she's very sensible on the roads.'

*Oh no. They've assumed Viv was driving. What will they say when I tell them…?*

Steph interrupted us to ask me my pain levels. 'Tell me how much pain you're in, on a scale of one to ten.'

'Oh gosh. Maybe about eight now.' The pain made it very hard to think. Steph added more pethidine to the drip and my head swam.

'Oh dear,' May said. 'Poor darling.'

'How's Viv today?' I asked in a croaky voice. My mouth and throat were dry.

May gave me a sip of water, saying with a break in her voice, 'Just a tiny sip,' then, 'Vivvie's more or less conscious but she's very badly hurt. They're going to operate on her leg tomorrow if she's properly conscious. But I think the hit to her head was the worst thing. She's starting to come round but she drifts back out of it fast. One of her legs is broken and it needs surgery. Dear Vivvie. Claire ... I had Viv on my mind yesterday. So I prayed for her. Just as well or she might have ... well, you both might have ... anything could have happened to you both.' May's voice wavered and she blinked away tears. 'Claire?'

'Mmm?'

'Would you mind praying for Viv tomorrow at ten o'clock in the morning when they operate? I'll ask them to tell you if it's not going ahead then. Please pray for no complications and she'll come right through, you know—that she'll be well and able to walk and everything normally.' May's voice wobbled and she blew her nose on a tissue from beside my bed.

*Does she think I'm a believer like them? What has Viv told them?* Well, I could pray even if there was no god to hear my prayers. It would do no harm. I certainly wanted Viv to come through. I wanted her to be well so we could walk and swim together like we used to. That part was selfish motivation, I realised. 'Sure,' I told May.

Bert's head poked around the doorway. 'Claire, how are you?'

May replied for me. 'She's just had an op, Bert. I think we'd better leave her to recover in peace for now.'

'We'll be praying for you, Claire,' Bert said. May leant over and kissed my cheek, then they went out the door.

I drifted in and out of sleep that day and was able to eat a very small, light meal in the evening. I found it hard to sleep that night. I was just starting to doze when the night nurse came around. She shone a bright torch on my face and asked, 'Still awake?'

Well, I was then! 'I can't sleep properly. I suppose I've slept all day.'

'You need it at the moment. Take this.' She handed me a small tablet and a glass of water. I swallowed the tablet, sipped some water and lay back, hoping for sleep. Viv's face swam before me. I was terrified she wouldn't come through all this properly. Or at all. My mind tormented me, replaying the horror of the accident and not knowing what to do as the white car headed towards me.

I must have slept because the next thing I knew, a nurse wheeled a huge rattling trolley around and handed plates of food to some of the other patients. She came into my little room and asked, 'Ready to eat breakfast?'

'I guess so, thanks.' She set up my bed with a tray across it and I ate a bit of porridge and a few mouthfuls of toast. I still felt too sick to eat much. Then I remembered. Today was the day they operated on Viv. Although it was only her leg. I'd had my ankle done and it was no big deal although I still had a lot of pain. I wanted to see Viv again before her operation but Carol said she had enough on her plate.

I tried to read for a while. Mum had brought me a new book. *Voss* by Patrick White. I always enjoyed his writing. That morning my head was a bit woozy, though, and I gave up after a few minutes.

At five to ten I decided to pray. *Well, God, if you're there, I* began, *I suppose this counts as prayer with you. I'm so sorry about the accident. It was my fault. I'm not strong enough to stand up to Vivien when she puts the pressure on. It was just so hard. I didn't know what to do when she panicked and went hysterical. And I panicked too. I made a quick decision and it was the wrong one. Sorry. I really am incredibly sorry. I hope Viv and her parents can forgive me. The car was probably a write off and Viv's ... well, I won't say she's a write off too*—I choked back a sob—*but you know what I mean.*

I paused and thought for a minute. My head was still dopey. *Anyway, God, please bring her safely through this operation and help her to get back to the bubbly, healthy person she used to be. And please don't let everyone blame me if ... well, if things don't go well. I know that's selfish but I do desperately want her to come through whole and well for her sake mainly—I really care about her —but I'm scared about her family if she doesn't, when I was the driver. It was my fault and I'm sorry. Very sorry.*

I sniffed and blew my nose. *Well, God, that's a lot of bits and pieces. And Viv was pregnant. I don't know how it's okay to pray about that. Please look after the baby whether it's inside Viv still or if it's gone to heaven. If that's what happens. Please do bring Viv safely through today. And—I know this is selfish—but please make her get properly well so we can go walking and swimming together again when we're through this. I want everything to be the way it used to be. Things used to be so good. Amen.*

I was crying as I finished praying. What if ...? *Will* Viv be all right? Would they realise she was pregnant during this op, if she still *was* pregnant? Would it have shown up in her blood tests? I reached out to the bedside drawers, grabbed a tissue and blew my nose. I was so desperate for us both to come through well and for life to go on as it had been before. Except now I had Mark properly in my life. We'd be married at last. But Nate. What would Viv do about him?

Words kept beating at the edges of my mind, around and around. '*Someone musta bin lookin afta ya, someone musta bin lookin afta ya.*' It was the man at the accident site. He'd seen the crushed door where I'd been sitting. Theoretically I should have been killed. Someone probably did look after me. I suppose that would have to be God.

My mind slipped sideways to Viv's parents. Such lovely people and so happy. Sincere Christians. Viv was too in her own quaint way. So why did God let this awful thing happen to her? Then I decided things like that could happen to anyone. It'd be different if she'd caused the accident. Maybe. Or *had* she caused it, indirectly?

I frowned at nobody and decided life was too complicated. My head was aching again. And yet, I had this odd feeling niggling at my mind: I'd rather be a believer and be happy than be a non-believer and try to work out what was what. Nobody was perfect, anyway, not even Christians. Like Viv. Perhaps

May could explain a few things to me before I committed myself to a belief I'd avoided for so long. I'd kept putting it off, afraid of becoming narrow-minded.

So when Bert and May popped in again on their way to check on Viv after her surgery, I asked, 'May, can I ask you something important as soon as you have a few minutes?'

'Why not now? The little blonde nurse said Vivvie's still sound asleep so I've got a few spare minutes.'

'Thanks. May, why doesn't God prevent bad things happening to good people? Well, even Christians?'

'Darling, God gave us all freewill. We make our own decisions. If we're sensible, we ask God to lead us as we make big choices. But we don't always think to do that and we really do reap the consequences of our choices.' She gave a wry smile. 'Not always fun. Perhaps like Vivvie and her drive that morning. She must have been overtired although the policeman assured me it was the other man's fault.' She sighed. 'That's enough for now, I think. We'll talk more another time.' She stood up, brushed some pollen from my flowers off her skirt, then said, 'I'll go and see if Viv's awake.' She kissed my forehead and headed off with Bert, who had hovered in the corridor.

So two important things came out of that, I figured. I *did* want to be a Christian. And I still had to tell May and Bert I was the one driving. Somehow that scary piece of information had escaped them.

I told God I wanted to be a Christian and I was sorry I hadn't believed in Him before. Viv had mentioned about confessing your sins. I couldn't think of any real sins. Maybe not believing in the God who created me was a sin. I was still trying to work out what to do when Steph came in and topped up my pethidine. Soon I was drifting, then dozing.

When I woke I was happy. Alive with real joy. And I sensed a gentle presence around me, like a living cloud. I remembered trying to become a Christian. It must be the presence of God! It felt wonderful. *Jesus?* I asked silently. The presence intensified and I felt sure God was with me in a special way. *Will you lead me to become a real Christian?* Again the presence grew stronger and there was a bubble of joy inside me so strong I nearly burst out laughing. This must be it! Him!

'Just heard from the boyfriend?' Steph asked me. I hadn't noticed her there.

I laughed out loud. 'No. Something better.' She looked puzzled and checked my drip. 'And guess what, Mark and I are actually engaged now! We've been going together on and off for years but now it's the real thing.'

'Well, congratulations!' Steph looked genuinely pleased for me. 'But there's actually another boy here to see you today. He wanted to see Vivien but I said she's not ready so he wants to see you.'

Who would it be now? Was I like a receptionist for all Viv's admirers? Steph went out and in walked Tom. His blond hair and tanned skin all looked so healthy in this pale hospital environment, he looked terrific.

'Claire, heck, I'm sorry to hear about this.' He handed me a bunch of flowers. 'They're just from the garden. I brought enough to give some to Viv too but they won't let me yet.'

He wanted to hear all about the accident. His big eyes were even wider as he heard the scant details I assumed were okay to tell.

'By the way,' he told me, 'I thought you'd be interested to know I'm going out with one of Ruth's friends at the moment.' His eyes twinkled. If ever there was a guy who deserved to find the right girl ...

Soon Steph told him it was time to go. As he waved goodbye from the doorway, I thought what a shame it was Viv had fallen for Nate instead of Tom. But Tom wouldn't be exciting enough for Viv's temperament and he'd only be happy with a contented wife. A good guy.

I resumed thinking about being a Christian and married to Mark—a double blessing—and how good it all felt.

But then my thoughts catapulted into something else. What would Mark think about my being a Christian?

# Chapter 37

Viv had come through her leg surgery well but still had a permanent headache and at times lost consciousness briefly, so she had little blackouts. It was scary seeing her like that but she seemed quite at peace.

The first time I saw her after her surgery, she was very subdued. She lay there with tears streaming down her cheeks as we began to talk. 'Claire, I've lost my baby,' she sobbed. 'I wanted her.'

As she was so upset about it, I tried to disguise my mixed feelings but had no idea what to say.

'The hospital counsellor came and talked to me for a while and told me I'd been pregnant. She asked me whether I'd known I was pregnant and told me I'd lost the baby. She suggested I have more counselling. I won't though. Oh Claire, I wanted that baby.' She took a deep breath. 'Thank goodness, they're not going to tell my parents. I'm an adult, after all, and it would only upset them.'

I tried to be caring and compassionate about the baby but I honestly felt Viv was better off. But how could I chatter on with my own good news when Viv was so miserable? I did it anyway. 'Viv, I'm a Christian now! I'll tell you all about it when you're feeling better.'

Her face lit up. 'Claire, that's wonderful. Did Mum talk you into it?'

'No, but she helped.'

Viv looked happier. I decided to leave telling her about Mark and me until she felt a bit better.

I'd been wheeled around to visit her a few times now. I loved seeing her but it was also upsetting. She was miserable about the baby. And I felt guilty about the accident. Viv didn't blame me at all, but I was at fault and I knew it. Okay, God had forgiven me, but I hadn't forgiven myself yet. I'd been rash—unlike me. If this was where expressing my emotions led me, I'd be better off getting safely back under my mask. But then I thought of Mark and how he loved the real me. Perhaps I just needed to get back to using more wisdom in the future.

'Viv,' I said the next morning, 'Nate wants to see you. He's still your fiancé, you know. I realise it won't be easy but I think you should face him and get it out of the way.'

Viv's eyes were closed and her eyelids flickered. 'No,' she sighed. 'I can't, Claire. I'm not ready to face him. I don't know what to think about him anymore. And Claire, the baby. He never knew and I guess he wouldn't specially have cared.' Tears ran from beneath her eyelids. 'I'm not going to tell him.' Her voice dropped. 'You know, Claire, I still do sort of love him. But I feel like ...' She paused and cleared her throat '... like something inside me is broken and he's not the right person to mend it. I'll have to see how I feel after I get better. I don't know whether I want to marry him now.'

The next time I saw her, she asked, 'Will Mark cope with you being a Christian?'

I shivered. 'Gosh, I hope so. I *really* hope so. Because we're actually engaged now. We're getting married as soon as I'm home and up and running enough to organise it.'

'That's wonderful. Congratulations!' She giggled. 'After all this time. Fancy!—It took a car accident. Nate's shown his true colours too. That Sally relationship was the cause of the accident, I suppose. There'll always be a good excuse with Nate. "His last fling" and all that. Shame—he's such fun. But I could never trust him now.' Tears trickled down her cheeks again and I felt embarrassed at being so happy.

A few hours later, Mark arrived again. My hand was shaking as I sipped tea with him. 'Mark,' I said tentatively, 'I need to tell you something.'

He frowned. When Mark frowned properly, his whole forehead folded up into a concertina of wrinkles. 'What's wrong?'

'I've decided to become a Christian. I'll tell you more about it later but please keep in mind, God saved my life. The car door where I was sitting was all crumpled in. I should have been dead.' I took a deep breath. 'So how will you feel about having a Christian wife? Are you still okay to go ahead and get married?'

Mark looked shocked.

My insides quivered.

'Hell, Claire, what do you think I am? Of course we're getting married. And of course it's fine for you to be a Christian. I'll have to give it some thought for myself but I'm totally happy for you to believe like that. It seems to make for happy people. And I respect you for having the guts to make that decision.'

Relief must have shone all over my face. 'Oh, Mark, you're gorgeous.'

We talked for over an hour before Carol came and told me it was time to have a break.

Surprisingly, it was my parents who gave me the most resistance. Mum in particular was quite against it. 'Claire, how can you believe in a good God when your father came home from the war like this? How *can* you? And you so intelligent too. I wouldn't be so shocked if Julie made a silly decision like that, but you with all your brains! I just can't believe it.' She burst into tears.

I looked at Dad. He looked grim but calm. 'It's your life, Claire. Just be sure before you go too far with all this stuff. There are some very strange people out there, selling Bible stories like fish and chips. Give it some thought, love.'

'Dad, I've been thinking about this for years now. I've made my decision. It's what I want for my life. And Mark's happy about it.'

Mum frowned. 'But he's never going to marry you now, you'll have to face that. Nobody wants a religious wife.'

'Mum! He's fine about it and—we're engaged now! He loves me.'

*Poor Mum.* What a lot of shocks for her in a few days after years of fairly steady life. I was sure she'd come around, though, when she'd had time to think about it. She often reacted badly to surprises.

Viv was out of Intensive Care but they were keeping a close eye on her. I managed to wheel myself around to visit her a few times a day, once my drip was detached from my arm and I was on oral painkillers. They weren't as effective as the drip but were still strong enough to dull the pain and make my head feel strange. I felt peculiar using a wheelchair but it was great to be able to get around again.

Viv was sitting propped up against a mound of pillows when I next saw her. She looked tired but quite happy, to my surprise.

'Viv,' I asked cautiously.

'Mmm?'

'Have you decided for definite if you'll go ahead with marrying Nate after all that's happened?'

She sighed deeply. 'You know,' her face twisted in pain as she talked, 'I wasn't going to tell anyone at all but it's different with you. This amazing thing happened. I suppose I would've forgiven Nate and married him, even though he'd hurt me so badly. Crushed me, I guess. I still feel like that. Sort of crushed. But something happened.'

'What?'

'I was out to it, unconscious, and yet I was aware of some things, like I knew when people were talking to me. And then there was silence and a clear voice in my mind. I somehow knew it wasn't any of you guys visiting me. This was different. The words were so clear in my head, I thought it was God. I still think it was, you know.'

'Wow, lucky you!'

'Yeah, but what He said wasn't easy for me at first.' She shivered. 'He said, "I don't want you to marry a man like Nate." So how about that! I felt sure it was right. And it didn't mean just Nate but anyone like that. That type of bloke. It was so clear and all of a sudden I was conscious and completely alert straight after it. But I thought, "Well, I'll have to stay single." I *like* "men like Nate." Even if Nate himself did the dirty on me. But that's the kind of guys I'm attracted to.'

She sniffled. 'But you know, I'd already sort of decided about Nate. When I was first in hospital and I had awful cramps in my stomach ...' She turned away and I realised she was remembering the baby she'd lost. '...I felt so sick, I wondered if I was dying. And thought, *I can't face Nate. He's the last person I want to see when I'm maybe dying.*' Tears trickled onto her pillow. 'He was using me. I don't feel safe with him.'

She closed her eyes. 'Anyway, I need to have a sleep. We'll catch up more soon. But don't worry.' Her face twisted again. 'This whole accident is basically Nate's fault. But I'm finding it hard, *really* hard, to imagine life without "a man like Nate".'

So Viv considered Nate the cause of the accident. And I felt it was at least partly my fault. I'm usually intelligent enough to have handled that awful night better. Sooner or later, I'd have to tell her parents the truth. There'd be lots of questions. And I'd have to be very careful.

I knew Viv's secrets.

# Chapter 38

Viv had to stay in hospital after I'd gone home as she still had brief black-outs and the doctors were concerned. They told her to be careful once she went home and not to swim out of her depth. Perhaps never again.

My heart sank. All our blissful times swimming together in the river, then lying on the sand on the far bank while we dabbled our feet in the water and the sun warmed us through. The only easy way to that far bank was by swimming across the deep hole.

Way, way out of our depth.

I remembered the day I'd had that strange feeling there. As if time had stopped. At one stage I'd decided it related to Nate and the drug drama but that was only the beginning. The sharp, menacing tip of a vicious iceberg.

I hastily pulled my thoughts back to Viv. Here was I bemoaning my loss of time on the river with Viv, while she still lay in hospital with an unknown future. Dear Viv. She was coping well, considering.

I had to go home to my parents' place after hospital as the doctor was adamant I couldn't drive yet. I was lucky to get an excellent physio and enjoyed getting to know her. Mum loved having me home, even though I was concerned I was adding to her load.

*Poor Mum!* I truly did feel awful about being another burden to her.

'Darling! Don't be silly. As if I'd want you to be anywhere else while you're recovering after such a terrible accident. I'll be delighted to look after you. It'll give me time to catch up with you—you're always so busy. And the other girls can help me sometimes.'

Soon my physio had me walking most of the time without crutches. She said I'd be able to drive in a week or two at that rate.

Nate appeared at the front door one day. 'Viv's broken it off,' he told me in forlorn tones. 'For good, she reckons.'

I was relieved she'd had the courage to do that. Apparently he was playing his flute in a local orchestra as well as farming, so I figured he'd be all right.

I watched him when he headed off—a lonely figure with his lurching gait, facing life without the girl he declared he still loved. His eyes were dull despite his claim that flute playing made him so happy.

When I phoned Viv in hospital and told her, I was surprised and a bit relieved about her response. 'Claire, I'm not going on a guilt trip over Nate. Unless his drugs mess him up too much, he'll be fine. Not only with his flute but he's doing a philosophy course next year, Tom told me. And girls love Nate. He's attractive. He's fun. He'll find a way out of his loneliness.'

Despite what Viv said, I still sensed in Nate an inherent solitude that sometimes haunted me. Nate—our former friend.

'Guess what! I'm going home tomorrow,' Viv's voice sounded cheerier than it had for ages.

The next day I rang her just before she was due to leave, to wish her well. To my surprise, the almost-vibrant girl of the former day was gone. Viv sounded miserable.

'What's wrong?' I asked.

'Would you believe Alan's on holidays too and he's coming home for a while and bringing a group of friends with him.'

'So?'

'I don't want to meet any men while I'm looking so pathetic.' She groaned into the phone.

'Viv, you look just fine.'

'Yeah, with crutches or even a wheelchair for a while.'

'Oh well, I'm sure you'll be okay. You always manage so well.'

A few days before Christmas, to my surprise Suzanne arrived at the door and Mum let her in. 'Visitor for you, Claire.' Then Suzanne was on the back porch with me.

'Well, this is a surprise!' I managed.

'Claire, I've always found you so easy to talk to. I need to say something.'

My heart raced.

'I did take that bracelet of Vivien's. It was the day I popped in for a cuppa. I heard you'd been blaming Sally for a while and I felt awful. Sal's okay.'

'Suze, why on earth did you do it? You've got enough money to buy your own. Well, so you tell me.'

She sighed. 'I loved it so much and Vivien didn't need it. She's got everything and she doesn't share any of it with me—she's never even invited me home to that farm. She's spoilt. I was actually short of cash. Jeff had run up a few bills.'

I suspected what they'd have been.

'When I was at your place,' Suze continued, 'the bracelet was lying on the bathroom bench. I knew it was hers because I'd seen it on her. It was just what I wanted for my wedding so I slipped it in my handbag. I figured it might have sentimental value to Vivien and—well, I wanted to hurt her. So there, I've told you.' Tears were running down her cheeks and she handed me Viv's bracelet. I put it away ready to take to her next time I saw her.

Against all odds, I was sorry for Suzanne. She was not a very likeable girl but, up to a point, I still esteemed her in some ways.

Viv was discharged from hospital to have Christmas at *Riverside*.

I was missing Mark, who was on holidays with friends in PNG. Missionaries, to my surprise. I wondered if they'd have more influence on his believing than I'd had so far.

Christmas Day was fun. Mum amazed me by cooking a full-scale traditional Christmas dinner—turkey with cranberry sauce, baked veggies to go with it and a plum pudding with custard and ice cream. It was delicious. To avoid the intense heat, we had the meal in the deep cool shade of the magnolia tree.

Christmas evening brought a surprise. Mark! He'd come home from PNG a bit earlier than expected and had spent most of Christmas Day with his family.

He handed me a carefully wrapped parcel. 'Careful, it's fragile.'

It was a beautiful vase. 'Bit of a selfish pressie actually,' Mark laughed. 'It's for our home when we're married.' He kissed me. 'We're going shopping for that engagement ring in a few days, when the shops are open again.'

I almost jumped for joy and I caught Mum looking surprised and thrilled.

I'd asked Julie to buy some exotic chocolates for Mark. He was delighted.

The next morning I was woken by the phone ringing. Mum knocked, then poked her head around my door. 'Claire, there's a phone call for you. You've slept in. It's already nine o'clock and Mark's been talking to your father for ages. Dad wanted to hear all about Papua New Guinea.'

'Who's the phone call?'

'Mrs Barlow. Vivien's mother.'

Oh no, I'd blown it. I should have rung her first. Perhaps she was just ringing to wish me happy Christmas. If I were lucky.

I wasn't.

'Claire, darling, I hope you had a lovely Christmas. Claire, Bert and I were just wondering about that terrible accident. Vivvie said she wasn't driving the car when we asked her how it happened. So you were, I gather. So ... we just need to understand how you came to be driving Viv's car and how the accident happened. The policeman told us it wasn't your fault but there are parts we don't understand.'

'Well I ... um, Viv ...' I groped for words. How on earth could I explain it to them? Viv had been hysterical. I'd panicked too, seeing her like that. 'Well, it's actually hard to explain but ...'

She cut across me. 'Darling, how would it be if you came up here for a night or two? We could talk it through and you could have a nice relaxing time as well. And of course, catch up with Vivien. She's lonely. If you're not up to driving yet, perhaps Mark could come too.'

So the following Tuesday saw Mark driving me to *Riverside*. I wore a yellow mini sundress to keep cool and tied my hair back in a ponytail.

'Wow!' said Mark when he picked me up. 'Terrific colour on you.' And he helped me and my crutches into the car. Soon we were on the familiar highway to the Sunshine Coast. We talked eagerly about our future until needles of nervousness jabbed my stomach when we pulled in to *Riverside*.

We parked under the fig tree near the kitchen. May greeted us with her usual warm hugs, then led us inside. Viv was waiting there, sitting on an armchair they'd pulled into the kitchen corner. She had one leg up on a stool and cushions packed around her. 'Claire! It's been so long! You look terrific—but crutches still.'

'Just a bit tired, I think. I've been walking without them quite a bit.'

Mark had bought a simple but classy diamond ring which I loved and I showed it off to the whole family.

'Congratulations, darling!' May hugged me. They left me to talk to Viv, while Mark made some coffee.

I smiled my thanks.

'How are you recovering, Viv? And where are your brother and all his friends you were concerned about? And Alan's fiancée?'

She paused. 'I'm pretty well okay but the doctor still says no swimming out of my depth—probably ever again. Because this weird thing happens—don't get a fright if it happens while you're with me—I still go unconscious for a few seconds quite often.' She pulled a face. 'I don't think I'll be allowed to drive if it continues.' She took a deep breath. 'Alan and his mates are out canoeing and Pamela, his fiancée, is having time with her family at home down at the Gold Coast.'

'Viv, look in my handbag. I've brought your bracelet back.' I'd told her on the phone about Suze.

Viv thanked me. Suddenly she burst into tears. 'Oh, poor Suzanne!'

After lunch under the fig tree, we all chatted in a superficial way. Bert looked stern. Soon May brought out tea and coffee and we all sat back, theoretically to relax. My stomach was in a knot.

'Darling,' May said, 'Bert was wondering how you came to be driving Vivien's car. It's a big car and it must have been hard for you to manage it. No wonder things went so badly wrong.'

I stared at her. They still had no idea what had actually happened. Perhaps they hadn't even known Viv had always liked me to drive her car at times. My mind was screaming again, *I shouldn't have been driving it. I should have told Viv to go to bed so she'd be at least able to drive us up in the morning.*

I was guilty.

But ... in that atmosphere of panic and trauma, I'd found it impossible to make a clear decision.

Viv interrupted. 'Dad, I more or less *made* Claire drive. It was totally my fault.'

Bert looked at me and I understood what Viv had meant about his grim look. 'Claire?'

I cleared my throat, as my voice had become croaky. 'Well, Viv was very upset and she desperately wanted to go home straight away. She was too upset to drive—she couldn't have driven safely in that state—so I said we could go if I drove. And she wanted me to.'

'Bit presumptuous of you, wasn't it?' Bert's eyes were assessing me.

'I'm sorry. I can't tell you how sorry I am. Maybe it was presumptuous, I don't know about that. But we were both upset then. I was upset to see Viv so unhappy and, well, almost hysterical.' *Should I have said that? Oh dear.* 'I wanted to help her out of that mess so it seemed the thing to do.'

'Well, obviously it wasn't.'

'You mean, because of the accident?'

'The policeman told me it was not your fault. He recounted the scene when I talked to him. Nice bloke. But Vivien would have handled it better. She's a country driver.'

I was shrinking inside myself. Suddenly it all seemed unfair and anger welled up inside me until I was furious on the inside. How dare he assume Viv would have handled it better? But it was one of those situations where I thought I'd better mask my emotions. 'I'm very sorry. I did what I thought was best in a difficult situation but this awful thing happened to us.'

'Hell, Bert,' Mark interrupted. 'Claire's a clear-headed, sensible girl. I'm marrying her, for goodness sake. She did her best in a messy situation. Can't you just forgive her and lay off her now?'

Bert frowned and cleared his throat. 'We'll leave it at that. I'm just very sorry it all happened to two lovely young women.' He stood up and walked away to the house.

Tears were streaming down my face. Mark had his arm around my shoulders. May began to clear the table.

I needed to go and sit by myself in my spot beside the river. 'Mark, I need a few minutes to myself. Would you mind if we get together again in about half an hour?'

'If you're okay. I'll be in the kitchen if you need me.' Mark went to the house.

Feeling shaken up, I needed my crutches. I found it hard with them, though, walking on rough, bumpy ground covered in cushiony grass down to my spot under the jacaranda. At last I was there and somehow, with the help of an overhanging branch, sat down under the tree and gazed at the river. It was singing today. Rushing along, carrying twigs and bits of debris, high but not really rising.

I sat there, letting little gusts of sobbing well up from inside me, waiting until I was calm. Waiting to feel some wisdom about these hurting people. And trying to cope with the way Viv still, in spite of her God interactions or whatever, looked shattered. Shattered like I'd never expected to see her, with her former glowing resilience.

*~ Part Ten: May ~*

## CHAPTER 39

MAY WATCHED CLAIRE struggle her way down to the riverbank and walked down herself, keeping away from Claire. *Poor dear.* Bert was upset and he didn't express it as easily as he might have. Poor Claire obviously needed a little bit of time to think. May felt uneasy about Vivien too.

Bert had said last night as they settled into bed, 'It won't matter if Vivien doesn't marry. We've all been too focused on that. She'll always have a home here at *Riverside* and she makes friends easily so she won't be lonely. I suppose it's just that you and I have been lucky to have such a happy marriage and I'd like to see the same for Viv. She usually likes her men.' He laughed. 'I realise that too. But May, it won't be the end of the world if she ends up single.'

May sighed. Perhaps Bert was thinking of Viv's injuries and he had a point. Viv seemed to be avoiding Alan's friends. She must be embarrassed about having to limp. Still needing crutches at times too. Most of the time, actually. May believed Viv would have a good life, no matter what. But it would be wonderful to see her with a nice suitable man.

It was relaxing sitting here by the river. The water sang as it trickled over the rocks and her mind wandered as she sat there. A picture, almost a vision, slipped into her mind. First she was listening to the water. Then, with the tinkle of the water, she thought she heard laughter. She remembered it—little Vivvie's happy laugh when she was about eight— the innocent joy of a child. May remembered Viv playing in the shallow water when she was little. There she was, in technicolour, throwing showers of water into the air and laughing as silver droplets splashed down over her, cooling her hot skin. Such a pretty child, she'd been.

May sighed as the picture faded. Viv was still lovely looking but it wasn't the same—she had crutches! And no husband to look after her or to father little children who would bring back that innocence and laughter. A sudden nostalgia for the past, with small children in all their guilelessness, gripped May. Life was so beautiful, so happy, back in those days. Her life was still wonderful but ... When had it all begun to change? Perhaps that was just life. Seasons. She pulled her mind to the present and the future. Even if Viv stayed single, there were the other girls. There would be another season of little children playing in the water, she felt sure. But Viv ...

May took a deep breath and pulled her thoughts into the present. Life wasn't easy at the moment. But the World War had been terrible too, yet they'd come through that and they would come through this as well. Not all the men had come back from the war. And that had left some women, lovely girls many of them, single. Their fiancés had been killed. They'd managed, but life was easier being married. Well, May thought so anyway. Perhaps it wasn't everyone's cup of tea. One day she might talk about it all with Claire. Claire had turned into a strong and insightful friend to Viv and to the whole family, as well. After all the doubts Bert had had initially. As long as she survived this latest tirade of Bert's. Claire might be feeling like having a chat now. May frowned. Perhaps she should give the girl a bit more time to herself first.

She went back and helped clear the table, then decided Claire had had long enough by herself.

# CHAPTER 40

FOOTSTEPS CRUNCHED THE LEAVES behind me. *Mark? No, too slow.*

'Are you all right, darling?' It was May.

I half-laughed. 'I love coming here to think, even pray, I guess. I hope you don't mind.'

May's voice was gentle. 'Oh Claire, I do the same thing. So are you all right? Bert can be a bit abrupt but he'll get over it, you know. I'm glad you feel free to use our property to sit and think. Like I do.'

She left me sitting there. *So May's a thinker too. Great that she doesn't mind me making myself so at home like this.*

Mark was like that. Gave me space to think. He was a bit of a thinker himself despite Viv's declaration he was not 'deep'. He wasn't as messily complex as Nate, that was for sure. But he valued time alone or with his violin, to think or express himself. Yet he was often the life of the party. Most people didn't realise how much there was to Mark. Genuine depth.

It was time I went back to the others. Viv waved me over to her as I approached the veranda. 'Claire, I need to tell you something.'

'Sure. What?'

'We finally let Nate come up and see me last week, even though I'd broken it off. It was awful, Claire. Just awful.' Her voice was wobbling. 'Would you believe he says he still wants to marry me? I told him, no, it's over for good this time but he wouldn't accept it. He reminded me I'm a Christian and asked me to forgive him. So ... well, I did and I can, sort of, but forgiveness doesn't equal trust. I could never trust him again. He just didn't get it. He was nearly crying. He left soon after that, but first he tried to persuade me *again*. Reminded me we were in love. He even reminded me of *That Night*. That hurt. And he reminded me I'd said *Yes, I'd marry him*. But honestly, Claire, I knew I had to keep it broken off. It really is finished. Like I said ...' Her face twisted, '... something inside me's broken—apart from any bones—and I don't trust Nate to fix me up.' Viv's face crumpled. 'Not to mention what I certainly didn't tell him. What God said about not marrying a man like him.'

I hoped Viv had been right in believing that was God and not some weird thought from her battered head. I tried to encourage her without resorting to platitudes. So I didn't tell her it would all work out for the best or that God had someone more suitable for her. But heck, I hoped He did.

Later that afternoon I noticed Viv had a twinkle back in her eyes. I wondered what could be causing it at such a time, when she still hobbled along on crutches and occasionally even used a wheelchair. That would certainly cramp her style if she planned any Viv-style escapades.

We were sitting under the fig tree where we'd had lunch and she was looking tired—so unlike the Viv I'd known all those years. But her eyes were alight.

'Tom's got a group of boys doing rehab on his farm at the moment.'

'That's great. But—um—do you still find Tom boring?'

She looked at me, embarrassed. 'Actually, I do. I get a little bit bored with him, even when he's talking about interesting stuff. He's a great guy but just not my kind. I'd always hoped he'd end up with one of my sisters but I think he's keen on a friend of Ruth's.'

I smiled to myself. A bit keen, perhaps, but I'd seen the way he and Ellie looked at each other. 'By the way, you know Mark and I are getting married soon?' I asked her.

'Course I know. You showed me your ring.'

'Well, I would have liked to have you as one of my bridesmaids but you're not physically ready for that sort of thing.'

'Who says I'm not? I'll be a bridesmaid even if I go down the aisle on crutches.'

I laughed. 'Great. I shouldn't have doubted.'

Suddenly her face fell. 'You don't mind, do you? About having a bridesmaid on crutches?'

'Viv,' I flung my arms around her. 'Of course not. I was only thinking of you.'

That night Mark was shown to a room in the wing and I had 'my' old room back. Just as I began to doze, the murmur of voices in the kitchen jerked me awake. Those big cracks between the wide red cedar boards allowed voices to travel through unhindered so I heard every word. 'Claire's been a bad influence on Vivien.' Bert's gruff voice sounded angry still.

'Oh, I don't agree, Bert, and I don't think it's that simple,' May's voice replied. 'Vivvie can be very erratic and even a bit volatile, in her quaint way. Yes, darling, I know she's a gentle girl, but she's been a bit all over the place all through her teen years and now through her twenties. There was her relationship with Nate, you know. He might have influenced her more than anyone else. I've always found Claire a stable, reliable sort of a girl. Vivvie could have done a lot worse in her friendships. I just hope she finds a man who's strong and stable. Not another Nate.'

'Mmm.' Bert's voice still sounded grim. 'I'd still like to see her and Claire have a break from that friendship. They lead each other on.'

'Oh, Bert ...' At this point they must have taken mugs of milo and moved away into the lounge room as their voices faded.

Hot tears streamed down my face and my throat tightened. Bert still considered me the guilty one. And up to a point, I definitely was. But who could control Viv when she was having a panic attack? How could I live with my own share of guilt for such a horrible thing? Viv on crutches. I gulped down a sob.

The next day Mark wanted to get home early so we left before lunch. May came out to the car and enveloped me in a soft, warm hug. Tears ran down my cheeks again. She handed me a tissue and we both half-laughed.

We bumped our way back along the little driveway to the avenue and the gateway. The jacarandas were covered in green foliage and cast gentle shade over the entrance. A cluster of silky oaks were still in bloom as we turned onto the road. It was like driving out beneath a golden halo through the almost magic entrance that, for me, had always been the way into an enchanted world. Perhaps the Barlows' Christian beliefs lent a special fragrance to the property.

Mark wanted to know more about the accident and he too was curious about why I'd been driving. So I told him. Even about the party and Nate and Sally. And Viv's hysteria. 'Hell, Claire, you managed well, considering. But couldn't you have just tipped some cold water over Vivien or something? They say that's what you do when someone goes hysterical. Or slapped her face. Not that I can see you doing that.'

'I don't think it would have made much difference, Mark. She was in an emotional tangle and seriously traumatised. Nate really did the dirty on her.'

'I'm surprised she went as far as getting engaged to him without realising he's like that. That's who he is, no matter what excuses he might make. He'd make a lousy husband. He'd be eyeing up some other chick on his honeymoon.'

I groaned. 'I guess so. Well, it's all over now anyway.'

'Vivien's a pretty girl. And she's fun. I don't think she'll find it hard to get together with another man. As long as she heals up well enough to get out and about, I suppose.'

He squeezed my leg gently. 'Let's get married as soon as you can walk without a crutch. Oh heck—if it's going to be long, let's get married, crutch and all. But I know you want to get all dressed up. You're already walking well by yourself some of the time. How long do you reckon it'll be?'

I began to unwind as Mark and I drove home. I felt so relaxed with him now. And soon we'd be married.

'Do we have to ask Nate to the wedding?' Mark asked me.

'No way. Not after all he's done. You know, I'm still quite fond of him but I don't want him there at such an important time.'

Mark had managed to save enough money to buy our own house straight away. An uncle had left him an inheritance too, so we could afford a nice house in a pleasant area. He'd been looking at houses in Chelmer, a suburb we both loved. He enjoyed doing home carpentry and creating bits in the yard so there'd be plenty for him to do at home when he wasn't busy lecturing.

My stomach gurgled with a mixture of nerves and excitement when I thought about being married to him.

So … late that summer, I was dressed in a surprisingly flattering white lace dress with an underlay of pearly silk material. I actually felt glamorous. And I didn't need my crutch. I was walking properly again.

Would Mark like my dress? I'd never appeared in lace before.

Viv had helped me choose it, bravely coming in to the city with me and walking with just one crutch now. She, Lee and Julie were wearing a pretty shade of violet.

My stomach was nervy all the way in the car to the church. Mark had surprised me by wanting a church wedding. Perhaps it was for me, since I'd become a Christian. Any doubts I'd had about whether he would like me in this un-Claire-like attire disappeared when I began to walk down the aisle after Viv on her crutch and my two sisters. Mark turned around and his face lit up with joy when he saw me. Excitement and happiness filled me. For once in my life I felt beautiful.

We were both calm and sincere all through the ceremony, only to have Viv burst into emotional sobs as we signed the register. She continued to weep and May handed her a tissue, then stepped up and hugged her. When we walked back down, Viv was leaning heavily on her crutch and blowing her nose with her spare hand.

Mark raised a quizzical eyebrow at me. I resisted an urge to raise my own eyebrows, and smiled at him. By the time Mark and I began to walk back down the aisle, Viv was calm and smiling. 'It's like a fairy tale,' she said. 'Almost too good to be true.'

'It's true,' I said.

She hugged me. 'I know it is. I'm just being me.'

I found the reception fun. A reunion of so many old friends and my family and cousins.

'Guess what!' It was Viv, of course.

'What?'

'Ellie saw Nate slinking in at the back of the church. He wanted to be there in spite of you not wanting him.'

'Is that why you cried so much?'

She laughed. 'No way. That's just me. You all looked so beautiful! And after all this time. I had no idea Nate was there, luckily. Ellie just told me a minute ago.'

Mark leant over and whispered in my year. 'Emotional chick, isn't she?'

I shrugged. She was whimsical and full of life but Nate's antics the past few years had taken her on an emotional rollercoaster.

I was tired by the time we left amid flowers thrown all over us. Viv cried again as she hugged me but assured me she was thrilled and it was about time. We were flying to New Zealand that night and staying in a hotel in Auckland before touring the South Island.

From start to finish, my wedding and honeymoon were among the happiest times of my life.

# Chapter 41

WE'D BEEN BACK only two days when Viv turned up on the doorstep of our new home, an old Queenslander in Chelmer. She still had a crutch under her arm. To my surprise, she was radiant. She leant towards me and whispered, 'I'm not by myself. I'm banned from driving.' She hugged me. 'Marriage suits you. You're already glowing.'

'Who drove you, Viv?' My insides were suddenly churning as I realised it would probably be Bert or one of her sisters.

'Oh, just one of Alan's mates.' She avoided my eyes. 'We're on our way to see a movie. He decided I needed a bit of time out in the city for a change. And I wanted to have a quick look at your house. It's beautiful.' She smiled. I wished she'd say more but she had an enthusiastic look around our house, then managed her way down the steps despite the difficulty with her crutch.

I was glad Viv was seeing other men now. She had lost that lonely look at last. But was that enough to make her genuinely happy?

A few weeks later Mark and I were arriving at *Riverside*, visiting Viv and her family again. When we turned in to the property, again I sensed a hint of that other-worldliness as we passed along the avenue in its gentle shade. My cares began to slip away in spite of my impending encounter with Bert. 'Go slowly, Mark!'

We parked under the fig tree and I expected May to run out and greet us. Instead Bert came up to us and took one of my bags. 'You can have the room at the end of the wing,' he told Mark.

'Bert, we're married now! You were at our wedding. Don't we get to share a room?' Mark was laughing.

Bert chortled. 'Sorry. Habit! You can both have Claire's old room. And Claire, I'd like a word with you.'

My insides tightened.

'I'll see you in the lounge room in a few minutes,' he said.

So I went and sat in the antique-filled lounge room. I tried to look relaxed as Bert came in. Did I actually call him Bert to his face, or Mr Barlow? My mind had gone blank. May had always been May to me but ...

I decided to play it safe after our last awful interaction. 'How are you, Mr Barlow?' I asked as he stooped his tall frame under the low doorway.

'*Bert* to you, Claire, and I'm fine. But I did want to apologise for my attitude last time you were here. I was upset about Vivien's injuries and the accident. And of course the car was a write-off. But I had no business to blame you like that. Vivien has explained it all to me and it wasn't your fault.'

My heart was racing. 'I do actually feel I was partly responsible,' I told him firmly. 'I made a wrong decision in driving up here that night. I should have insisted Viv go to bed and we should both have had a good sleep before Viv drove up here.'

'Well ...' he stroked his chin as if checking whether he had stubble there. 'Claire, I think you did make an error of judgment but I know how difficult and headstrong Viv can be. And of course, life throws us these challenges and we all make wrong choices at times. Well, I assume we all do. I certainly have, myself, in the past. I think you should accept it was a wrong decision but don't blame yourself. These things happen. Give yourself a bit of rope.'

To my embarrassment, I felt tears running down my cheeks.

Bert cleared his throat. 'We'd better go and rescue that nice husband of yours.' As he walked out to the kitchen, I pulled a tissue from my handbag and blew my nose, then followed.

'I'll just have a bit of think time,' I told Mark when I met him outside the kitchen. 'I feel as if everything's changing again. Apparently Viv's out for an hour or so.'

'I'm going to get changed for a swim. Do you want one?' Mark asked me. 'You'll join me in the river soon, will you? By the way, if you're having some of your "think time", here's something for you to think about: I'm planning to come to church with you on Sunday. Perhaps even every Sunday. We'll be able to discuss what the preacher says at home that way.'

My heart raced. Was this his way of telling me he had become a Christian?

He chuckled. 'No big decisions yet, Claire. Don't forget how long it took me to marry you. But I figure if you're going to have a head full of some preacher's stuff, I need to know what he's telling you so we can discuss it.' He looked just a bit embarrassed and I suspected there was a little more to it than that. I was delighted. Imagine! To have Mark at my side in church! And wanting to discuss the Christian gospel at home.

*Back soon.* Viv had left a message on a scrap of paper on the bench.

Mark wiped a strand of hair off my forehead and headed into the homestead to change into his swimming shorts.

I went down and sat under the camphor laurels where I relaxed in their fresh, tangy fragrance. In the distance I could hear the musical trickle of water gurgling over rocks.

The river gleamed white in the late light, beneath me. Great pale cloud reflections glowed and billowed on its surface. Small birds twittered in the trees above me. I remembered the day Viv and I had swum in the river and I'd had that strange feeling, almost like a warning. A premonition. It was tempting to wish I could have aborted the troubles that followed, starting right back with Nate's disappearance, but ... a lot of wonderful things had happened too. I let the river enchant me until Mark's crunchy footsteps rustled through the leaves behind me. He helped me up and we headed back to the house where I changed. Soon we were enjoying the refreshing water and swimming across to the far bank.

We scrambled back across the paddock and showered and changed before going to see everyone in the kitchen.

'Hurry up!' It was Viv's voice.

I tidied my hair quickly and we went into the kitchen.

Viv limped over to me and gave me a hug. Her face was shining with—was it *joy*? 'Guess what!' she said.

My heart galloped. Was the old Viv back? The Viv of 'guess what' and all her quaint sayings.

'What?'

'Do you remember that gorgeous guy who lectures in psychology? Pete Rogers?' She was blushing.

Hope leapt inside me. 'Yes.'

Pete came in from his car, walking with a long, loping stride. He was quite good-looking with his reddish hair and ready smile, tall and thin but very agile.

Viv held out her hand. There on her ring finger sparkled a pretty sapphire set in tiny diamonds. 'Look!' she appeared ready to burst from excitement. 'We're engaged. We're getting married in about four months. Just a tiny wedding in the garden here. You can be my bridesmaid—well, matron of honour, I guess it is—Claire, can't you? I might have all my sisters too or else keep it very small.'

'Pete, I thought you were in a hurry to get married years ago when Viv first got to know you.' I watched his face with its crinkly smile.

'A moment of truth, I suppose. She was worth waiting for.' Pete put his arm around Viv's shoulders.

As the morning went on, over many cups of tea and slices of May's homemade sultana cake, we both enjoyed talking and laughing with him and Viv. A likeable man, about midway between Nate and Tom in personality, just like Viv had hoped, perhaps even prayed for. Trustworthy and intelligent but lots of fun.

After a long, happy day, knowing Mark was ready to leave, I slipped away to the riverbank by myself. It was still awkward walking with a limp over springy grass tufts but I managed. The sun was sinking towards the horizon, sending great hazy shafts of light that lay in slanting golden sheets across the paddocks.

I thought again of the day, years ago, I'd felt everything was somehow different. So much had changed since then. And now, at last, Viv had found the right man. She'd always liked Pete.

I thought about the baby, Viv's baby. I assumed God had taken her to heaven. She would never grow up here in this earthly paradise with Viv as her—or his—mother. Perhaps it was, in a weird way, God's will for the baby to leave Viv so early so Viv was free to start a whole new life without any link with Nate. Viv would be happy in spite of grieving over the baby, I knew that now.

Heavy footsteps rustled though the grass behind me. *Mark.* His hand was on my shoulder.

'Ready to share your "me time" and have a few minutes of "us time"? Okay if I sit here too?'

'Sure.'

It was different with someone else there but I still felt bathed in that tangible peace and Mark brought a strong sense of security and love. Despite the upheavals and all the changes I hadn't wanted at all, I felt sure everything would turn out for the best.

The river lay, glowing white and quiet beyond us, swishing a little when it reached the rocks and whispering its gentle eternal song.

# BY THE SAME AUTHOR

Mirage
Amelia's Island
Lantern Light
Healing Song
Songs in the Night
Jodie's Story: The Life of Jodie Cadman
Glimpses *(Journey Writers Anthology)*

facebook.com/jeanette.grantthomson